GONE BUT KNOT FORGOTTEN

"I want to do one last favor for an old friend."

Lucy narrowed her eyes. "Uh oh. Please tell me you're not going to get involved in another one of *those* again."

Lucy's voice sounded more than a tad disapproving as she alluded to my recent penchant for discovering dead bodies and getting sucked into murder investigations. And both times the killers came after me.

"This is way different, Lucy. First of all, the attorney never said anything about murder here. Second of all, being the executor of someone's estate only involves signing papers and selling stuff. There's nothing to worry about. What could be more straightforward?"

My redheaded friend shivered a little. "You know, Martha, I'm getting a strong feeling about this." Lucy swore she possessed ESP and could tell when something bad was going to happen.

In the past, I'd dismissed her feelings as some kind of displaced anxiety. But if I were honest, I'd have to admit that in the last several months her warnings turned out to be valid. Still, the lawyer gave no indication poor Harriet's death was anything more than tragic and premature.

"For heaven's sake, Lucy. Don't you think I've learned my lesson? Don't you think I'd run straight to the police at the first sign of something suspicious?"

Without hesitation, Lucy and Birdie responded in unison, "No!"

Books by Mary Marks

FORGET ME KNOT

KNOT IN MY BACKYARD

GONE BUT KNOT FORGOTTEN

Published by Kensington Publishing Corporation

GONE
BUT KNOT
FORGOTTEN

MARY MARKS

KENSINGTON PUBLISHING CORP.
http://www.kensingtonbooks.com

KENSINGTON BOOKS are published by

Kensington Publishing Corp.
119 West 40th Street
New York, NY 10018

All Kensington Titles, Imprints, and Distributed Lines are available at special quantity discounts for bulk purchases for sales promotions, premiums, fund-raising, and educational or institutional use. Special book excerpts or customized printings can also be created to fit specific needs. For details, write or phone the office of the Kensington special sales manager: Kensington Publishing Corp., 119 West 40th Street, New York, NY 10018, attn: Special Sales Department, Phone: 1-800-221-2647.

Kensington and the K logo Reg. U.S. Pat & TM Off.

ISBN-13: 978-0-7582-9209-4
ISBN-10: 0-7582-9209-0
First Kensington Mass Market Edition: September 2015

eISBN-13: 978-0-7582-9210-0
eISBN-10: 0-7582-9210-4
First Kensington Electronic Edition: September 2015

10 9 8 7 6 5 4 3 2 1

Printed in the United States of America

*This book is lovingly dedicated to
my big brother, Sgt. Major David Terry Marks,
and my cousin Mark Levy Rosenberg,
both of blessed memory.*

ACKNOWLEDGMENTS

As always, I'd like to thank those people so essential to writing this book: my mentor, Jerrilyn Farmer, and my critique partners (in alphabetical order) Lori Dillman, Lindsey Fenimore, Cyndra Gernet, Carlene O'Niel, and Rochelle Staab.

I'm also indebted to a variety of awesome experts. Thanks to my legal guru, Linda Greenberg Loper, Deputy DA (retired) LA County; Lisa Holzer, computer maven; Grant David Brown, a most excellent gamer; Dr. Shelby Sanett, preservation specialist; Sofia Leiva, Salvadorian food expert; Britt Heymann, consultant on Swedish culture; and Shelley Piser, yoga instructor. An extra thanks to Rochelle for the tarot tutorial.

I always save the best for last. Heartfelt thanks go to my agent, Dawn Dowdle, at Blue Ridge, and my editor, John Scognamiglio, and his incredibly able staff at Kensington.

CHAPTER 1

So far, the morning mail only yielded credit card invitations, an interesting flyer for yoga classes, and now that I belonged to AARP—another postcard advertising the Neptune Society. I picked up a white number ten envelope, glanced at the unfamiliar return address, and almost tossed it in the junk pile, but something stopped me.

First, my full legal name, Martha Rivka Rose, appeared above my address. I never used *Rivka*. Second, the envelope looked official, not part of a mass mailing. The law offices of Abernathy, Porter & Salinger of Los Angeles, California, paid full price for the stamp.

I reached for the white plastic letter opener, a prize I received from the UCLA Department of Internal Medicine after having my first colonoscopy. The envelope tore neatly along the top fold, and I pulled out a one-page letter.

Dear Ms. Rose,
   We regret to inform you of the death of Mrs. Harriet Gordon Oliver. You have been named the

*executor of her estate. Please contact me personally
at your earliest convenience to initiate the process
of probating her will.*

*Very truly yours,
Deacon "Deke" Abernathy, Esq.*

Harriet died? I hadn't heard from her in over twenty years. We'd been best friends in high school. She moved to Rhode Island with a scholarship to Brown, while I lived at home and attended UCLA. Years later, she returned to Los Angeles with her husband, Nathan Oliver, a fellow Brown graduate. I had married Aaron Rose, a local boy finishing his psychiatric residency at LA County Hospital. Harriet and I reconnected at our tenth high school reunion in the late 1980s.

Since we all lived in Brentwood, a tony part of the west side, we met a few times for dinner. Harriet and her East Coast husband collected wine and art, while Aaron and I focused on raising our three-year-old daughter and paying the mortgage on our much smaller home. Eventually even the dinners stopped. By the time I divorced Aaron and relocated to a not-so-tony part of Encino in the San Fernando Valley, Harriet and I had already drifted apart.

Now, sadly, she was dead at the age of fifty-five. What took her so young? What about her husband? Children? The more I thought about the letter, the more questions I had.

I telephoned the number Deacon Abernathy gave me.

"Deke here."

"Mr. Abernathy? My name is Martha Rose. I just received your letter about Harriet Oliver."

"Oh, right. Thanks for calling, Ms. Rose. We have

some details to go over, including Mrs. Oliver's funeral instructions. How soon can you come to my office?"

"Wait a minute. Please slow down. When did Harriet die? How did she die?"

"I'm sorry. Got ahead of myself. Has it been awhile since you spoke to Mrs. Oliver?"

"Decades, actually."

"That explains our problem locating you. We only had your old Brentwood address to go by. Under the circumstances, I guess I'm not surprised."

"What do you mean, circumstances? What's going on?"

"There's no delicate way to say this, Ms. Rose. We discovered Mrs. Oliver's body in her home about three weeks ago. The coroner estimated she'd been dead for at least ten months."

Thank goodness I was already sitting. My ears started ringing and a black circle closed out my peripheral vision. I envisioned horrible pictures of desiccated corpses and skulls with gaping jaws. "Ten months? Didn't she have family? What about her husband?"

"It's too complicated to explain over the phone. The thing is, Mrs. Oliver hasn't been buried yet. We needed to wait until we located the executor to make certain, ah, decisions. So, you can appreciate, Ms. Rose, the sooner you get here, the sooner we can, ah, lay her to rest."

Poor Harriet. How was it possible nobody missed her? She'd been such a vibrant and pretty teenager with long black hair she ironed straight every morning before school. During our sleepovers we whispered about our plans for college, our hopes for the future and which girls slept with their boyfriends. When she left for Brown, we hugged and cried and promised to write letters every day. But time and distance slowed our friendship. With the exception of our brief reunion in Brentwood, we moved into completely separate lives.

I shuddered at the thought of her body lying unattended for ten months. It really bothered me that nobody missed her. Didn't the neighbors notice any bad odors? I agreed to meet the attorney at the Westwood office of Abernathy, Porter & Salinger later in the afternoon.

After ending my conversation with Deacon Abernathy, I gave my shoulder-length gray curls a once-over with a wide-toothed comb. Then I stuffed my Jacob's Ladder quilt, sewing kit, and an emergency package of M&Ms into a large red tote bag and headed for my best friend Lucy Mondello's house. Today was Tuesday, and I never missed our weekly quilting group. I drove in a daze, trying to make sense of the shocking news about Harriet's death. What a horrendous way to go—alone and evidently forgotten.

I maneuvered my way across Ventura Boulevard and wound around a couple of side streets before pulling up in front of my friend's house. The boulevard served as a natural dividing line between classes in Encino, one of the many small communities in the San Fernando Valley. Small homes, condos, and apartment buildings sat on the valley floor north of the boulevard. That was where I lived, in a tract of medium-priced midcentury houses. Residences south of the boulevard—especially those constructed in the foothills of the Santa Monica Mountains—tended to be large, custom-designed, and *très* expensive. Lucy lived somewhere in between: south of the boulevard but not in the hills, gracious home but not a McMansion.

She smiled and greeted me as I pushed open the front door. "Hey, girlfriend. You're a little late. Everything okay?"

Lucy always dressed with a theme. Today she wore canary yellow twill slacks, a yellow-and-white-striped long sleeved T-shirt, and dangly citrine earrings. Her bright orange hair looked freshly colored and her eyebrows perfectly drawn. Even at sixty-something she could have been a model. I, on the other hand, wore my usual size-sixteen stretch denim jeans and T-shirt straining under my ample bosom.

"I just dealt with a last-minute phone call. Give me a sec and I'll tell you all about it." I settled down in one of the cozy blue overstuffed chairs in Lucy's casual living room.

Every few years she changed the décor in her home the same way she changed her daily outfits. This latest version evoked an elegant cabin: furniture upholstered in richly colored woolen fabrics, Navajo rugs, and a coffee table made of polished burled tree roots. Above the fireplace hung a reproduction of a yellow Remington painting of longhorn cattle. The room screamed Wyoming, where both Lucy and her husband, Ray, were born and raised.

"Did the call upset you? You look a bit peaky, dear." That was Birdie Watson, Lucy's across-the-street neighbor and the third member of our small sewing circle.

"I got a letter from an attorney in LA this morning asking me to call." I fitted my multicolored

Jacob's Ladder quilt in a fourteen-inch wooden hoop. The Jacob's Ladder block featured lots of little squares and larger triangles of contrasting light and dark materials. The more fabrics, the more interesting the quilt, and this one featured dozens of different cotton prints. I threaded a needle with red quilting thread and related the story about Harriet's death and my surprise at being named executor of her will. "The creepy thing is, she died more than ten months before they discovered her body."

"How awful!" Birdie, naturally predisposed to worry about people, frowned and twisted the end of her long white braid. In her mid-seventies, Birdie looked like an old farmer. She always wore the same thing: white T-shirt (short sleeves in summer, long sleeves in winter), denim overalls, and Birkenstock sandals (with socks) to accommodate her arthritic knees.

Lucy handed me a cup of coffee with milk. "You must have been close for her to make you executor. Yet, I don't think I've ever heard you mention her name before."

"We were best friends growing up." I told them how our teenage friendship failed to survive our adult lifestyles. "After I moved to Encino, everyone in West LA forgot about me, including Harriet."

Lucy shook her head. "Well, obviously she didn't forget about you. Do you know what happened to her husband?"

"I wish I knew more of the details. I have an appointment with the lawyer this afternoon to get poor Harriet buried. He said he'd explain everything then."

Birdie tilted her head. "So you've decided to go through with becoming the executor? Not knowing what's involved?"

How could I say this without sounding morbid? "I want to do one last favor for an old friend."

And I'm curious.

Lucy narrowed her eyes. "Uh-oh. Please tell me you're not going to get involved in another one of *those* again."

Lucy's voice sounded more than a tad disapproving as she alluded to my recent penchant for discovering dead bodies and getting sucked into murder investigations. And both times the killers came after me. "This is way different, Lucy. First of all, the attorney never said anything about murder here. Second of all, being the executor of someone's estate only involves signing papers and selling stuff. There's nothing to worry about. What could be more straightforward?"

My redheaded friend shivered a little. "You know, Martha, I'm getting a strong feeling about this." Lucy swore she possessed ESP and could tell when something bad was going to happen.

In the past, I'd dismissed her feelings as some kind of displaced anxiety. But if I were honest, I'd have to admit that in the last several months her warnings turned out to be valid. Still, the lawyer gave no indication poor Harriet's death was anything more than tragic and premature.

"Oh, for heaven's sake, Lucy. Don't you think I've learned my lesson? Don't you think I'd run straight to the police at the first sign of something suspicious?"

Without hesitation, Lucy and Birdie responded in unison, "No!"

CHAPTER 2

The law offices of Abernathy, Porter & Salinger were located in a black glass high-rise on the corner of Wilshire Boulevard and Federal Avenue in West LA, where parking cost five dollars for every fifteen minutes.

I stepped off the elevator into a plush suite of offices occupying the entire tenth floor. The reception area, situated in the south side of the building, revealed spectacular views of the Pacific Ocean all the way down to Palos Verdes and west to Catalina Island. The late-afternoon December sun striped the horizon in shades of pink and gold. Harriet must have been very well off to afford an attorney in this luxury setting. I was glad I wore a dress for the meeting.

"May I help you?"

I tore my eyes from the stunning view and approached a male receptionist sitting behind an antique walnut desk. A head of short, bleached hair appeared almost white in contrast to his latte skin. He blinked his eyes once, and a flash of black eyeliner caught my attention. Another part of LA's rich diversity I loved so much.

"Martha Rose for Deacon Abernathy."

He pressed a button on a console and spoke into a headset, then smiled warmly and gestured toward the waiting area. "Mr. Abernathy will be free in a couple of minutes. Please make yourself comfortable. May I get you some water? Coffee? Soda?"

"No, thanks." I returned the smile.

I sat in a chair upholstered in plum leather and gazed at the sunset, calculating how much each minute of waiting would cost me in parking fees. I had reached three dollars and forty cents when a slender woman wearing glasses walked efficiently toward me.

"Ms. Rose? I'm Mr. Abernathy's assistant, Nina. Sorry for the wait. He's most anxious to meet you. Will you please follow me?"

We moved down a long corridor decorated in original art to a huge corner office with a jaw-dropping view not only of the sunset but of the Veterans Administration to the east and the UCLA campus beyond. Vivaldi played soothingly in the background. If your name came first on the door, you could command the best office.

A thickset man with a receding hairline stood and came round his desk with his shirt sleeves rolled up, and shook my hand vigorously. "Ms. Rose, I'm Deacon Abernathy, but everyone calls me 'Deke.'" Abernathy looked like a former athlete gone soft around the middle, probably thanks to decades of steak dinners and martini lunches. He led me to a comfortable sofa and sat in a chair facing me, across a coffee table with two glasses of ice water. Something about this guy seemed familiar, but I couldn't quite place him.

I took a deep breath. "Please tell me about Harriet."

He tented his fingers and pressed them against his lips. "I've been Harriet's attorney for years. Our firm handled both her legal and her financial affairs. I tried contacting her recently. Some investment transactions needed her signature. When she failed to return my calls, I became alarmed and drove to her house. Nobody answered the door, so I went round to the back. Nothing looked out of place. The gardener still tended the grounds, but everything was quiet. Too quiet. I suspected something terrible had happened and called the police. They forced their way into the house and found her dead."

My skin crawled. "How did she die?"

He coughed and covered his mouth. A slight tremor rippled through his hand. Was the poor man trying to hide his emotions? "The coroner couldn't determine the cause of death because of the state of her body. The police found no obvious sign of foul play. She could've suffered a heart attack."

"Oh God." My mouth felt dry; I reached for a glass of water. "What about her husband, Nathan? Did they have children?"

"One son, Jonah, was born in 1990 but died at the age of five in a tragic accident."

This story grew worse and worse. "How?"

"Nathan took him on a charter boat to Catalina Island for a father/son fishing trip. Apparently the boy wasn't wearing a proper life jacket. He fell overboard and went under. Some fishermen dove in the water, but by the time one of them could find him and pull him out of the ocean, the child was dead."

Poor Harriet. The death of her son was the second tragedy in her life. At nine, her twin brother, David, died under the wheels of a bus. Now she'd faced a similar horror years later with her son.

Nina, the assistant, materialized with a bottle of Pinot Grigio on a large silver tray with two wine-glasses, platters of tapas—mini open-faced sandwiches—and ceviche served with tiny forks. She set the tray on the coffee table and offered me a glass, but I shook my head. I had to drive back home.

Abernathy handed me a napkin. "We offer happy hour to our clerks and associates on Tuesdays. Go on, help yourself."

"Thanks, but I'm not hungry." I usually enjoyed a warm and fuzzy relationship with food. However, as Harriet's story unfolded, I lost my appetite. Abernathy, on the other hand, shrugged and poured himself a generous drink and tucked into the raw fish with gusto.

My grandmother, who raised me, may she rest in peace, would rather have poked her eye out with a fork than eaten in front of someone else. She communicated through food. If any guest of Bubbie's refused to eat, she coaxed, cajoled, and wheedled until he gave in. *Just a small sliver. You need your strength. What. You don't like my cooking?* It worked every time.

Nina slipped quietly out of the office and I waited until Abernathy had washed down the food with more wine.

"What happened to Nathan?"

He wiped his mouth with a cocktail napkin and once again his hand trembled. Maybe he suffered a neurological problem.

"About two years after the boy's death, Nathan disappeared. Must've been the guilt. He left behind a note saying he intended to go back out to sea, to the place where Jonah died and join his son. We never found his body."

I thought about all the episodes of *Cold Case Files* on TV. "What if he didn't kill himself? What if he just wanted to run away?"

"Naturally, we thought of that and hired detectives to search for him. But Nathan Oliver vanished. After seven years, without a trace, and on the strength of his suicide note, we had him declared legally dead."

"What about her parents?" Herschel and Lilly Gordon, both Holocaust survivors, had been older when Harriet and her brother, David, were born. They avoided mentioning the aunts, uncles, and cousins who died in the camps. And like most survivors, they were overprotective.

"Both dead. No other living relatives."

"Well, what about friends? A social life?" When we were teenagers, Harriet often spent the night at my house. She rummaged through my closet, changed into my torn jeans and leg warmers, and—unbeknownst to her parents—we hung out with our friends at the mall.

Abernathy shook his head. "Harriet became a recluse. She seldom left her home and rarely received visitors."

My heart squeezed in pain at the thought of

Harriet's devastating losses and her self-imposed isolation.

"Did she say why she chose me to be her executor?"

Abernathy spread his hands and shrugged. "Up until he disappeared, Harriet made her husband, Nathan, the executor. Then she selected her father until his death ten years ago. After that, she named her college roommate, Isabel Casco. Two years ago, Harriet changed her will again and appointed you."

"You said you handled her financial affairs. How could she lay in her house for ten months without anybody knowing? With no one to pay the bills, didn't the overdue warnings from the utility companies raise a red flag?"

"Good questions. All her household bills were sent directly to our office. We routinely sent out monthly payments. As far as we knew, nothing raised a flag." Abernathy popped a small slice of baguette, topped with an olive tapenade, in his mouth. "You sure you won't try one of these? You're missing out."

Did nothing spoil this man's appetite?

I cleared my throat. "No, thanks. I hate to bring this up while you're eating, but I can't help wondering why the neighbors didn't detect a foul odor coming from the house."

He put his small plate of tapas back on the table.

Maybe he does have limits.

"Yeah, I wondered that too. But, as the coroner explained, Harriet's house stood on a large lot. Any odor would dissipate long before reaching the surrounding homes. And her location inside the house, well, not much of the smell would've traveled outdoors."

"Where was she?"

"Upstairs off the master bedroom inside a windowless walk-in closet. The worst odor would've been pretty much confined."

My stomach lurched. I tried not to think about the poor cop who first entered Harriet's closet. "Had anything been stolen? Could she have been killed by an intruder?"

Abernathy shifted his weight forward and studied me intently. His frown deepened the creases between his eyes. "You sound like a police detective, Ms. Rose."

I maintained eye contact and said nothing.

He poured himself another glass of wine, relaxed back into the chair, and smiled slightly. "To tell you the truth, I didn't know what to expect when I contacted you, but it's clear you're both smart and, ah, insightful. I think Harriet chose her executor wisely. To answer your question, I couldn't tell whether anything was missing. I did notice a general messiness, as if someone might've been looking for something."

I pictured the young Harriet going through my closet hunting for cool clothes. I tried not to picture the grown Harriet lying in her closet for ten months. She deserved to be in her final resting place as soon as possible. "So, what does being Harriet's executor involve, Mr. Abernathy?"

"Call me Deke. We're pretty informal around here. May I call you Martha?"

"Sure. Okay."

He briefly reviewed the details of the will—she left everything to charity—and explained the process of probate. "It'll be your job to dispose of her assets and distribute her bequests. We'll take care of filing the court papers. The first thing you must do is make some practical and religious decisions regarding her burial. Harriet owned a plot at Gan Shalom Memorial Park next to her son, but she never specified any final details.

He stood and retrieved a bulging accordion file from his desk, reached inside, and handed me a handful of papers and a bulky envelope. "This is a copy of her will. Here are keys to her house and automobile." He indicated the file. "The rest of these papers include copies of her death certificate, a financial summary, insurance policies, and an investment portfolio. Anytime you're ready, my accountants will give you full access to her records, statements, and whatever else you need to settle her estate."

"Where is Harriet's body now?"

"Still with the coroner. Info's in the file. Let me know what arrangements you make."

I glanced at my wristwatch. An hour had passed. I gathered up the documents and stood. For the first time, I spotted a silver trophy with a football on top of an art deco pedestal. I walked over to read the inscription: UCLA ROSE BOWL JANUARY 1976.

Now I remembered why he looked so familiar. In 1976, my senior year at UCLA, we won the Rose Bowl when star quarterback, Deke Abernathy, threw the winning pass. His face appeared regularly in the *Daily Bruin*. We sat in the same geography class, although I was sure he'd never remember a married student like me. Deke Abernathy hung out with the jocks and sorority girls. I was, frankly, surprised to see this guy had been smart enough to become a lawyer.

"I thought I recognized you, Deke. We attended UCLA at the same time."

He grinned wide enough for me to observe a mouth full of capped teeth. "Did we ever meet?"

"Well, we sat in one class together, but I'm certain you wouldn't remember."

He put a meaty hand on my shoulder. "What a shame. I'm sure I would've liked you, Martha." His hazel eyes crinkled at the corners and his teeth flashed.

Oh, brother.

"Probably not. I was married at the time."

He winked and gave my shoulder a little squeeze. "Never too late."

Really? Is he really trying to go there? "Great. In that case, I have a question to ask."

He chuckled. "Anything for a friend."

I pulled out my parking ticket. "Do you validate?"

CHAPTER 3

The next morning I woke with a fibromyalgia flare-up. My neck and shoulders were stiff, and every part of me hurt. All the dampness and weather changes turned winter into the crappy time of year for me. My sensitive body could predict rain three days before the first drops fell.

In the kitchen, my orange cat Bumper purred and rubbed his whiskered cheeks against my ankles as I poured star-shaped kibble into his bowl. I stood and spotted the yoga studio flyer from yesterday's mail. A flexible young woman sat smiling in the lotus pose, her palms pressed together in the prayer position. The last time I saw Dr. Lim at the UCLA Pain Clinic, he suggested I try yoga for the chronic discomfort of fibro. He pointedly looked at my hips. "It might help you lose a little weight while you're at it." I could have been so insulted.

I reached for the phone and called the number on the flyer, still unsure whether yoga was for me.

"Sublime Yoga. *Namaste.*"

"Hello. My name is Martha Rose and I'm calling about your trial offer."

"Great. I'm Heather. Let's set up an appointment to give you a tour of the studio and afterward we'll schedule you for a free class. When would you like to come in?"

A long list of chores waited for my attention, beginning with the task of reading Harriet's will and contacting Gan Shalom Memorial Park. "I'm pretty busy today, but how about tomorrow morning?"

"Perfect. Give me your phone number and I'll schedule a tour for nine on Thursday. And, Martha? Be sure to wear something loose and comfortable."

An hour later I showered and dressed in black slacks and a gray pullover. Ever since my hair turned salt-and-pepper, I discovered gray clothes complemented my coloring. With the accordion file next to me on the sofa, I prioritized the papers by the most immediate task first. The contact info for Gan Shalom Memorial Park, located in West LA, sat on the top of the pile. I punched in the number on my phone and after two transfers, a Mrs. Deener came on the line.

"Hello. I'm calling about Mrs. Harriet Oliver. My name is Martha Rose, and I want to make arrangements for her funeral."

"Oh, yes." Mrs. Deener spoke in a pleasantly modulated, almost unctuous voice. "The lawyer's office told us to expect your call. You'll need to come and sign release papers so we can transport the deceased from the county morgue. Although Mrs. Oliver is a prepaid, there are still a few decisions to be made.

A prepaid? I bristled at the way the woman just reduced Harriet to a commodity.

I looked at my watch. "It's ten now. I can drive over the hill and meet you at twelve."

I got off the 405 Freeway at Howard Hughes Parkway and wound my way across Sepulveda Boulevard. A long driveway lined in Italian cypress trees meandered up the hill to the white marble administration building and chapel. Gan Shalom, one of several Jewish cemeteries in LA, had become a popular local destination. It was the first to offer "green" burials—not only politically correct but good for the environment. Here, according to ancient Jewish customs, the deceased could be wrapped in a shroud and placed in the ground without a casket or cement vault. Who knew that thousands of years of Jewish burial practice would become so LA hip?

I pulled up to the complimentary valet parking, surrendered my car keys, and walked inside. I checked in at the reception desk at eleven fifty-five. At twelve sharp, and not a moment later, the middle-aged Mrs. Deener appeared in a baby blue wool suit and a brown wig drooping slightly forward. She clasped her hands together in front of her bosom and gave me the slightest smile. "Good morning, Mrs. Rose. I am so sorry for your loss. Shall we get started?"

In her cozy peach-colored office, I signed papers and filled out forms. I insisted on reading everything and she didn't rush me. I admired Mrs. Deener's skill and patience in performing her slightly creepy job.

Harriet specified she wanted to be buried next to her son in a section called *Ayelet Ha Shachar*, literally "Gazelle of the Dawn," or "Morning Star." Since this wasn't the "green" section, Mrs. Deener asked me to choose a casket. She led me to a room full of coffins. As Bach played softly in the background, I briefly wondered how it felt to be dead.

I didn't know Harriet's preferences, but I remembered her parents had been religiously observant. So, to be on the safe side, I chose a strictly kosher casket—a box made with soft pine wood and plant-based glue and held together with wooden dowels instead of nails. Jewish custom required an easily biodegradable coffin that would return the deceased to the earth as quickly as possible.

Harriet's body was far beyond the stage where she could undergo another custom, a ritual washing called a *tahara*. However, I did hire a *shomer*, a "guardian" to sit with her remains from the time she arrived at Gan Shalom until she lay in the ground.

Mrs. Deener picked up a large datebook. "Because Shabbat begins in two days, on Friday, I've scheduled the funeral for the first thing tomorrow morning, Thursday. It's customary to bury the dead as soon as possible. Given the circumstances of Mrs. Oliver's demise, I'm sure you're anxious to move forward."

"I'm sorry, but tomorrow isn't feasible. We'll have to delay her funeral until I've had a chance to notify people. Harriet has waited over ten months. A little more time won't make a difference now."

We settled on Monday morning, allowing me four days to go through her address book and call everyone. Maybe Abernathy's office could provide further guidance.

I asked Mrs. Deener to take me to see Harriet's plot. We drove in a golf cart to a pleasant expanse of lawn bordered by willow trees, waving delicate fingers of green. The nearby lilac bushes, now bare in winter, would burst with fragrant blue blossoms in the spring. She directed me to a quiet spot in the back near a rock wall. I read the engraving on a pink travertine square slab: JONAH DAVID OLIVER 1990–1995. Elegantly curving letters told his story in Hebrew. The foot of his grave pointed east toward Jerusalem.

Poor little boy, there's nobody alive to mourn you. Tears blurred my eyes as I lifted a small pebble from the stone wall and placed it on Jonah's grave in an ancient symbolic gesture.

I left a message for Abernathy, advising him of the time of Harriet's funeral, and headed home. On the drive north through the Sepulveda Pass, the beginnings of a migraine started over my right ear and curled around my temple to my eye. The stress of the last couple of hours was taking a toll. The clock on the dashboard read nearly three and by the time I reached my house in Encino, my whole head throbbed. I stumbled inside and went straight for the medicine cabinet.

A couple of pills, a hot cup of tea, and a half hour later my headache had subsided. I sat on my cream-colored sofa and studied Harriet's will, shocked to discover she provided me with a financial stipend of $10,000 a month until the closing of probate. *What is this?* In addition to the generous stipend, Harriet invited me to choose one item from all her belongings as a keepsake. No restrictions.

I never would have considered paying my daughter, Quincy, or my best friend, Lucy, to carry out my last wishes. However, Harriet and I hadn't seen each other for a couple of decades. Maybe she thought she owed me something for my trouble.

But really, how much trouble can this be?

Harriet financed the Jonah David Oliver wing of the new Children's Hospital through a major bequest of thirty million dollars. The rest of her assets would be divided between a number of charities, including the LA Regional Food Bank and Haven House, a battered women's shelter.

Where did all this money come from?

A rider attached to Harriet's insurance policies listed her treasures, and a flash drive contained photographs of each item. Among her assets were some very good pieces of jewelry, including a diamond bracelet worth over a hundred thousand dollars. Her eclectic tastes led to an accumulation of fine porcelain, rare books, a group of antique American pocket watches valued at a quarter of a million dollars, and a stellar collection of American folk art.

Holy crap! According to Harriet's will, I could become the owner of any one of several very valuable items.

Abernathy mentioned Harriet's house looked messy, as though someone had rummaged around looking for something. I'd have to make an inventory of every item in her house to cross-check with the rider. That way I'd discover if anything was missing. Clearly, I needed to hire security as soon as possible, and I knew the perfect person to call.

My jaw dropped as I read Harriet's financial summary. She owned rental property, including a couple of commercial buildings in Westwood, had an investment portfolio in the eight figures, and had interest in a couple of small business franchises. How in the world did someone go about liquidating such a complicated estate?

Even with the thirty million destined for Children's Hospital, Harriet's remaining net worth added up to much more. How did a sweet girl from a middle-class family in the Pico-Robertson area of Los Angeles end up with so much money? Who was Nathan Oliver, exactly?

All of a sudden, "selling stuff" seemed like a huge task. I began to understand why Harriet had provided me with a generous allowance. Settling her estate had just turned into a full-time job. What had I gotten myself into?

My stomach rumbled and complained of neglect. I pulled a Trader Joe's Southwestern salad from the refrigerator and emptied the measly contents of the plastic container into a bowl. With Weight Watchers in mind, I added a quarter of an avocado and tossed in two tablespoons of low-fat dressing. I put my feet up to watch the six o'clock news when the phone rang.

"Hey, babe."

"Hi, Yossi. What's up?" I met my biker friend Yossi Levy, also known as Crusher (don't ask), a few months ago. We helped prove a mutual friend innocent of murder.

"I'm at Brent's. Do you want me to bring over a couple pastramis on rye?"

Oh my God. Brent's Deli sold the absolute fattest, tastiest, most mouthwatering pastrami on the planet. I'd save the salad for tomorrow. A person needed a little protein, didn't she?

"Heck yes. I'll open some red wine."

Thirty minutes later the roar of a Harley engine pulled up in front of my house. The bearded Crusher filled the doorway with his six foot six, three hundred pounds of solid muscle. He wore his leathers against the December chill. A blue bandana covered his graying red hair.

He grinned as he handed me a large paper bag like a present. By the weight and smell, I realized with a frisson of guilty pleasure the bag held more delicious things besides two sandwiches.

We sat at my kitchen table and I poured two glasses of a hearty Chianti. I pulled apart my sandwich and smeared brown mustard on the spongy rye bread. Then I helped myself to kosher green tomatoes, crispy coleslaw, and *kasha varnishkes,* a warm dish made of buckwheat groats and egg noodles. I never said I did Weight Watchers perfectly.

Between bites I told Crusher about Harriet Oliver's tragic life and death and how I became involved in settling her estate. "You know, Yossi, I can't get over the dreadful way she died. Nobody missed her."

He fixed his blue eyes on me. "How come?"

"That's one of the questions I hope to answer. Anyway, I scheduled her funeral for Monday, so my next task is to notify people."

"Do you need me for a *minyan*?" Crusher referred to the quorum of ten Jewish men necessary for the recitation of certain prayers during the mourning period. To be part of a minyan was considered a *mitzvah*, a good deed.

"Thanks for the offer. I'll know more when I get a sense of how many people will be attending." I took a sip of wine. "When we were teenagers,

Harriet loved being with friends, but she died a recluse. I'd sure like to know more about why."

Crusher chewed a bite of sandwich and poked an errant string of pastrami back into the corner of his mouth. "Seems to me you'll get to know a lot about her by the time you're through. Need any help? We made a great team investigating the murder of the baseball coach."

How could I forget? Crusher protected me from a knife-wielding psychopath, guarded me against death threats, and then proposed marriage two weeks after we met. He and the guys in his motor cycle club, the Valley Eagles, helped me out a couple of times.

I grinned. "Actually, yes. Some really valuable things are sitting in Harriet's unoccupied house. I want to hire some of the Eagles to protect the place until her stuff can be sold or relocated."

"Anything you want, babe."

I put the leftovers in the refrigerator and wiped the table clean. Crusher stood watching me as he drank a glass of wine. "How about some dessert?"

"Sorry, I don't think I have anything sweet. I do have a little fruit if . . ."

Crusher laughed. "I'm not thinking of food."

My love life tanked three months ago. My boyfriend, LAPD Detective Arlo Beavers, dumped me when he learned his dog was seriously injured defending me. Crusher briefly stepped in to take Beavers's place. Each of them decided they wanted a permanent, exclusive relationship with me. So I did what any right-thinking woman of my generation would do. I turned them both down. Crusher and I agreed to be just friends, at least until I figured out what I wanted to do with the rest of my life. Beavers, not quite as sanguine, dropped out of sight.

Crusher looked at me expectantly.

Remembering the one night we spent together made my toes curl with desire. I took a deep breath. "Not tonight, Yossi."

"I'll wait," he smiled.

That night I dreamed I sat behind Crusher on his Harley, speeding in the dark down the 405 Freeway. Closing in behind us was *Malach haMavet,* the angel of death.

CHAPTER 4

Thursday morning I rummaged through my closet, looking for appropriate yoga clothes. The flyer from Sublime Yoga pictured a slender blonde in a blue halter top and skinny black tights. No way could I ever put my size sixteen thighs into tights. I finally located a pair of L.L. Bean dark knit trousers, with an elastic waist, folded in a pile destined for a small church in Van Nuys that ministered to the homeless.

I pulled on the trousers and an old red T-shirt and drove to the yoga studio on the boulevard in nearby Tarzana. In the middle of a sunny reception area stood a round counter and shelves full of yoga supplies for sale. Fit young men and women with rolled-up mats streamed toward the receptionist, who electronically scanned their little plastic ID tags before they disappeared into a classroom. I felt as out of place as a pork chop on Passover.

The blonde from the flyer stood behind the desk.

"Hi. My name's Martha. I'm here for a tour."

She put her palms together and dipped her head. "*Namaste.* I'm Heather."

After a quick circuit of the classrooms and locker room, Heather and I sat in a lounge where she poured me a demitasse of hot green tea. "I suggest you start out twice a week in a class for seniors."

Octogenarians sitting around on chairs waving their arms? "I think I can handle something a little harder."

Heather just smiled and walked me over to an open classroom doorway. "This is our Vinyasa Flow class."

I could have been observing an audition for Cirque du Soleil. The instructor called out, "Warrior two." Everyone took a wide stance and lunged sideways with arms parallel to the floor. "Triangle." Still in a wide stance, they all bent sideways at the waist and shot an arm straight up. "Tree pose." The students effortlessly balanced on one leg and reached their arms straight overhead. I got the picture.

Ten minutes later Heather settled me on a borrowed orange rubber mat on the bamboo floor of classroom two. Two men stuck out in this class of mostly senior women of every body type, including a white-haired former ballet dancer and me.

The short, buxom teacher in her forties with wild cherry-colored curls stood in the center of the classroom and knocked together two delicate brass bells to get everyone's attention. "Hello, class!" she said in a thick Russian accent. "This is Yoga for Seniors, and I am Dasha. Do we have anyone new today?"

I raised my hand.

Dasha walked over and smiled. "Do you have physical problems I should know?"

I told her about my fibromyalgia.

"You're in the right place. Welcome."

An hour later, after breathing deeply through leg, hip, and spine stretches, we assumed the corpse pose, *Shavasana,* and rested quietly on our backs for the last five minutes of class. My muscles protested against all the unaccustomed exercise, but I was energized. Maybe Dr. Lim at UCLA knew what he was talking about. I walked out of Sublime Yoga with a new pink rubber mat, a six-foot-long woven strap, and a little plastic tag with my membership number.

After a shower at home, I changed into jeans, a long-sleeved T-shirt, and sweater and demolished the leftover coleslaw and *kasha varnishkes* from the night before. By twelve thirty I headed on the 405 south toward Harriet's house in Brentwood.

I took Sunset Boulevard west to Bundy Drive, turned right for a half mile to her large Tudor style home, and parked in a circular driveway hidden from the street by lush landscaping. Not one flyer, throwaway paper, or business card lay on the ground. By the moisture in the soil, I guessed the gardener recently watered and cleaned up, just as he had been doing for the last ten months.

I braced myself before turning the lock with the keys Abernathy had given me. What would I find? What would I smell? Poking my head inside, I took small, cautious sniffs of the air. Thankfully, the house harbored no unpleasant odors.

At least a couple weeks of mail, dropped through the slot in the door, littered the hardwood floor. Several months' worth of envelopes and papers sat in cardboard boxes on a round table in the middle of the walnut paneled foyer, waiting for me to sift through them.

I closed the door and flipped a light switch. An

iron chandelier with alabaster globes turned golden in the gloom. Directly in front of me a dark staircase led straight to the second floor. A powder room stood opposite the stairs. A painting hung on the foyer wall of a fair-haired toddler holding a toy fire engine. He bore Harriet's smile and sensitive eyes.

The living room to the right gave off an English vibe, with hand-rubbed plaster and a ceiling coffered in more dark wood. Harriet loved Jane Austen and Paul McCartney.

A pair of overstuffed chairs, upholstered with red chintz roses, sat on either side of a game table, and two green leather sofas flanked a large stone fireplace. Photos of Jonah, Harriet, and Harriet's family lined the wooden beam serving as a mantel.

Where was Nathan's picture?

Framed paintings hung slightly askew on the walls as if shifted by an earthquake. Didn't Abernathy say he thought things looked a little messy?

Continuing on to the right, a door at the end of the living room opened to a library, which also served as an office. Books stuffed the floor-to-ceiling dark shelves on the far wall. An antique rolltop desk sat in one corner and a rectangular table with six oak chairs took over the center of the room.

Two volumes lay on the floor. I read the titles as I picked them up and placed them on the library table. *Communicating With Spirits: Contacting the Dead* and *Aura Reading for Dummies*. Poor Harriet. She must have been aching to be with her deceased family. Just how far did she take this obsession?

The papers and envelopes lying in the desk were carelessly mixed up, not the way I'd expect Harriet's desk to look. When we did our homework together, I used to tease her about the precise way she organized her notebook by subject and date. She never turned in an assignment with sloppy handwriting. She wrote round, neat cursive and dotted her I's with hearts. Someone else had disturbed Harriet's desk.

I sorted through the mess, looking for an address book, and finally found a small one bound in blue leather with only a few names. No person on this list missed her for ten months?

The left side of the foyer led to a formal dining room. Two heavy branched silver candelabras, now tarnished, stood in the center of a long table covered in dust. A massive china cabinet with a curved glass front displayed dozens of pieces of fine porcelain. I winced at the thought of having to inventory each and every item.

A vintage design hid a state-of-the-art kitchen with white AGA appliances, black granite countertops, white cabinets, and a black and white checkerboard floor. A person could easily prepare meals for a hundred people in this space. When we were teens, Harriet and I baked package brownies in my bubbie's small kitchen. Heaviness gripped my chest as I guessed Harriet seldom used more than one of the eight burners on her fancy range.

Beyond the laundry room sat a maid's room and bath. About twenty cardboard cartons full of God knows what sat in the middle of the area. I'd have to open and catalog the contents of each one.

Something niggled at me.

Obviously Harriet didn't employ live-in staff, but she still needed someone to take care of this big house. Did the cleaner carry a key? Why hadn't she discovered Harriet's body?

I moved into a family room on the other side of the kitchen, filled with comfortable furniture and a large-screen television. Next to a VCR stood a neat stack of old video cassettes: *Pinocchio, Willy Wonka and the Chocolate Factory, Pippi Longstocking,* and *The Muppets.* Apparently Jonah's movies.

I steeled myself to go upstairs. Who knew what sort of unpleasant surprised awaited me? The finial on top of the newel post wobbled a little in my hand as I began to slowly sniff my way up the stairs. On the second floor, I peered down the wide hallway in both directions. Through an open door on the far end, directly above the living room and library, I spotted the large master suite, the place where Harriet's body lay for ten months. I'd go there last.

In the opposite direction, rooms sat on either side of the hallway. Another door at the end turned out to be a long, narrow linen closet. The shelves inside held piles of neatly ironed white sheets and stacks of towels in pastel colors. Blankets and pillows filled the bottom cupboards.

A cheery yellow guest suite greeted me behind the first door. Abernathy said Harriet had become a recluse. When did she last entertain visitors?

I stopped in my tracks as I passed through the door across the hall. Children's books, stuffed animals, Legos, and toy trucks filled the light blue room. A car-shaped bed, painted with a red racing stripe, sat in the corner under Lindberg's famous painting of an angel guarding two children crossing a bridge.

Harriett had preserved Jonah's bedroom for

more than fifteen years, but this shrine to the boy's memory appeared disarrayed. One drawer gaped slightly open, and the small mattress sat somewhat askew.

I steeled myself to enter Harriet's bedroom. A portrait of Jonah sitting in Harriet's lap hung in a gilt frame on the taupe walls. Opposite the doorway a queen-sized bed with a headboard upholstered in rose velvet dominated the space. Black polka dots covered the matching duvet. Black dots also covered the carpet and every other surface. I looked closer. Dead flies scattered like dark cornflakes around the room. My stomach revolted and I ran to the guest room just in time to puke in the white toilet.

At the sink I swished water in my mouth, rinsed my face, grabbed a yellow towel, and regarded myself in the mirror.

Calm down, Martha. Take a yoga breath. You can do this.

I moved down the hallway toward Harriet's room, noticing that the dead flies also littered the dark hardwood floor. I stepped gingerly across the dotted beige carpet to a door standing wide open and forced myself to look inside a closet as big as my bedroom. The shelves and hangers filled with women's clothes lined three of the walls. I found no trace of a man's clothes or belongings.

A built-in bureau stood in the center of the closet. Nearby, a huge section of broadloom had been removed where Harriet's body must have lain. A dark, greasy spot stained the exposed subflooring. Clearly I'd have to replace everything before the house could be sold.

At first glance, the closet seemed orderly, just the

way Harriet would have left it. When we were girls, she often borrowed the cool pair of jeans with the hole in the knee from my closet. She used to chide me for being disorganized and messy. "I can never find anything in here," she'd complain.

On closer inspection, a few items lay on the carpet, and a floor-length gown hung out of place between her jackets and coats. Someone had searched this area after Harriet's death. How long after?

I stepped carefully around the missing carpet. Some nice pieces of ladies' costume jewelry sat in the top drawer of the bureau, but the expensive pieces listed on the insurance rider were absent. Also missing were any items belonging to Nathan. Why didn't Harriet keep something of his as a keepsake—a watch or a pair of cufflinks? After all, she kept everything of Jonah's.

Harriet would've been mortified for anyone to see her home in such a revolting condition. I retrieved a vacuum cleaner from the linen closet at the other end of the hallway and spent the next half hour getting rid of the fly carcasses. Before I left the house, I gathered up the mail from the foyer and carried the boxes to my car.

On the drive back to Encino, I reviewed my next steps. Make an inventory of every item in her house. Arrange for the appraisal of her possessions. Hire an estate manager to organize a sale. Hire Crusher's guys to secure the house in case the intruder decided to return.

The question of the absent housekeeper bothered me. Why hadn't she discovered poor Harriet's body? I needed to call Abernathy.

CHAPTER 5

By the time I returned to the San Fernando Valley, Larry the Locksmith had locked his doors and I was too tired to hunt for another key shop. I headed straight for home and last night's salad from Trader Joe's.

Bumper meowed and scolded me for my late arrival, so I let him sit next to me on the sofa while I ate with a plastic takeout fork. He sniffed at my clothing, jumped up on the back of the sofa and nosed my hair. Then he yowled and leaped to the floor, staring from a distance. Bumper possessed a keen and discerning nose. Although I didn't detect unpleasant odors in Harriet's house, the scent of death must have hitchhiked home on my body.

After retrieving the boxes of mail from the car and dumping them in the living room, I headed straight for my second shower of the day. Then I climbed into my cozy blue flannel pajamas, sat on the sofa wrapped in a blue and white quilt, and wrote a to-do list with a call to Abernathy at the top. I reached his voice mail.

"Mr. Abernathy, Deke, this is Martha Rose. You

were right about Harriet's house being disturbed. Someone's been inside. The private Brentwood Security Patrol has been useless. I'm arranging for twenty-four-hour protection on the premises. And something puzzles me. Didn't Harriet employ a housekeeper? Why didn't she discover the body? Where is she now? Please call me at your earliest convenience. Thanks."

The measly salad wasn't enough, so I boiled a cup of spicy Indian tea with milk, sliced an apple, and cut a hunk of sharp cheddar cheese from an orange brick of Tillamook. Then I called Crusher at his bike shop.

"Hey, babe. Change your mind about dessert?"

Oh Lord, I'm tempted!

I laughed. "Not yet. Listen, Yossi. I inspected Harriet's house today."

"How'd it go?"

"Really creepy. Looks like someone searched through her things. Her good jewelry is missing, maybe more. Can I hire a few Eagles to secure the place?"

The playfulness left his voice. "I told you. Anything you want. How long will you need them for?"

"It may take a couple of weeks. The good news is, money's not a problem. I'll pay whatever you think is fair."

The sound of shuffling some papers came from the background. "Two shifts. Twelve on, twelve off. How's fifty an hour sound?"

"Totally doable. When can they start?

"Give me the address. I'll send Malo over tonight. Do you have a spare key to the house?"

"I'll get a duplicate made tomorrow." I gave him Harriet's number on North Bundy Drive.

"Need anything else?"

"I don't know, but this is good for starters. I'll be in touch. And thanks."

Next I telephoned my best friend, Lucy.

"About time you called me, girlfriend. I've been dying to ask what you've been up to. How did the meeting with the lawyer go?"

"Gosh, that was two days ago." I filled her in on my appointment with Abernathy and my trip to the cemetery. "Harriet's funeral is scheduled for Monday. I also visited her house today."

"Ew. Her body laid there for ten months. The place must have been totally disgusting."

I didn't want to think about the flies. "It wasn't as bad as I feared. Some jewelry seems to be stolen. I can't be sure. Maybe Harriet kept it in a safe. I'll conduct a more thorough search."

Lucy sounded worried. "If things are missing, do you think it's wise to stay in the house by yourself?"

"I've hired a couple of Eagles for security twenty-four/seven. I won't be alone."

"Need help?"

"Yeah, I need to create an inventory of every item in her house. Can you ask Richie to recommend some kind of database software I can use?" Richie, Lucy's middle son, trained as a computer engineer. He also happened to be gay and my daughter Quincy's best childhood friend.

"No problem. I can loan you the bar-code software Ray uses to keep track of inventory at his business." Lucy's husband, Ray, an auto mechanic, built a string of successful auto shops in LA. "I don't mean to be nosy or anything, but you know me and antique stores. I love going through old stuff. Want me to tag along?"

God bless Lucy, always willing to lend a hand. "Absolutely! Why keep all the fun to myself?"

"Okay. Birdie and I will meet you at your house tomorrow at nine with all the inventory stuff. Then we can drive to Brentwood."

"I'll have coffee."

I picked up Harriet's blue leather address book and opened it. Only fifteen names were listed. I found my name with my old Brentwood address and phone number. Lines were drawn through eight of the names, including Herschel and Lilly Gordon, Harriet's deceased parents. I looked under "O," hoping to find members of Nathan's family. There was a Henry Oliver, in Newport, Rhode Island. Written below was Estella Oliver in Pawtucket at the other end of the state. I decided to take the chance they'd still be up at ten Eastern time. I didn't know how they were related to Nathan, but I'd soon find out. I dialed Henry's number first and left a message on his voice mail. I got luckier with Estella.

She answered the phone with a certain Yankee straightforwardness. "This better be important, it's after ten at night."

I introduced myself as Harriet's executor.

Estella remained silent for a moment. "Harriet's dead?"

"Yes." I briefly explained the circumstances.

"Too bad. How long did you say her body just lay there?"

"Ten months." I informed her of the funeral arrangements on Monday.

"Don't know if I can travel on such short notice. Did she leave a will?"

Wow. Cut to the important stuff, why don't you? "She did. May I ask how you were related?"

"I'm Nathan's sister. Harriet got everything when the courts declared Nathan legally dead. Was I mentioned in her will?"

"Not specifically, no."

"Well, she kept some items belonging to our family. I'm sure Nathan would've wanted me to inherit them."

I'll bet. "There might be some leeway with things not earmarked for specific donation. What did you have in mind?"

Estella was all business. "A pair of silver candelabras, several place settings of antique Spode china, and an old quilt. Plus some silver serving pieces and maybe a few old books."

Even though Harriet didn't name Estella in her bequests, I felt the heirlooms should stay in the family. "Are there other relatives who might also have a claim?"

"Only myself and my younger brother, Henry, but I doubt he'd want those old things. I can fly out next week and pack everything up."

You're moving awfully fast, lady. You want to grab the heirlooms before anybody else can ask for them. And yet you can't make time to bury your sister-in-law?

"I won't be making any decisions until after the funeral."

"What funeral?"

I understood why Estella may have been overlooked in the will. "Harriet's," I reminded her.

"Oh. Right. So when do you think you'll decide?"

"I'll be sure to let you know. And I'm sorry for your loss."

I should have saved my breath. Estella had already hung up.

I tried the four remaining numbers in Harriet's

small address book. I left three messages and talked briefly to a woman who turned out to be Harriet's old college roommate, Isabel Casco.

Isabel sounded like a habitual smoker because her voice registered ten octaves lower than normal. "I can't believe Harriet's dead." Cough, cough.

"I'm contacting everyone in her address book. When did you last speak to her?"

"Oh gawd, I'd say almost two years ago. Why?"

I tried to think of a polite way of asking why nobody cared about Harriet. "I'm wondering how she lay dead for more than ten months without anyone knowing. Do you have any ideas?"

Isabel took a long drag off a cigarette. "I moved to Los Angeles in the mid-nineties just before Harriet lost her son. I did my best to help her through that terrible time. Then Nathan disappeared and she really needed a friend. But about two years ago, she stopped returning my calls and just slipped off the radar. Now I'm sorry I didn't try harder. How did she die?"

"Her body lay there for so long, the coroner couldn't tell."

Isabel went into a coughing fit lasting for several seconds. She finally came up for air. "Dear Lord. Bad luck followed Harriet everywhere. Just let me know when the funeral is and I'll be there."

Unless I heard from the others, Isabel and I would be the only ones from Harriet's address book to bury her. I'd ask Abernathy who else should be contacted. At this rate, I'd need Crusher for the *minyan* at her funeral after all.

I poured myself the rest of the Chianti from the bottle I opened last night and put the flash drive from Harriet's insurance packet into my laptop.

Dozens of photographs appeared and I scanned for the objects Estella wanted. Item number five listed a pair of repoussé sterling silver candelabras dated from fifteenth-century Spain. On close examination of the image, I realized they were the ones sitting on Harriet's dining room table, dusty and tarnished.

A brief caption under the photo stated the candelabras came to Newport, Rhode Island, from Spain via Holland with Jacob José Oliver and his wife, Estella, in the 1600s. A photo of an article written in the *Newport Mercury* mentioned the Oliver family loaned the candelabras to the famous Touro Synagogue in Newport for its dedication in 1763— thirteen years before the American Revolution.

The Olivers were among many Sephardic Jews who escaped the Spanish inquisition at the end of the 1500s and found shelter in Holland. Some of their descendants immigrated to the British colonies in North America in the 1600s. By the time of the American Revolution in 1776, the Sephardic community had been established in Newport for over 100 years. The Touro Synagogue, the first Jewish house of worship in North America, now stood as a national historic site.

Even though the candelabras would no longer be handed down from Nathan to his son, Jonah, this treasure belonged with a family member. If Estella spoke the truth and Henry didn't want them, I hoped she didn't intend to sell these precious artifacts for the fifty thousand they were worth.

Item number fourteen consisted of a set of antique Spode china. Another potential windfall for Estella. An image of a beautiful blue and white

Chinoiserie plate looked like the porcelain in Harriet's china cabinet. Another photo showed an old receipt with spiky cursive made out in 1833 to Henrique Adelan Oliver for the purchase of a service for fifty people. *Fifty people at a sit-down dinner? How many pounds of brisket would a person have to prepare?* On the bottom of the receipt a note in bolder cursive read, *"Para Sara, mi novia encantadora"* (for Sara, my enchanting bride).

Clearly the Olivers were both wealthy and prominent. Sara undoubtedly retained a staff to prepare and serve so much food. Although several pieces hadn't survived the intervening 170 years, the remaining collection appraised at $40,000.

Now I knew a little more about Nathan Oliver. He was a *Grandee*, a descendant of wealthy Sephardic Jewish colonists, among the first families in America. His roots ran deeper than most. At Brown University in Providence, Rhode Island, he met Harriet Gordon, a Jewish girl from California, whose family carried no such credentials.

Nathan may have loved Harriet, but I sensed Estella bore no such feelings. Perhaps she thought a sweet, middle-class girl from the Pico-Robertson area of Los Angeles and the daughter of Holocaust survivors didn't deserve the oldest son of an oldest son. I hated the thought of Harriet suffering her disdain.

I scrolled through dozens of shots cataloging Harriet's assortment of antique watches, a half million dollars in jewelry, and an impressive collection of priceless books dating back to the eighteenth century. Another group of images showed items of

American folk art, including rare Native American baskets and Early American wooden toys.

A tsunami of fatigue hit me and my vision began to blur before I reached the end, so I sent the whole file to the printer and started getting ready for bed. The phone rang and I hurriedly spit out a mouthful of toothpaste before rushing to answer.

"Deke here, returning your call. I hope this isn't too late."

"No, I'm glad you called me back." I wiped my mouth with a towel. "I went to Harriet's today and I think you're right. Someone rummaged through her place. Did the police search the premises and disturb things?"

"No. The coroner couldn't tell for sure because of the state of her remains, but he said Harriet probably dropped dead of a heart attack. So the police found no reason to search."

If the police didn't disturb the house, who did? "Didn't Harriet have domestic help?"

Abernathy cleared his throat. "Yes, a woman who came in five days a week."

"Yet she didn't discover Harriet's body?"

"Apparently Harriet let her go around the time of her death. Our accountant received instructions to cut her a final paycheck, which she sent to her via FedEx."

I began to get irritated. Nobody bothered to check on Harriet after that? Especially those who were responsible for her day-to-day maintenance and financial well-being? "Nobody became concerned when Harriet didn't hire another cleaner? A woman in her position would have needed help with such a large house."

Abernathy yawned. "Look. I would've been worried if I'd known. But our accounting department took care of the day-to-day matters of paying Harriet's bills."

I ran my fingers through my hair in exasperation. "Did the housekeeper have a key?"

"If she did, I assume she returned it when Harriet let her go."

Did the housekeeper come back with a key to loot Harriet's house?

I struggled to hide the irritation in my voice. "For heaven's sake. Has anyone spoken to the woman?"

"I gave the police her contact information."

I didn't like the casual way everyone wrote off Harriet's death. A very wealthy woman died from unknown causes and nobody seemed suspicious? Now some of her things seemed to be missing. My anger grew with my unease. What if something bad happened to my friend?

I understood from experience the people who knew the most were often those who worked behind the scenes. "Can you e-mail me the contact info for the housekeeper and the gardener?"

Deke sounded weary. "Sure, if it'll make you feel better."

Obviously nobody else really cared about Harriet, or the fact her house may have been looted. I cared. I'd find out the circumstances surrounding my old friend's death.

"I spoke with only two people in Harriet's address book. Are there others who should be informed about the funeral on Monday?"

Abernathy yawned again. "I'll ask my assistant,

Nina, to contact everyone connected to Harriet's finances and her philanthropy. Will that help?"

"Yes. Thanks for calling me back."

I crawled into bed pissed, worried, and exhausted. I closed my eyes and dark thoughts, like hundreds of black flies, buzzed in my head.

CHAPTER 6

Before Lucy and Birdie arrived Friday morning, I ran over to Larry the Locksmith and Bea's Bakery to pick up a chocolate *babka* for this morning and a raisin challah for Shabbat. They showed up at nine, just as the coffeepot stopped gurgling and blew out the last bit of steam.

Lucy wore her working clothes—jeans, with a crease pressed down the leg, and a dark blue cashmere cardigan over a blue and white gingham blouse. A red bandana covered her orange curls, and gold gypsy hoops hung from her ears. Under her arm she held a cardboard carton with an iPad and some electronic equipment.

I pointed to the box. "What did you bring?"

Lucy pulled out her tablet and waved it. "This has a bar-code generator app. You type in the name or data you want to use and a code is generated. Tap a button and the program sends the code wirelessly to this printer, which then spews out a label to stick on your item."

The simplicity of the system impressed me. "How do I decipher the code?"

She picked up a small metal wand. "You use the handheld scanner to read the bar code. You can print out a hard copy of the master inventory with all the details."

"I love technology. This'll save me a ton of work."

Birdie always dressed for work in her blue denim overalls and white T-shirt. She cut the *babka* while I poured three cups of Italian roast. We settled in the living room and my friends listened intently as I brought them up to date on my conversation last night with Abernathy.

Birdie tugged on her braid. "Heavens, dear, do you think the maid came back after Harriet's death and poked around her things?"

I shrugged and swallowed a bite of heavenly pastry laced with ribbons of hard chocolate. "The intruder must have been someone with a key because Abernathy said the police forced their way in."

Birdie sipped her coffee. "Are you sure there were no signs of a B and E?" My 75-year-old friend never missed an episode of *Law & Order* or *CSI* and spoke forensics as a second language.

"I didn't search very hard yesterday. Mainly I wanted to get a feel for the place. Today we'll go methodically through as many rooms as we can. We'll find out if any of the insured pieces are missing."

Lucy grinned and rubbed her hands together. "Oh, this sounds like Nancy Drew. Did Harriet have an attic? A basement? Shall we take flashlights?"

A half hour later we hit the 405 south toward Brentwood. We pulled up into Harriet's driveway in Lucy's vintage black caddy with the shark fins. Malo jumped out of his maroon SUV and headed our way, wearing a black leather jacket and heavy motorcycle boots. This pumped-up Latino sported a long black ponytail and a series of short black vertical lines tattooed on his cheeks. Crusher told me Malo operated an earthmover by day. At night he played drums in a pickup band. They occasionally performed in a biker bar called Bubba's—also known by the regulars as Tits and Tequila.

He sized up the three of us, then grinned at me. "You Crusher's lady?"

Although it's perfectly fine for me to tell Lucy and Birdie everything, I hoped Crusher never revealed we once slept together or that he wanted to marry me. On the other hand, who knew what guys talked about? If I did, I might not have so many trust issues. Or maybe I'd have more.

I offered Malo a handshake. "I'm Martha, and these are my friends Lucy and Birdie. Thanks for agreeing to work on such short notice. I'm sorry you spent the cold night in your car." I reached in my purse and handed him the duplicate key. "From now on, you can stay inside. Just pass this along when you go off shift."

The noisy guttering of an engine announced the arrival of a motorcycle.

"Sounds like my replacement is here."

Carl, the youngest member of the Eagles, parked his bike and removed a helmet from his sandy-colored hair. His black leather jacket had a purple "VE" on the back for Valley Eagles. Carl spotted Birdie and grinned. Without a word, he strode over to her, bent his six-foot frame, gently encircled her with his arms, and twirled her around as she whooped in delight.

Four months ago Carl helped clear my neighbor, Ed, from a murder charge. He met Birdie and immediately bonded with her because she reminded him of his grandmother. She, in turn, adored Carl and treated him as the child she'd never had.

Birdie patted the shoulder of his leathers with a blue-veined hand. "Put me down before I fall, dear."

Carl set her down gently and kissed her forehead. Birdie put an arm around his waist.

I walked over to them. "Hey, Carl, are you going to work this security day shift? Don't you have a job?" Carl earned a degree from Caltech in computer science. He developed fraud detection and prevention software for the SEC. He also carried a gun.

"Crusher said you need help, so I volunteered. I can hook up my computer anywhere." He stared at the ground. "So, you and Crusher. Are you two, you know, a thing now?"

Malo paid particular attention.

See what I mean? Who can tell what guys talk about?

I crossed my arms. "I thought Crusher was dating one of the Kardashians."

"Dude!" Malo howled with laughter and slapped his knee. "Crusher warned me you were tough."

Before he left, Malo wanted to examine the house in the daylight, so I took them all on a quick tour to get the layout. In each room, the two men checked the windows and doors. Everything was locked tight.

The five of us ended up in Harriet's large closet. I pointed to the hole in the carpet and the stain on the floor. "This is where she died."

Birdie turned green and walked out to the hallway.

Lucy followed her. "If it's all the same to you,

Martha, let's start downstairs first. I don't think Birdie's ready for this room."

Good thing I vacuumed up the flies. "Of course. Let's go back downstairs."

Two sets of biker boots clumped heavily down the stairs. One of them slowed down to help Birdie.

When we got to the foyer, Malo started to leave, then stopped. "What about the garage?"

I'd completely forgotten about the garage. "I've never actually been inside."

We walked to the kitchen and found a door I'd overlooked the day before. Malo flipped the dead bolt and turned the knob. Overhead lights flickered on in the ceiling of a spacious and nearly empty three-car garage. White cupboards lined one wall and held household cleaning supplies, a floor scrubber, a carpet cleaner, a shovel, a ladder, and a child's fishing pole. A late-model black Lexus sat in the middle of the nearly empty space. No matter how much money she enjoyed, Harriet never would have owned a German car.

My own garage bulged with junk. Piles of dusty sacks and boxes of stuff accumulated over the last twenty years reached the rafters, along with old furniture, household detritus, and half-empty paint cans. Before she moved to Boston, my daughter, Quincy, claimed half the garage as her free storage facility.

"The garage door locks electronically," said Carl. "Nobody can get in without a code."

Birdie twisted the end of her white braid. "Well, now we can be certain of the POE."

Lucy's head jerked up. "Huh? What's *POE*?"

Every eye focused on Birdie.

"Point of Entry, dear. The intruder must have used a key on the front door."

Carl chuckled and Lucy rolled her eyes.

We decided to work our way from one end of the downstairs to the other starting in the library. Carl set up his laptop on the table, and Lucy plugged in her equipment. I reached into my purse and retrieved the insurance rider listing every piece we needed to locate and label.

I shook my head. "I don't know how a private person can collect books like the ones we're about to look for, but these are truly treasures." I showed them the list.

Birdie gasped. "Are they real?"

I nodded. "I know, right? The insurance company says they're real."

Lucy said, "We're not going to be putting sticky labels on those."

We began to search the library shelves for the four-volume original edition of *Memoir, Correspondence & Miscellanies: From the Papers of Thomas Jefferson,* published in 1829; ten volumes of *The Works of John Adams, Second President of the United States,* published 1850-1856; and *The Private Life of the Late Benjamin Franklin,* French edition published in 1791.

Since Lucy reached nearly six feet tall, she took the job of reading the top shelves. "Was Harriet interested in Early American history?"

To accommodate her arthritic knees, Birdie sat on a chair and inspected the lower shelves. "Well, I guess so. Consider the books we're hunting for. All authored by the Founding Fathers."

I scanned titles on the middle shelves. "Harriet majored in history at Brown. She collected Early

Americana in general—wooden toys, watches, Native American baskets."

An hour later we had finished our search of the bookshelves and sat at one end of the library table while Carl worked quietly at the other.

My heart sank. "A fortune in first editions is missing."

Carl glanced up from his computer. "What were those titles?" I showed him the list and he started typing. "Give me a minute." He tapped at his computer and the three of us stared at him. He finally stopped. "Nothing with those titles has been submitted for authentication or sold in the last year through auction houses or any other legitimate venue."

"So the perp must be hanging on to the goods unless he took them to a fence." That was Birdie, bless her. "Shouldn't we call this in?"

Carl smiled and gazed down at his keyboard. "I'm going back to work."

The loss of such important books felt devastating. "This is just the first place we've explored. There are many other rooms to go through. Harriet might've kept them somewhere else in the house, somewhere not out in the open."

Lucy swept her hand toward the shelves. "So, what are you going to do with the rest of these? Your friend read everything from historical novels to books on spiritism. Looks like she was into the occult."

I shook my head. "It doesn't sound like the practical and pragmatic Harriet I knew, but profound grief can do weird things to people."

A metal clink and a *thwap* came from the foyer. Carl stood and motioned for us to be quiet. He took a gun out of his leather laptop carrier and walked through the living room, both hands on the weapon. He reached the foyer, relaxed, and tucked the gun into the front of his waistband.

Birdie whispered, "I sure hope he has the safety on."

"It's just the mail. Came in through the slot on the front door." He returned to the library and handed me a couple of invitations to open Visa accounts and a flyer for Pepe's Salvadorian restaurant on Wilshire Boulevard.

Lucy stood and moved along the wall, tapping with her knuckles. "Maybe there's a secret compartment in the library where she stashed the books."

Is Lucy serious? "I don't think so. Three of these are outside walls and the fourth shares a two-sided fireplace with the living room. Just where would such a compartment be?"

Lucy wouldn't give up. "It's true, the two outside walls with windows aren't thick enough. But the wall at the end, the one covered in bookshelves, could be hiding something." She pushed on the shelves and knuckled the dark paneling from one end to the other. After five minutes of knocking high and low, she gave up and shook her hand. "Yeah, maybe you're right."

Birdie sat at the desk and checked the drawers, gathering all the papers for me to sort through at home. Lucy and I went into the living room to examine and catalog the five framed paintings.

"Are these valuable?" Lucy asked.

"I think I read none of them are worth more than ten thousand."

The paintings hung askew. I lifted the first painting; nothing hidden on the wall behind it. I reached to put the painting back and my finger caught on a sharp edge.

"Holy crap, Lucy. Take a look at this. The paper seal on the back is slit open on the bottom edge."

Lucy helped me take down the rest of the art. "Someone tampered with all of them. What do you suppose was in there?"

I looked at my friend. At this point she knew almost as much as I did. "Obama's birth certificate?"

CHAPTER 7

On the way to the maid's room, Birdie picked up one of the candelabras from the table. "This is very old silver and very heavy. You can see it's been around for a long time by the nicks and dents along the bottom."

I examined the second candelabra. "This one has a big dent in the bottom. Someone must've dropped it."

We moved to the maid's room. Lucy set up the bar-code equipment. Then she pulled down the carton from the top of the nearest pile and set it on the floor. The top of the box had already been slit open. I pulled back the flaps to find well-worn and stained white linen tablecloths and napkins with the letter "G" monogrammed in white thread. I looked at my friends. "These would have been precious to Harriet. They were hand-embroidered by her mother, Lilly Gordon."

"They're old and stained," said Lucy. "What are you going to do with them?"

I sighed and wrote *Donate* with a Sharpie on the outside of the box.

Lucy lifted down the second box. "This is heavy. Feels like books."

The seal was broken on this box as well. Several oversized volumes of the Talmud rested inside. Harriet's father, Herschel Gordon, and my uncle Isaac belonged to a group that studied a different page of the Talmud each week. I wrote on the outside of the box, *Donate, American Jewish University Library.*

We discovered two sets of fancy Bavarian china. I once helped Harriet and her mother bring them out of storage for use during Passover week, one pattern for meat and one for dairy. Harriet had whispered, "Just more stuff to keep clean."

I marked each of the boxes and Lucy stuck bar codes on them.

Lucy knocked on every wall, looking for a hidden cache. She even tugged at the corners of the wall-to-wall carpeting, but nothing came loose.

Birdie laughed. "Heavens, dear. If I were going to hide something, I certainly wouldn't choose the maid's room."

We moved into the kitchen and opened every drawer and cupboard. Lucy threw her hands up. "Do you really want to bar-code everything in here? There must be a jillion items."

"You're right. I'll hire an estate manager to sort them into lots for appraisal and sale."

I noted a couple of boxes of package brownies sitting on the shelf of the walk-in pantry and remembered, with a pang, the times Harriet and I made brownies during sleepovers.

Lucy balanced on a wooden Windsor chair and reached into the back of every upper cabinet.

I put my hands on my hips. "What in the world are you looking for up there?"

"Dang if I know."

We drifted into the family room and Birdie pointed to the pile of video cassettes. "My, these are old."

"Jonah's movies," I said.

Birdie read the titles and shook her head sadly. "Heartbreaking."

The media wall held a large flat-screen television and video components. Native American baskets and antique wooden toys sat on open shelves around the room, valuable items from the insurance rider.

Carl's heavy boots thudded on the kitchen floor. "Anyone hungry? It's after one."

I found the flyer for the Salvadorian restaurant and ordered bean and cheese *pupusas,* fried yucca roots, chicken tamales in banana leaves, and fried *platanos* with sugar for dessert. A half hour later Pepe's delivered two huge grocery bags full of hot food smelling like cumin, garlic, onions, and a hint of cinnamon.

After stuffing our faces, we returned to the family room and carefully checked each basket against the list. I spotted a polychrome black on white basket shaped like a large pot with an opening just big enough for a hand. I carefully lifted it. "This was made over one hundred years ago by Dat So La Lee, a famous Washoe Indian weaver. It's valued at one million dollars."

Birdie softly touched the dried grass coils. "Amazing. This looks so well preserved."

Lucy picked up the printout. "A penciled note next to the photo says Dat So La Lee's main supporter and promoter was Abe Cohn, a distant cousin of Nathan Oliver's. I wonder how long this has been in the family."

I turned the basket in my hands and something slid around inside. "What's this?" My heart sped up as I pulled out a small key. I turned it over, looking for some kind of identification. "What do you think this is for?"

"It's too small for a door." Birdie furrowed her brow. "Maybe this opens a cupboard or a safe."

"Or a jewelry box," said Lucy.

I added the key to Harriet's key ring.

We carefully examined and cataloged the rest of the baskets. A photo of an auction receipt stated Harriet paid $350,000 for a Mono-Paiute polychrome basket, shaped like a large salad bowl and woven by Nellie Jameson Washington in the early twentieth century.

"Who knew baskets could be so valuable?" Birdie twisted her braid. "Don't you think it's odd your friend Harriet collected different kinds of Americana, yet she didn't collect any quilts?"

"Birdie has a point," said Lucy. "I'd at least expect to see a Baltimore Album. I heard one sold at auction about ten years ago for three hundred thousand." Baltimore Albums were a style of quilt popular among ladies of leisure in the nineteenth century with lots of intricate appliqués featuring flowers, baskets, and birds. Each block in the quilt featured a different usually symmetrical design.

"Yes, I do find that strange."

After we accounted for every basket on the list, we moved to the antique wooden toys. The more valuable pieces in Harriet's collection were a horse and wagon pull toy, a sailboat with some of the original paint and spinning tops, including an antique Hanukkah dreidel from Portugal with Hebrew letters painted on each of the four sides.

Birdie looked at her watch. "It's four, dear. We should get on the freeway and head home."

I nodded. "It's been a long day."

Lucy wagged her fingers in an air quote. "No problemo. I had fun, considering." She looked in the direction of Harriet's bedroom and her voice dropped a notch. "We still have the upstairs to do."

We said good-bye to Carl and headed for Encino. They dropped me off at my house around sundown. Shabbat had officially started. I rushed inside to phone my daughter, Quincy, who lived in Boston, and left a greeting on her voice mail. Next I called my uncle Isaac, my mother's brother. He took care of me, my mother, and bubbie the whole time I grew up. Uncle Isaac was the only father I ever knew.

"Shabbat shalom, Uncle."

"Good *Shabbos, faigela.* What's new?"

I briefly told him about Harriet, but left out the grisly parts.

"Oy! What a *ganze shandeh.* Such a nice girl. I knew her father, may he rest in peace."

"Will you come to her funeral? She needs a *minyan.*"

"Of course. I'll bring Morty and the boys." Uncle Isaac played poker every week with his seventy- and eighty-year-old friends. At their age they were experts at funeral prayers. Poker and Talmud. A person should live a balanced life.

"So, *nu*? What's going on with you? You still seeing the detective? What about that big Jewish fellow, Yossi Levy?" Uncle Isaac always referred to Crusher as "that big Jewish fellow." Crusher impressed my uncle when he confessed to using his do-rag as a religious head covering. At Shabbat dinner four months ago, we were impressed by Crusher's knowledge of Torah, his "hidden depths" as he called it.

"I haven't heard from Arlo in months, Uncle. He dumped me, remember?"

"But I thought he changed his mind."

Until he found out I slept with Crusher. "We had some issues."

"What about Levy?"

Ah yes, what about Levy? I didn't tell my uncle Crusher wanted to marry me. Knowing my uncle, I'd never hear the end of it. Uncle Isaac meant well, but I didn't want him to pressure me. Better to be alone than with the wrong person.

"I see Yossi from time to time."

"Okay, okay, I know when to stop asking. *A glick auf dir.*" Good luck to you.

I laughed. "I love you, too, Uncle."

The house seemed unusually quiet as I covered my head with a sequined blue scarf. Lighting two candles in my bubbie's silver candleholders, I recited the Sabbath blessing and thought wistfully about spending Shabbat with someone I loved. Did Harriet feel the same way in her isolation? Did she ever put pure white candles in those fifty-thousand-dollar candelabras and recite the blessing in her big, empty house? I felt lonely enough for both of us.

The doorbell pulled me out of my reverie. I looked through the peephole. Crusher smiled at me from the other side of the door. He wore a brown tweed sport jacket, a blue shirt open at the neck, and a traditional black skullcap instead of a do-rag.

Oh no. I didn't know if I was ready for this. The only other time he'd come over in nice clothes, they ended up on my bedroom floor.

I opened the door and he handed me a bouquet of pink roses and stepped inside. In his other hand he held a bag from Brent's. "I figured you'd be tired from working all day, so I brought Shabbat dinner." He noticed the Sabbath candles flickering on the dining room table and when he looked back at me, his eyes glistened. "You feel like home."

I sensed my defenses evaporating. "I'm all dusty and yucky."

He gently tilted my chin and kissed me softly on the lips. Electricity sizzled down my spine.

His deep voice cracked. "Go do what you have to do and I'll get dinner ready."

My heart sped as I rushed to my bedroom. After a quick shower, I blew my hair dry and rubbed my body with fragrant oils. I chose a pink silk blouse and a long black skirt. Twenty minutes later I took a deep breath and walked into the living room.

Crusher waited for me in one of the big chairs. When I walked in, he stood and looked at me for a full five seconds. "God, you're beautiful."

Dishes of food rested on a white tablecloth at my dining room table. We sat and he opened a prayer book with a scuffed black cover. According to tradition, he chanted in Hebrew the *Eshet chayil,* from the book of Proverbs. Heat rose in my cheeks as he began the love song. *An excellent wife, who can find? She is more precious than pearls.*

Then he raised the cup of wine for the *Kiddush,* the blessing that ushered in the Sabbath. He took a sip and handed the cup to me. The essence of all the Sabbaths and all the holidays for thousands of unbroken years lay distilled in the taste of sweetened Concord grapes. After he blessed the raisin challah I bought at Bea's Bakery, he tore off two pieces, sprinkled them with salt, and handed one to me.

A sense of peace slowly washed away the sadness. Everything felt right. A Sabbath table with familiar savory foods. A man who respected and embraced our common traditions. I studied his face in the candlelight. Gray flecked his neat red beard, and his startling blue eyes crinkled at the corners when he smiled at me. The places inside me, aching and empty only an hour before, filled with the honey of life. We didn't speak about Harriet. We didn't speak about much at all but ate in a contented silence. Without discussion and without negotiation, I understood and accepted where this night would lead.

CHAPTER 8

Saturday I woke to Crusher's beard tickling my face as he kissed me. I rolled into his arms.

"Babe, I want to wake up like this every morning. Marry me."

I wanted to wake up every morning like this too. I mean, who wouldn't? But what did I really know about this man? "We should get to know each other better."

"What's to tell? I'm forty-eight years old, never been married, and have no kids. I was born in Brooklyn and went to yeshiva until I turned eighteen. Then I left home, traded my black hat for red boots, and joined the Israeli Army Special Forces. I left the army and traveled around the world, working security for El Al. I came back to the States when I hit forty."

I stared at him with my mouth slightly ajar.

"What? You want more? I'm not a heavy drinker and I don't do drugs anymore. Five years ago I opened the bike shop. Sometimes the cops come around and hassle me. I've even been busted a couple of times, but they've never proved anything.

Why do you think that putz Beavers has such a hard-on for me? Trust me, babe, I'm a nice guy."

I propped myself on my elbow and looked at him wide-eyed. "You're seven years younger than me?"

His laughter rose from deep inside his barrel chest and shook the bed. "If age is the only thing you're worried about, we should call the rabbi tomorrow."

He pulled my body closer when the phone rang. I reluctantly picked it up.

"Hey, girlfriend," said Lucy. "You ready for another day at work? Birdie and I will be over in five minutes."

Holy crap! I'd completely forgotten about going to Harriet's. The clock on the dresser read nine. "Uh, Lucy? Can you come in half an hour instead?" I flapped my hands frantically, motioning for Crusher to get out of bed. "I just woke up and it'll take me awhile to get ready."

"Babe." Crusher reluctantly moved his six-foot-six body to an upright and vertical position.

"Who's there?" Lucy said. "Did I hear a man's voice in the background?"

Darn.

"No, no one's here. I just cleared my throat."

"I don't believe you. Birdie and I are on the way."

Before I could tell her to wait, she hung up the phone.

"My friends said they'll be here in five minutes, which means ten, fifteen if I'm lucky. If I take a really fast shower and get ready, maybe you can hide in the bedroom until we leave. I don't want them to know you were here. I could give you an extra key and the alarm code to lock up. Would you help me out here?"

The skin tightened around Crusher's mouth. "You ashamed of something?"

I hurried out of bed. "No, I'm just not ready to face questions I don't have answers for."

He thought for a moment and then looked at me. "No."

"No *what*, for God's sake?"

"No, I'm not that guy. I've already met your friends, remember?"

Time was slipping by. "Fine." I grabbed my bathrobe and huffed my way into the shower.

Three minutes later I toweled off while Crusher showered. The doorbell rang. "Just a minute," I shouted, even though I knew they couldn't hear me.

I jumped into my jeans and a T-shirt and ran to open the front door with wet hair. Two men wearing suits and serious expressions stood there. The older one was obese and the younger one seemed bored.

The fat one pulled out a badge. "Mrs. Rose? I'm Detective Gabe Farkas and this is Detective Frank Avila from the West LA Division of the LAPD. May we come in?"

I opened the door wider and stepped aside. "What's this about?"

"You're the executor of Mrs. Harriet Oliver's estate?"

I nodded. "You said West LA. Did something happen at Harriet's house?"

"No. The house is fine."

What, then? I led them to the kitchen. "I'm making a pot of coffee. My friends will be here shortly."

"Go ahead. This will only take a minute."

I filled the carafe with water.

"We received a call this morning from the mortician at Gan Shalom Memorial Park. He used to work as a coroner's assistant and noticed something suspicious about Mrs. Oliver's remains."

I put down the carafe so abruptly water spilled over the edge. "What did he find?"

Farkas glanced quickly toward Avila and then back at me. "As he laid out the bones in the coffin, he noticed a crack in the hyoid. The bone split apart when he tugged the ends. He got curious and looked at the fracture under a magnifying glass. He believes the break occurred before death, so he notified us."

I knew it. Something bad happened to Harriet. I shuddered at the vision of her body reduced to bones. Although I knew the answer to my next question from watching a hundred cop shows on television, I needed Farkas to confirm it. "What exactly is the significance of a broken hyoid bone?"

"The bone in the throat breaks when someone is strangled." Crusher had walked into the kitchen in time to hear the last part of the conversation. He wore clean clothes from an overnight bag: jeans, a black T-shirt, a red bandana on his head, and his feet were bare.

I looked at Farkas. "Is he right?"

He measured Crusher with a surprised glance and nodded.

"Are you telling me Harriet Oliver was strangled?" I felt woozy and wobbled a little.

Crusher reached me in two steps and put an arm around my shoulders, supporting me like a huge bear, smelling faintly of lemon verbena soap. In real life I stood five feet two inches and wore a size sixteen, but standing next to him, I became a petite size four.

Farkas cleared his throat. "The coroner picked up her remains an hour ago. He wants to examine this new evidence."

"It's not new evidence," I said. "It's evidence he missed in the first place. And anyway, her funeral is scheduled in two days. Monday. You can't make her miss her own funeral."

Farkas scratched the side of his head with his finger. "Well, yeah, the coroner can do pretty much whatever he wants."

I jammed my fists on my hips and thrust my head forward, preparing for a fight. He raised a calming hand. "But the exam won't take long. He just wants to confirm the mortician's findings. He assured us Mrs. Oliver will be returned by Monday."

"Well, what about the stupid coroner? With three whole weeks to examine her body, how could he miss such an obvious clue?"

Farkas took out a handkerchief and wiped the sweat off his forehead. Now, far be it from me to criticize the overweight. They are my people, but this poor man needed to lose some serious pounds.

Detective Avila opened a file and looked inside. "The autopsy report shows an unknown cause of death. The coroner wrote cardiac failure as a probable cause."

"I know what the report says, Detective. I have a copy. Just so you know, your heart *always* stops beating when you die. Cardiac failure occurs in one hundred percent of deaths. What the report doesn't say is why everyone assumes she died of a heart attack. The coroner didn't have an organ to examine. Were there medical reports in the file indicating she suffered heart problems?"

The detectives looked at each other but didn't respond.

I put my hands on my hips and leaned forward. "Exactly. Someone at the county coroner's, who should have known better, got lazy and screwed up. At least the mortician paid attention, thank God. Otherwise, evidence of Harriet's murder would have been buried along with her body."

Farkas closed his eyes briefly. "Look, I can understand your frustration. The shooting at the LA airport happened around the time Mrs. Oliver's remains were discovered. The coroner processed an unusual number of bodies that week. Stuff happens. Things sometimes get overlooked."

I opened my mouth to complain, but he kept on talking.

"Right now we consider Mrs. Oliver's house to be a crime scene. Nobody can go inside until we're through investigating. I'm asking you to please give me the key to the house."

"How long will your people be there?"

"Probably a couple of days."

"Some very valuable items are sitting in her house. I hired private security guards to watch the premises twenty-four/seven. I don't want to leave the house unprotected."

Avila took a wide stance and hooked his thumbs in his belt. "We've already talked to Hector Fuentes. He can stay, but he can't enter the house."

I blinked. "Who the heck is Hector Fuentes?"

"Malo," Crusher said.

"Oh."

I pulled Harriet's house key out of my purse and held it up. "I want you to call the minute you're finished with the house."

"Yes, ma'am, I will."

I wasn't through with him yet. "And good luck with your crime scene, Detective. You're ten months too late. We've been all over the house and our fingerprints are everywhere. But I did save you the job of vacuuming. Your forensics people will find a million dead flies to process in the vacuum cleaner."

He handed me his business card. "Can you give me the key now?"

As Farkas and Avila walked toward their car, Lucy and Birdie arrived at my front door. Lucy pointed to the detectives. "Is one of them the man's voice I heard over the phone?"

"No," said Crusher from the kitchen.

Lucy and Birdie stepped inside. He stood in his bare feet, chopping potatoes.

Lucy raised her eyebrows and looked at me. "Okaaaay, then."

While Crusher cooked, we drank our coffee and talked at the kitchen table. .

Lucy said, "I've been thinking. You know the three of us took one whole day to search the downstairs. We'll probably spend another day going through the upstairs. If the killer came alone, how many days do you suppose he spent rummaging through Harriet's house?"

I put my cup down. "I see where you're going, Lucy. While the killer searched the house, Harriet's body lay in her closet. He could've hunted for several months after he killed her, returning multiple times."

Birdie grabbed her braid. "Mercy. While the body decomposed?"

Crusher put a large plate of scrambled eggs, cottage fried potatoes, and half a loaf of challah, dotted with little black raisins, in the middle of the table. He took one look at our faces. "Come on, ladies. Forget the gory details for now and have something to eat."

My grandmother always used to offer food as comfort. "You remind me of my bubbie." I smiled. "Thanks for going to all this trouble, Yossi."

He bent and kissed me. Right in front of my friends. So much for keeping our relationship on the down low. Crusher had just marked his territory.

I blushed, Lucy raised her eyebrow, Birdie tittered, and Crusher sat and ate. A lot. So did I, in spite of the disturbing new information that my old friend, Harriet Oliver, had been strangled to death.

CHAPTER 9

Since Farkas had barred us from returning to
Harriet's, Lucy and Birdie went home.

When we were alone again, Crusher said, "I like
your idea this morning about becoming better
acquainted." He put his hand up the back of my
T-shirt and fiddled with the snaps on my 36 DD bra.
"Let's spend the rest of the day getting to know
each other a lot better."

My body vibrated like a violin string, but duty
called. Now that I knew Harriet had been murdered, I wanted to examine her personal papers. I
pointed to the cartons of mail on my living-room
floor and the stack of papers Birdie had gathered
from Harriet's desk yesterday. "I have to sort
through all this."

Crusher grunted and withdrew his hand. "Okay,
I'll be back later." He put on his boots (at least a
size sixteen) and a flannel shirt against the cold (a
lot of plaid for a man his size).

I frowned. "How do you know I'll even be here
later? Are you trying to move yourself in? Call me

conservative, Yossi, but aren't we jumping into this relationship a little too fast?"

"Too fast for who? I told you four months ago I wanted you to be my woman."

"Yeah, but we'd only known each other for two weeks."

"Look, Jacob loved Rachel the moment he set eyes on her. Then he worked for fourteen years before he could have her. As far as I'm concerned, I'm ready. If you're not, then I'll wait. I'm your Jacob." He pulled me onto his lap and kissed the crease in my neck, sending chills through my body. "Just please don't make me wait fourteen years. I'll be an old man by then."

I knew the biblical story well. Even as a little girl I'd hoped for a Jacob of my own, someone who'd love me forever. However, starting with my divorce from Aaron Rose, through a couple of failed relationships, to my breakup with Beavers, I scored 0 for 4 in the lifetime commitment department. I was so over the notion of undying love.

I kissed him and then stood. "I guess I'll see you later." I smiled.

After Crusher left, I went in the bedroom to straighten up. I noticed, with some irritation, he'd hung his good clothes in my closet and left his grooming kit on my bathroom counter. I picked up his double-edged razor and studied the little red hairs sticking to the blades. I squirted some of his shaving foam on my fingertips and breathed in the lemony masculine scent so different from my oils and sweet perfumes. Could I make room for him in my closet? In my life? By leaving his stuff here,

Crusher, aka Yossi Levy, invited me to consider the answer.

Back in the kitchen, I emptied the first cardboard box of mail on the table and sorted through the pieces one by one. Catalogs, ads, and obvious junk went back into the carton for recycling. Only five pieces of mail looked important. I put those in a keep pile. The next two cartons yielded a similar result. When I finished sorting through the mail and the papers from her desk, the keep pile contained seventeen letters.

I used my white plastic UCLA letter opener on the first envelope. Correspondence from Abernathy, Porter & Salinger dated November 3, about a month ago, advised Harriet her signature was due on some investment transactions. This must have been the letter Abernathy first told me about. He'd become concerned when Harriet didn't respond. He drove to her house and discovered her body.

Ten large manila envelopes dating from February through November were sent by Abernathy et al. They contained monthly financial summaries, including income and expense statements. Who was to say those statements were accurate? Harriet's isolated lifestyle made her an easy target for fraud and embezzlement. I'd hire a forensic accountant to go over all her financials.

In June, Harriet received two birthday cards. One from a dentist in Beverly Hills and another from Isabel Casco, her college roommate. My eyes stung as I realized how small Harriet's world had become. Only one friend cared enough to wish her a happy birthday, and it hadn't been me.

I came across three pieces of mail dated around

the time of Harriet's death. Although they were in the boxes with the unopened mail, they'd already been opened. The first envelope came from the International Quilt Study Center in Lincoln, Nebraska. Lucy, Birdie, and I once visited the museum there. We'd flown to Paducah, Kentucky, to attend the American Quilters Society annual show. Afterward we rented a car and drove in a big circle through Missouri, Kansas, Nebraska, and Iowa, looking to buy vintage quilts. We made a special trip to the IQSC in Lincoln. Why did the IQSC send Harriet a letter?

January 17

Dear Mrs. Oliver,

Thank you for sending the photo of this fascinating quilt. I won't be able to authenticate either the age or provenance until I can examine the quilt. Afterward, I can provide you with an appraisal.

Judging by the signatures on the red and white blocks, you appear to have a friendship quilt. The central block with a circle of thirteen stars on a blue square is especially intriguing. This may indicate the quilt dates back to Colonial times. As you know, the first American flag featured the same design.

I will send the photo to a friend of mine, who is the curator of American Quilts in the Smithsonian, for her opinion and let you know what she says. You may have something rather unique.

Very truly yours,
Anne Smith, Curator
International Quilt Study Center

Birdie had observed an avid collector of Early Americana should have owned some quilts. According to this letter, Harriet did have at least one and had sought an expert appraisal. A quilt made so long ago would be quite valuable.

Friendship quilts had been made in some form or another since Colonial times. Occasionally, when a new bride left home or when a friend or relative moved away from their community, loved ones gave them a quilt as both a remembrance and a practical gift. Each friend contributed a block for the top. Sometimes the blocks were signed, like a going-away card, only in fabric. When the industrial revolution and the westward expansion created a mobile population, friendship quilts were assembled for those preparing to travel far from their roots.

Was this the "old quilt" Estella said she wanted?

As soon as the police permitted us to return to Harriet's, I'd search the upstairs thoroughly. The quilt might be stashed in some drawer or closet. Or maybe it lay on one of the beds underneath the duvet, especially if Harriet knew the best way to store a fragile old quilt was unfolded and out of the light. If the quilt hid anywhere in her house, I'd find it.

Dr. Anne Smith sent another letter a week later.

January 28,

Dear Mrs. Oliver,

I enjoyed our conversation yesterday regarding your remarkable quilt. Today I consulted with my friend, Dr. Naomi Hunter, curator of American Quilts at the Smithsonian. She is most anxious to examine this possibly historic item of great

*significance. I will call you to arrange a time when
we may come to Los Angeles to visit you.*

*Warmest regards,
Anne Smith*

Judging from the date of this letter, Harriet was still alive on January 27 when she spoke to Dr. Smith. Another letter arrived two weeks later from the Smithsonian.

February 13

Dear Mrs. Oliver,
*Dr. Anne Smith faxed me the photograph of
your friendship quilt, and I am very eager to
examine it. This quilt may be a priceless
American treasure. Perhaps you have heard of
the Declaration Quilt? Mrs. Abigail Adams
mentioned it in some of her correspondence with
Mrs. Sarah Franklin Bache, Benjamin Franklin's
daughter. Historians know this quilt existed, but
its whereabouts has been lost to history.*
*I understand Dr. Smith was unable to reach you
again after your conversation. I urge you to call
Dr. Smith or myself. I will gladly provide you with
more information when we meet.*

*Yours truly,
Dr. Naomi Hunter, Curator*

The letter from the Smithsonian indicated Harriet failed to respond to Anne Smith's second letter, so Harriet must have been murdered sometime between January 28 and before February 13. If she lay dead in her closet, who opened the letter from

Dr. Hunter? Who else had hunted for this "priceless American treasure"?

I'd never heard of the Declaration Quilt, but I'd call Dr. Hunter on Monday to find out more. How long had the Oliver family owned the quilt? How did they acquire it? Did Estella know the true value?

The rest of the papers from Harriet's desk yielded only one interesting item, a checkbook she kept for personal use. The register indicated she wrote weekly checks for five hundred dollars to Paulina Polinskaya, a name I recognized from the blue address book. The woman never returned my call.

The checks began two years ago and continued on a regular basis until January 5, about three weeks before Harriet's death. Who was Paulina, and why did Harriet pay her with a personal check, rather than having Abernathy take care of it? Wouldn't Paulina have been concerned about Harriet when the checks stopped coming? If so, why didn't she call the police? I needed to pay the woman a visit.

I got up to stretch and filled the tea kettle with water. A few minutes later the phone rang.

"Mrs. Rose? This is Emmet Wish returning your call." Emmet Wish was another name from Harriet's blue address book.

"Mr. Wish, thanks for calling me back."

"I was shocked and saddened to hear about her death. I'll be at her funeral, of course. You're Mrs. Oliver's executor?"

The knob on the stove *clicked* and the flame jumped to life under the kettle. "Yes. Are you a friend of hers?"

"I'm her insurance agent, but I'd also like to think I was her friend. I worked very hard to protect her property. She owned several extremely rare and valuable items, which she insured separately at great expense. Are you aware of the pieces I'm talking about?"

I put a bag of Scottish breakfast tea in a cup while I waited for the water to boil. "Yes, I've been making an inventory using the insurance rider and photos from a flash drive. I'm afraid some of the items are missing."

"Are you sure?"

"Well, I haven't done a complete search of her house yet, but I'm pretty sure."

Wish moaned a little. "This is very bad news. I mean, we insured everything. Art, baskets, books, a quilt, antique toys, and a pair of candelabras that had been in the family for generations. You'll be filing a claim, of course."

The tea kettle whistled. I turned off the stove and poured the water in my cup. "Yes, after I'm through taking inventory of the things still remaining."

"Damn disturbing news. Please call me right away if you do find them."

I stirred some milk in the cup. "Of course."

Later in the afternoon I sat on the sofa with Crusher, eating apple fritters he brought back from Western Donuts. I pulled my feet up onto the sofa and reached for a paper napkin. "I think we're looking for a killer with specific tastes. Rare books, possibly a priceless quilt, and good jewelry are missing, but valuable pieces of art are still sitting on shelves and hanging on the walls."

He brushed away some sugary flakes of glaze from his beard. "What do you mean *we* are looking for a killer with specific tastes? Let the cops handle this. Remember what happened four months ago? You almost got whacked."

I raised my eyebrows. "Trust the cops to handle the investigation? Like the coroner handled Harriet's remains? I don't think so."

"Babe, you live in the wrong country."

"What do you mean?"

"*Shin Bet* could use someone like you."

The Israeli Secret Service? Why would he mention them?

We sat in companionable silence for a few more minutes. Then he said, "I want to be with you again tonight."

"You're moving too fast for me, Yossi. I need some time to sort things out in my head."

"Let's talk, then."

"We will. I promise. But not tonight. Tonight I just need space."

After a lingering kiss, I almost asked him to stay. I reluctantly closed the door behind him and settled back on the sofa with my unfinished Jacob's Ladder quilt and my sewing kit. The slow, steady rhythm of pushing the needle in and out of the fabric always calmed me. A lump formed in my throat when I remembered the birthday card Harriet received from Isabel Casco. Didn't she deserve to know about Harriet's murder? I put down my sewing and called her.

Isabel picked up on the second ring. She must have been well into happy hour because ice tinkled in a glass as she slurred her greeting. "'Lo?"

"Hello, Isabel, this is Martha Rose. I have some bad news and I wanted you to hear it from me first."

"'Smatter?"

I told her about the mortician discovering

Harriet's murder. "Do you have any idea who might have wanted her dead?"

"Nathan."

"Her husband? He died in ninety-seven."

Isabel snorted. "I can't talk right now. I'm watching a marathon of *The Mentalist* on cable. Come over tomorrow an' I'll tell you all about it."

Click. Dial tone.

Oh Lord. Did she believe Nathan Oliver was still alive or was the booze talking? That was weird. Isabel Casco just accused a dead man of murdering Harriet.

CHAPTER 10

A tickling on my cheeks woke me Sunday morning. I opened my eyes. My cat Bumper's face sat about three inches away from mine. We stared at each other and I blinked first. "You hungry or what?"

He jumped off the bed, ran to the kitchen, and sat by his food bowl. The clock read seven-fifteen.

I made a cup of tea with milk, sat at the table, and opened Harriet's blue address book. Isabel Casco lived in an apartment in Santa Monica on Eleventh Street. Paulina Polinskaya, the woman who received five hundred dollars a week from Harriet's personal account, lived not too far away on Venice Boulevard in Culver City. I needed to talk to both of them. Paulina never returned my call, so I planned a sneak attack. I figured everyone would still be at home on a gloomy Sunday morning in December.

The southbound 405 Freeway was wide open at seven forty-five, and I reached Culver City in thirteen minutes. I drove west toward the ocean on Venice Boulevard, looking for Paulina's address, while a light drizzle sprinkled my windshield. A mixture of one-story commercial structures and gray office buildings lined both sides of the street.

Paulina's place, wedged between a strip mall and an auto body shop, turned out to be a small, pre–World War II yellow bungalow, the last domestic holdout on a street transformed into commercial buildings. A black BMW sat in the driveway next to a miniscule front yard that looked like the last blade of grass died when Nixon occupied the White House. A sign, with huge purple letters, stood on the cracked concrete:

PSYCHIC
TAROT READINGS
PAST LIVES
SPIRITUALIST

Well, this explained the books about contacting the dead on Harriet's library floor. Harriet must have paid Paulina to talk to her dead family. What else would account for the weekly checks for five hundred dollars? I began to understand why Paulina the Psychic didn't return my calls. She milked nearly $25,000 from Harriet over the period of a year.

A spindly hibiscus bush barely clung to life in a painted Mexican pot on the front porch. White paint peeled off the front door where a sign announced business hours and displayed an emergency number. I knocked, but nobody answered. Someone must be at home because of the car in the driveway. I dialed the emergency number on my cell phone.

A sleepy voice answered. "Nnnhullo?"

"Is this the Psychic?"

"Who's this?"

"Someone who needs help."

She yawned. "What time's it, anyway?"

"Eight. Can I see you? It's really important."

"You woke me."

"I'm sorry, but I really need your help. I'm right outside, but I guess you didn't hear me knocking."

A hard East Coast accent emerged. "I charge extra for emergencies."

"Okay I'll pay whatever you want."

"Gimme five minutes." She hung up.

Ten minutes later the door opened. I expected a wily old con artist. Instead, a plump young woman stood no taller than five feet. She had pulled her long black hair back into a hasty bun and wore a silk tunic with purple flowers. Her eyes, heavy with kohl, resembled the portraits painted on the walls of Egyptian tombs. The skin on her face padded high cheekbones and she smiled with lips painted fuchsia.

"I'm Paulina. Enter." Her eyes darted toward my purse.

I walked into a room painted a deep terra-cotta with one small lamp shining in the corner.

Paulina gestured for me to sit at a round table covered with a purple satin cloth and walked around the room lighting sandalwood-scented joss sticks and twelve white candles. Then she perched atop a burgundy velvet pillow she'd placed on the seat of the chair facing me. "Your aura's off."

"Off?"

She nodded solemnly. "Something bad's happened recently."

Well, duh, why else would I need an emergency visit?

Before I could respond, she shifted in her seat and stuck out her hand. "I charge a hundred dollars an hour, hundred fifty for an emergency session. You pay up front. Any questions?"

I leaned forward with my elbows on the table. "Yeah. What did Harriet Oliver get for five hundred dollars a week?"

The reflection from the lamp glittered in her black eyes, but she didn't flinch. "You're the woman who called the other night, aren't you? About Harriet's death."

The fragrant smoke from the joss sticks curled through the air. "I'm Martha Rose, the executor of Harriet's will."

She crossed her arms. "Whaddaya want with me?"

"I want to talk about Harriet. She was murdered."

Paulina raised her eyebrows. "Murdered? So that's . . ."

Just then the tea kettle whistled. Paulina turned toward another room. "Wait here."

I studied the blue flowers in the red Turkish carpet and the geometry of the inlaid Moroccan table across the room. Three minutes later she returned with two teacups painted with pink flowers. Without asking, she put sugar in both cups and handed one to me. "You like sugar."

It didn't take a psychic to figure out you didn't get my kind of curves without having a few extra treats now and then.

Paulina sipped her tea, leaving a fuchsia-colored lip print on the edge of the cup. "Your aura is pink. You are honest, are determined, and thirst for truth, so I'm gonna help you."

Should I be grateful my aura isn't green? "What exactly did you do for Harriet?"

"I was her spiritual adviser. And her death coach."

Did I just hear her right? "Her *what?*"

Paulina smiled and lowered her eyelids halfway. "I helped her communicate with the souls of the departed. Especially her little boy."

"Is this what she gave you five hundred a week for?"

Her eyes flew open. "I'm a skilled and highly sought-after medium. I spent a lotta time helping that poor woman. Making house calls when she became hysterical—sometimes in the middle of the night. Not once did I ever refuse to see her. Harriet insisted on paying me a weekly retainer."

I swirled my cup. The tea leaves eddied in the bottom. "Weren't you alarmed when the checks stopped? If you cared so much for her, if you were so helpful, why didn't you try to find out what happened to her?"

Paulina sighed. "When did you say she died?"

"I didn't say. Somewhere between January twenty-eighth and February thirteenth."

She relaxed back. "Harriet stopped coming to see me in the beginning of January."

"Why?"

"I worked with her to contact her son. She also talked to a twin brother who died when they were kids, and to her deceased parents. Harriet always felt calm and relieved whenever they came through with messages. Her father advised her to pay me a retainer."

I rolled my eyes. "Of course he did."

Paulina looked at me wearily. "I'm used to skeptics.

But I'm telling the truth. Do you wanna hear the rest or no?"

"Okay, go on."

"Harriet was definite. She didn't wanna communicate with anyone else, only those specific four people. I started getting some strong signals from her dead husband. He kept trying to break through and talk to her. I told her I sensed great turmoil, but Harriet insisted. She didn't want any contact with Nathan."

I drank the cooled tea. "Did she say why?"

"No, but during our last session I went into my usual trance, and Nathan managed to breach the barrier. When Harriet heard him speak, she screamed and broke the connection. Then she said she didn't want to see me anymore. I tried to warn her and reassure her, but she didn't wanna risk any further contact."

The smell of sandalwood smoke almost overpowered me. I fanned my hand in front of my face. "Warn her about what?"

Paulina placed her palms on the purple tablecloth. "When a soul suffers as much turmoil as Nathan Oliver, there's a lotta unresolved issues. Anger. Frustration. Regret. Until his soul can settle those issues, he's doomed to wander in a in-between world. A soul in such a state can wreck havoc on the living, cause torment and even violence."

"You really believe all that?"

She nodded vigorously. "Oh, yeah. I've helped many of the departed pass over. I promised Harriet if Nathan could communicate whatever he needed to tell her, he'd let go and never bother her again. But I warned her, if she refused to speak to him, well . . ." Paulina turned her palms up and shrugged.

My jaw dropped. "Are you saying Nathan Oliver could have killed Harriet?" When Paulina didn't respond, I shook my head. "Someone with human hands killed Harriet. No ghost could strangle her to death."

Paulina reached her hand across the table. "Gimme your cup."

I handed my empty teacup and saucer to her. She looked at the pattern the brown leaves made on the sides and bottom. "The one you thought you loved before will ask to come back into your life."

Beavers? Is she talking about Detective Arlo Beavers?

"The one you're with now loves you deeply."

Crusher? How does she know about my love life?

Paulina smirked. "Believe me yet? Lemme read your cards."

Shock and curiosity got the best of me.

Paulina shuffled the tarot deck and turned over a beautifully illustrated card picturing a queen sitting on a throne, holding a sword. "Just as your aura revealed, the queen of swords. You are honest and forthright and seek the truth."

The second card she turned over pictured a man holding five swords with two more stuck in the ground. Paulina frowned. "The seven of swords. Beware of a deceiver and a thief. Someone's been covering his tracks."

I hated to admit it, but Paulina was right. A clever thief did enter Harriet's house, and I wasn't even close to knowing his identity.

Darkness covered her face when she turned over the last card showing a tower being struck by lightning and people jumping or falling off the top. "This is very bad. The tower indicates chaos, an explosive crisis of some kind. Please believe me, Martha, you're in great danger. You must be very, very careful."

Right. She probably said that to everybody. But she did kind of nail the Crusher thing. Could she be right about this too?

Paulina looked up. "If you wanna come back, we could schedule an appointment."

CHAPTER 11

I left Paulina's by nine. I figured Isabel should be up by now, so I called her on my cell phone as soon as I got into my car. She answered on the third ring. Her voice raked through her throat. "Hello?"

"This is Martha Rose calling. Remember we talked last night?"

Isabel cleared her throat. "Vaguely."

"I'd really like to come over. I happen to be in the area right now. Are you free?"

"What time is it, for God's sake? I just woke up."

"Around nine. Let me take you out to breakfast. We can go to Harvey's Deli. It's not too far from where you live, and I can pick you up in ten minutes."

Isabel coughed. "Does anyone ever say no to you?"

"Sure," I laughed. "But I'm hoping you won't be one of them."

"Okay. Give me fifteen. Takes me awhile to put my face on."

I drove slowly on the surface streets from

Culver City to Santa Monica. Traffic became denser, especially around the big box stores, where people were no doubt doing their Christmas shopping.

Isabel lived in a condo near Wilshire on Eleventh. Her second-floor unit faced the front of the building with a view of the street lined with magnolia trees. For a fifty-something woman whose voice had been wrecked by cigarettes and booze, Isabel Casco looked stunning. Her brown hair had been cut a youthful and hip half inch from her scalp. Silver hoops hung from her ears, emphasizing her long, slender neck. A distinctive diamond cocktail ring sparkled on her right hand as she shook mine.

"Nice to meet you, Martha. Any friend of Harriet's is a friend of mine. Come on in. I'll make us a batch of mimosas." Her house smelled like stale cigarette smoke and Chanel N°5.

"Oh, no, thanks." I took in the mainly white furniture and latte walls. "I've got to drive home."

She waved her hand dismissively, flashing her shiny ring. "Don't be such a nervous Nellie. By the time we finish breakfast, you'll be fine."

"Can I take a rain check? I'm actually starving and need food."

She shrugged into her jacket. "Okay."

I drove us the short distance to Harvey's and, considering we hit the Sunday brunch crowd, we had to wait for a table. Harvey's Deli connected at the far end to a bowling alley. In the background, hard balls rolled noisily down polished oak alleys and struck pins with loud pops. An open bar separated the restaurant from the bowling alley. Isabel ordered a mimosa while we sat at the bar and waited for our table.

"So you and Harriet were roommates in college?" I smiled.

"Yes, Brown was very laid-back, and if you were smart enough, you could get by without too much effort."

"I remember Harriet as a serious student in high school."

Isabel played with the stem of her glass. "Oh, yeah. She loved her classes. I, on the other hand, loved to party. Since we were both history majors, I copied Harriet's notes when I didn't feel like going to class. Still, we managed to enjoy our share of the fun."

Several balls rolled heavily down the alleys and struck the pins almost simultaneously. "And you kept in touch after you graduated?"

"Oh, yes. I found a job in Southern California and reconnected with Harriet."

"When we talked last night, you said something remarkable. I asked if you knew anyone who might have wanted Harriet dead, and you said, 'Nathan.' What did you mean?"

Isabel put down her empty glass and signaled to the bar man to bring another. A lot of wooden pins cracked together and a cheer went up from the bowling alley. "Did I say that?" She looked away. "I must have been speaking metaphorically. Everyone loved Harriet. Besides, Nathan is dead."

"Well, something must have prompted you to say that. Were they not happy together?"

We sat in silence while Isabel finished her second mimosa and finally looked at me. "I had good reason to say what I did. Nathan was a pig and a mean drunk. I saw big bruises on Harriet more than once."

A waitress came to the bar and told us our table was ready. Not bad. We only waited twenty minutes. We followed her back into the restaurant and flipped through a ten-page menu. Harvey's featured typical deli food, along with dishes influenced by the diverse cultures of LA, including brisket burritos and spicy egg rolls.

Isabel ordered an egg-white omelet. I settled on scrambled eggs with lox and onions and the waitress left with our orders.

"Nathan abused Harriet?"

A busboy brought a basket of challah rolls and rye bread to the table and poured each of us a cup of coffee.

Isabel waited for him to leave. "He physically and emotionally abused her. He threatened to take Jonah someplace where she'd never see him again. With his money and resources, Nathan could have easily disappeared with the boy. Poor Harriet lived in constant fear. The only person Nathan treated halfway decent was his son, Jonah. And even then he managed to kill the boy."

I didn't think Isabel's story could get any worse. I peeled the foil off a pat of butter and spread it on half a challah roll. "Nathan killed Jonah? I thought the boy fell off a boat and drowned."

Isabel took a sip of coffee. "Oh, he did, all right. Thanks to his father. Nathan got drunk, as usual, and forgot to bring a life vest for Jonah. The captain didn't let them come aboard at first, but he finally scrounged up a small life vest under one of the bench seats, a couple sizes too big for the five-year-old.

Nathan promised he'd watch Jonah the whole time. What a crock. Instead of paying attention to the boy, Nathan kept drinking and started a card game with a couple other men."

"So, how did Jonah drown?" My heart sank as I thought of the five-year-old wandering the boat on his own.

"The boat stopped somewhere between here and Catalina so the fishermen could cast their lines in the water. Jonah had brought his little fishing pole. Apparently he went to the side of the boat and crawled up so he could put his line in the water like he saw the big men doing."

I clutched my coffee with both hands, willing the heat from the cup to warm the chill spreading inside me.

"When Jonah fell overboard, he gave a little cry. Then his body slipped out of the life jacket and he sank like a stone. A couple of the men dove into the water. They couldn't find him for several minutes. When they did, he was dead."

"What did Nathan do?"

"He stood at the edge of the boat shouting orders to the men in the water and swearing at them each time they came up for air without Jonah's body."

"What? He didn't dive into the water? Not even to save his son?"

She took another sip of coffee. "See what I mean? The man was a pig."

"Isabel, how do you know all these details?"

She leaned toward me and lowered her voice. "After the funeral, when all the mourners went back to Harriet's house, I shared a few drinks on the patio with the captain of the boat, Nico Grimaldi. He told me the whole story. The authorities immediately shut down his charter boat business for the safety violation leading to Jonah's accident. They refused to reinstate his license until he could pay a hefty fine or prove he wasn't at fault."

I buttered another piece of roll. "So why did he show up at the funeral?"

"The poor guy felt really bad and came to pay his respects to Jonah's mother. He even brought back Jonah's fishing pole. He also tried to talk Nathan into testifying on his behalf so he could get his license back, but Nathan refused. They got into a shouting match and Nathan ordered the captain to leave."

"How did Harriet take all this?"

Isabel shook her head sadly and her eyes filled. "She became so dead inside, even Nathan lost interest in hurting her."

The waitress brought two steaming plates of food to the table and refilled our coffee cups.

My heart ached for Harriet. "Did you ever tell her what you learned from the boat captain?"

"Yes, about two years later. I thought if she knew the truth, she'd find the strength to leave Nathan."

"Did she?"

Isabel took a bite of bread. "She didn't have to. Nathan must have finally found a conscience, because he jumped in the ocean and killed himself. For once in his life, he did the right thing."

I wondered. Abernathy said Nathan's body never turned up. Could he still be alive? Could Nathan Oliver truly have killed Harriet?

I dropped Isabel at her place and drove back to the valley. I kept thinking about the flashy ring on her finger. When I got home, I checked the pictures from Harriet's flash drive. The three-carat canary yellow diamond surrounded by a starburst of clear baguettes on a filigreed platinum band had, indeed, belonged to Harriet.

The gray, damp weather made my fibromyalgia flare up, and the muscles in my neck and hip throbbed. Instead of taking a Soma, I was determined to practice my new yoga moves to see if they would help with the pain. I rolled out my pink rubber mat and lay on my back on the hard floor.

I put one leg straight up in the air, wrapped the six-foot-long strap over my foot, and held on to the ends with both hands. I stretched the leg first to one side and then to the other, keeping my knee straight. *How did Isabel get that ring?* I repeated the moves with my other leg. *Did she steal it?* Then I did the same stretches with both my legs together. *Does she have the other missing pieces of jewelry?* The tightness released in my hips.

Still lying on my back with my legs in the air, I bent my knees and stretched my arms up to grab the arches of my feet in the *happy baby* pose. Muscles I didn't even know existed started burning with the stretch. I tried to breathe deeply, sending my "intentions" (whatever that meant) to the pain.

In my head I heard Dasha, my instructor, "Take a long, slow breath from the bottom of spine to the top of head. Now hold for four counts. Slowly release breath until there is no more air in lungs. Now hold for another four counts."

Air. Air.

The burning in my muscles actually subsided, but I started breathing rapidly to make up for the four counts without oxygen.

I finally gave up and just lay quietly with my eyes

closed in the corpse pose. I tried to picture Harriet on the floor of her closet with my third eye.

Paulina Polinskaya said Harriet refused to communicate with Nathan's spirit. According to Isabel Casco, Nathan was mean and abusive and directly responsible for Jonah's death. No wonder Harriet refused Nathan's collect calls from the dead. She must have hated and feared him with every fiber of her soul.

According to the suicide note he left behind, Nathan killed himself. According to Abernathy, a search at sea failed to turn up a body. On the theory Nathan might have faked his death, Abernathy said Harriet paid for private detectives to find him. However, after seven years and dozens of fruitless searches, the courts agreed that Nathan Oliver was deceased. If Paulina's claims could be believed, Nathan's spirit really dwelt with the *Malach haMavet.*

What if Nathan didn't die at sea? What if he deliberately disappeared? If so, a living, flesh-and-blood Nathan could have returned to kill Harriet.

However, the more I thought about it, the more the whole scenario made no sense. What would motivate a self-indulgent, wealthy man like Nathan to abandon his lifestyle and his fortune to a wife he didn't love or respect?

No matter how I examined the people in her life, not one person I talked to seemed likely to have murdered Harriet Oliver. I'd just have to keep looking. Maybe Estella and Henry would show up to bury their sister-in-law tomorrow. Maybe they could shed some light.

When I got home, my daughter, Quincy, called

from Boston. "Hi, Mom. Sorry I missed you Friday night. I had a hot date."

I sat on my cream-colored sofa and covered myself with my blue and white Corn and Beans quilt, enjoying the sound of my daughter's voice. Quincy, a reporter for NPR station WGBH in Boston, constantly met interesting men who were attracted to her intelligence, her long legs, and the coppery ringlets framing her beautiful face.

"Tell me about him."

"He's a physics professor at MIT. Young, brilliant, and very hot. We've been out every night this week, and he says he's ready to get serious."

Crusher proposed marriage two weeks after we met. I became worried for my daughter. "How serious?"

"He wants an exclusive relationship."

"How exclusive?"

"Oh, Mom, don't read anything more into it. He doesn't want us to date anyone else. He says he thinks this relationship can go somewhere."

"What do you think?"

"I'm willing to try. He's nice and funny and great in bed."

I gasped. "Stop! TMI. You're still my little girl."

Quincy laughed. "Mom, don't you know I love teasing you? And besides, I know you're way past all of that."

Past? If she only knew. "Quincy, honey, I only want your happiness. Just go slowly and be careful."

Quincy sighed. "Okay, Mom, but sometimes, when something good comes your way, you just have to let go and trust. Right?"

The million-dollar question.

Around seven in the evening I got a call from

Detective Farkas. "The coroner just released Mrs. Oliver's remains to the mortuary. You can go ahead with her funeral tomorrow morning like you planned."

"Did he confirm Harriet was strangled?"

"Yes," Farkas wheezed. "He also found a fractured wrist bone. She probably struggled with the killer before she died."

"Oh God. Poor Harriet must have been terrified. Will you be at the funeral, Detective?"

"Why? You think the killer will show up after more than ten months just to gloat?"

"I think it's possible. Strangulation suggests a crime of passion to me."

"You got anyone in particular in mind?"

I thought about Nathan Oliver. Although I didn't see one photograph of him in Harriet's house, maybe one existed in his missing person's file. "You might keep your eye out for a man in his fifties who looks a lot like Harriet's husband."

"The dead guy? You've gotta be kidding."

"Maybe not so dead, Detective. Remember, no one ever saw Nathan Oliver's body."

CHAPTER 12

Monday morning I called Kresky's Kosher Market and Catering near Uncle Isaac's house in West LA to deliver a couple of platters to his house at noon. Uncle Isaac would be hosting the mourners after the funeral.

Birdie, Lucy, and I drove to Gan Shalom Memorial Park in Lucy's vintage black Caddy. The nine a.m. southbound traffic crept slowly over the Sepulveda Pass. Neither of my friends knew Harriet, but they were determined to support me; not to mention they were also curious about the mystery of her death and the theft of her treasures. Both of them committed to return to Harriet's house and finish searching for the missing items.

I sat in the backseat in a gray Anne Klein woolen skirt suit and knee-high gray leather boots against the December chill. I told them about my visits with Paulina and Isabel.

Today Lucy wore all black, like the grim reaper. "Don't just write the psychic off, Martha. Maybe Nathan reached out from the dead."

Birdie pinned a stray piece of hair back on top of

her head. "Or maybe Nathan isn't dead after all. Maybe he returned in the flesh to kill Harriet."

I sighed. "Well, she didn't go without a struggle. When the coroner examined her the second time, he found a broken wrist."

We pulled up to the valet parking and an attendant helped Birdie from the car. For once she hadn't worn her overalls but opted instead for a lavender skirt and pullover sweater. Wisps of white hair flew around her face like fairy wings.

Lucy stood over six feet tall in her black leather heels. When we entered the mortuary, she draped a black lace mantilla over her orange hair.

I spotted Mrs. Deener, the funeral planner, and walked over to her. "Is everything ready?"

She nodded and her wig shifted slightly. "Yes, everything is taken care of. Rabbi Adler will officiate, and I've printed your uncle's address and directions to his house to hand out to the mourners. Will you be delivering the eulogy?"

I nodded. "One of them. I'm sure there are others who'd like to say something about Harriet."

"I'll let the rabbi know." She looked at her watch. "The service is scheduled to begin in half an hour."

Dark wood paneling covered the walls of the chapel, and plain wooden pews sat on thick blue carpeting. A bronze sculpture mounted on the front wall depicted an eternal flame formed by Hebrew letters. Harriet's plain pine casket sat on a bier in front of the wall. The *shomer,* the guardian of her remains, sat discretely on one side of the room, reading from a small prayer book.

Lucy and Birdie sat in the front row near Harriet's casket while I stood next to them and watched people drift into the chapel. Abernathy showed up with his assistant, Nina, and another woman. He reached in a wooden box next to the door and put on a white silk yarmulka. His hand shook again. *Definitely a neurological problem. Old football injury?* He came over to me and introduced the smartly dressed Bunny Friedman, fund-raiser for Children's Hospital.

"You'll want to talk to Bunny when you're ready to settle the estate," Abernathy said.

The poised Bunny handed me her business card. "Call me anytime, Mrs. Rose. I'm eager to help you finalize Mrs. Oliver's bequest to Children's Hospital. I know we both want to see her dream of the Jonah David Oliver wing come true as soon as possible."

Bunny must be the one responsible for persuading Harriet to donate thirty million dollars to Children's. Under ordinary circumstances, her bequest might not have become available for another thirty or forty years, but Harriet died prematurely. Of course Bunny would want to expedite the transfer of funds. Scoring such a large contribution would ensure her a place in the fund-raisers' hall of fame. Would Bunny's desire to sit at the big boys' table be enough motive for murder? And just how tight were she and Abernathy in all this?

I shook her well-manicured hand. "Thank you."

Crusher walked in with Uncle Isaac and his friend Morty, followed by a troop of several men in their seventies and eighties. They wore suits, prayer shawls around their necks, and their own head coverings. They shuffled to the front of the chapel, ready to take their positions as part of the *minyan*, the quorum of ten Jewish men. Uncle Isaac smiled and patted my hand. "You see, *faigela*? I promised you a *minyan,* and I brought you one." He gestured toward the others. "There are nine of us. The rabbi makes ten."

"I knew you'd come through. And thank you for offering your home for the reception afterward."

"Well, you said the police locked you out of Harriet's house. I remember her as a nice little girl. It's the least I could do for the daughter of my old friend Herschel Gordon."

I looked at the group of old men, most of them long past driving. "How did you all get here?"

"The senior center provides a shuttle." He stroked the side of his face. "We come here a lot."

Crusher hovered near me, wearing a crocheted white head covering and a black suit. He let the collar of his white shirt gape slightly open without the constraints of a tie. He hung his tallit a fine white woolen prayer shawl, like a huge blanket over his shoulders and down his back. "You okay, babe?"

My heart raced a little. He looked so handsome in the familiar religious garb. "Thanks, Yossi. I'm fine."

He gave me a probing look. "Want me to stay here with you?"

I shook my head. "I'll be okay. I've got Lucy and Birdie."

He sat next to Uncle Isaac and bent his head toward the old man while the two of them engaged in a serious conversation I couldn't hear. Soon Morty and the others joined in. Someone put their hand on my arm. I recognized the Chanel N°5 and turned to look at Isabel.

"I can hardly bear this." Her perfect makeup melted under copious tears. She hugged me and wept a little, shoulders shaking. A faint whiff of vodka tickled my nose. Finally, she pulled away, took a tissue from her jacket pocket, and blew her nose.

I patted her on the back. "I don't want to be the only one speaking today, Isabel. Will you say something when the time comes?"

She nodded and sat down in the front row next to Birdie.

Next, a short, middle-aged man in an expensive-looking pinstripe suit came up to me. A large gold class ring with a red stone sat on his right hand. "I'm Emmet Wish. Are you Mrs. Rose?"

I nodded at the insurance agent. "Thank you for coming today."

"Very sad. She was so young." He handed me his card. "I've written down my private number. Let's touch base soon."

Paulina Polinskaya materialized in the doorway wearing a long black dress and a purple velvet cape, with a printed scarf tied around her head like a turban. She took a lot of care with her appearance today. Diamonds sparkled in her ears and on her fingers. Her Egyptian-painted eyes scanned the room until they found me. She floated up to the front, every eye following her. Then she laid her right hand on Harriet's coffin and briefly closed her eyes. A stunning diamond bracelet peeked out from under her sleeve.

She spoke softly. "The killer's not in this room."

"How do you know?" I whispered.

"Harriet just told me."

"Right."

She ignored me. "Your aura's blue today. That's the color of sadness. But there's something else in there. Some purple." She looked around the room and stopped when she saw Crusher. She looked at me again and smiled. "Good choice." Then she sat down.

Hello?

As far as I could tell, Harriet's in-laws, Estella Oliver and her brother, Henry, didn't bother to show up.

Detectives Farkas and Avila slipped into the back of the room and stood on either side of the door, watching. Farkas gave me an almost imperceptible nod right before I sat. Then the rabbi came in.

The urbane and middle-aged Rabbi Adler recited psalms and read from the Torah. "'Earth you are and to earth you will return.'" Today Harriet would finally be returned to the earth, and the first part of my job as her executor and friend would be over.

When the time came for eulogies, I spoke about my childhood friend and how we made late-night brownies in my bubbie's kitchen. Isabel spoke about her college roommate and how Harriet used to cover for Isabel when she cut classes. Abernathy spoke about the generous philanthropy of Harriet Oliver. Then we proceeded to the graveside and buried her.

The rabbi led us in the kaddish, the mourner's prayer. Everyone formed a quiet line behind me. I dropped a shovel full of dirt on her coffin, near her son's grave.

My Catholic friend Lucy pointed to the shovel. "Am I supposed to do that too?"

I could barely speak through the lump in my throat. "You're not required to, but it's an act of kindness to make sure a person is buried properly."

Without another word, Lucy took the shovel, then Birdie. We were the first to leave the cemetery and drove to Uncle Isaac's house ten minutes away.

Lucy pointed to the basin with a pitcher of water Uncle Isaac left on the porch. "What's that for?" I showed them how to wash their hands in a symbolic gesture of washing away death before entering the house.

At five minutes to twelve, the catering truck arrived with deli platters and a case of chilled Dr. Brown's cream soda. Lucy unwrapped packages of paper goods and plastic forks. Birdie opened the plates of food and spread them on the table. "Oh my, these cold cuts smell delicious. And look at those nice nutty pastries."

I plugged in a twenty-cup coffee urn and opened one of the bottles of Baron Herzog kosher cabernet Uncle Isaac had put on the kitchen counter. Soon the house filled with mourners.

After blessing the wine and a loaf of fresh sesame challah, Uncle Isaac bustled around making sure everyone received something to eat and drink. Crusher stayed with the old men, earnestly discussing something. Every once in a while, one of them would look at me and smile or wink.

What is that all about?

Paulina swept around the room, discreetly handing out her business card. Uncle Isaac's pal Morty stood when she got to him. In his eighties, Morty still drove a gold Buick and had an eye for the ladies. He slicked back his sparse gray hair with his hand. "Hiya, doll."

Paulina smiled. "Hi, yourself."

He gave her his widest smile, treating her to a

view of all twenty-eight perfectly matched ceramic teeth. A diamond stick pin glittered on his wide blue silk tie. "I couldn't help noticing you earlier." He sidled up to her and put his hand underneath her elbow. "Did anyone ever tell you you're the spittin' image of Liz Taylor?"

She frowned and tilted her head. "Isn't she dead?"

"Yeah. But when she was your age, she was bee-you-tee-ful." Morty's dentures clacked a little. "Exotic, like."

Paulina chuckled and patted his chest right over the diamond. "And you look just like my grampa Leo."

Morty steered her by the elbow to the empty love seat. "Oh, yeah? Tell me about your grampa Leo. I'll bet he's quite a guy."

They sat down.

"Give me your hand and I'll read your palm."

He lifted his right hand.

She touched his gold and diamond pinkie ring. "You have a nice ring. I just love diamonds, don't you?"

"What's not to love? Liz went in for the really big rocks, you know."

Paulina rubbed her fingers lightly down his palm. "Your lifeline is very, very long."

Oh brother, I hope he's not falling for this.

Morty leaned closer and winked. "I feel like a young man, if you know what I mean."

Paulina continued to stroke his hand. "I see diamonds, maybe a Russian cut. Pearls. And a dark stone, maybe emeralds? Sapphires?"

"Oy! Sounds just like my Esther's jewelry, may she rest in peace. The family brought some nice pieces from the old country. I gave her a string of pearls for our tenth anniversary. She liked rubies."

Paulina held his hand and leaned closer, lowering her voice. "Would you like to talk to her some time? I could arrange it." Apparently she drummed up business by hitting on grieving people at funerals and hooking them with promises to contact their dead loved ones. Unfortunately for Paulina, Morty had moved on from Esther's death years ago.

He leaned in close. "Maybe I'm more interested in the living, if you know what I mean. Say, why don't you let me take you out to dinner tonight?"

I caught Paulina's eye and shook my head rapidly.

She ignored me. "Sure. Why not? We can go back to my place until dinnertime and I'll read your tea leaves."

Morty straightened his tie and wiggled his eyebrows. "Hot cha cha."

Before I could intervene, the two of them left. What did the much younger psychic plan for the eighty-eight-year-old Morty?

Paulina wore some very expensive-looking jewelry, including a diamond bracelet half-hidden by her sleeve. I needed to figure out a way to get a closer look. Could it be Harriet's $100,000 bracelet? Did Paulina take the missing jewelry? Did she kill Harriet?

CHAPTER 13

When I got home from the funeral, I traded my suit for a comfortable pair of jeans and slippers, made a cup of apple cinnamon tea, and unwrapped some cookies. Then I phoned Dr. Naomi Hunter at the Smithsonian and introduced myself as the executor of Harriet's estate.

"Mrs. Oliver's dead? I wondered why she never contacted me about the quilt, especially since she seemed so keen on getting an appraisal."

I swallowed some tea. "Your letter to Harriet really fascinated me. I'm an avid quilter myself and have studied quilt lore and history. But I've never heard of the Declaration Quilt. Can you tell me more about it?"

"Oh, the story of this quilt is fascinating. In June of 1776, Benjamin Franklin, John Adams, and Thomas Jefferson met in Philadelphia to draft the Declaration of Independence. What most people don't realize is Abigail Adams and Martha Jefferson also traveled to Philadelphia with their husbands."

The little devil on my left shoulder persuaded me

to pick up a cookie. "Yeah, history often overlooks the women."

"Exactly!" Dr. Hunter's voice became animated. "And these women did something extraordinary during the weeks their husbands worked on the document. Benjamin Franklin's daughter, Sarah Franklin Bache, also lived in Philadelphia. So, she played hostess to Mrs. Adams and Mrs. Jefferson. In the long hours of waiting, they created a quilt to commemorate the historic event."

I dunked the cookie in my tea. "They were quilters?" In those days, women in the upper classes often turned to fine needlework as a creative and social outlet. Unlike their poorer sisters, however, women like Abigail Adams and Sarah Jefferson might have left the utilitarian sewing and quilting to their servants and slaves. "How did you find out about the quilt?"

"From subsequent correspondence between Abigail Adams and Sarah Bache. They mentioned the quilt in their letters."

"Dr. Anne Smith suggested in her messages to Harriet this might be a friendship quilt."

"Right. The ladies made six-inch snowball blocks out of white muslin with red triangles in the corners. Then they coaxed a page at the legislature to gather autographs of the various members of the Second Continental Congress on each block."

"No kidding. All those important men signed blocks? Exactly how did the page accomplish that?" I couldn't imagine a modern-day legislator agreeing to sign a piece of cloth, especially if he knew someone on the other side of the aisle had signed a similar one.

"We don't know, but in one of her letters, Abigail

refers to Robert Treat Paine, congressman from Massachusetts, who spilled two drops of India ink on his block. Anyway, they collected fifty signatures. The women reserved four more blocks for their own names, which they placed in the corners of the quilt."

"Wait. I thought you said only the three of them met. Abigail Adams, Martha Jefferson, and the Franklin daughter, Sarah Bache."

"The fourth quilter was a friend of Sarah's, who also lived in Philadelphia, the widow Elizabeth Griscom Ross."

I gasped. "Do you mean *Betsy* Ross?"

"The same. Benjamin Franklin charged her with sewing the first American flag in secret, which she did while sitting every day with the other three ladies. Sarah convinced Betsy to reproduce the flag's design for the central medallion of the quilt. The eighteen-inch block depicted thirteen white stars appliquéd in a circle on a blue field."

I smiled as I pictured the quilt. Those ladies sat together, just like my friends and me, sewing and chatting and eating cake. They wore long dresses; we chose jeans and overalls. They penned letters; we used the telephone or e-mail. Otherwise, the passage of centuries had changed nothing. Our quilting connected us through time. Lucy, Birdie, and I often helped each other with projects. Did Abigail, Martha, and Sarah help Betsy sew the flag? Did they, like their husbands and father, debate among themselves what should be written in the Declaration of Independence?

"How big was this quilt?"

"About the size of a modern-day throw. Four

experienced needle women would've easily finished all the stitching."

I took the last bite of my cookie. "Who got the quilt?"

"The ladies sewed it specifically to raise funds for the Continental Army led by George Washington. On the twelfth of July, a week after the congress voted to adopt the Declaration, the quilt was auctioned off at a gala dinner held in Philadelphia. Stephen Hawkins, representative from Rhode Island, prevailed on a member of 'The Hebrew congregation Yeshuat Israel of Newport' to come up with the highest bid for the cause. Unfortunately, the trail ended there for historians. The buyer insisted on remaining anonymous."

The Hebrew congregation she referred to worshipped at the Touro Synagogue. Did Nathan Oliver's ancestor make the winning bid? Had the Declaration Quilt always been in the Oliver family?

Dr. Hunter lowered her voice a notch. "The Smithsonian will need to authenticate the quilt, of course, but we've located a private donor prepared to pay Mrs. Oliver's estate two million dollars to hand over this American treasure to the National Archives."

"My God, two million is a lot of money, but I can see why you'd pay so much. The Declaration Quilt is an important part of American history, ranking right up there with the signed copies of the Declaration of Independence. Only this national treasure was created in fabric by the founding mothers of this country."

I dreaded breaking the news. "The only problem is, I haven't found the quilt among Harriet's things."

She took a sharp breath. "The quilt is gone?"

"We're still looking. Several items have disappeared after Harriet's murder."

Dr. Hunter paused for about five seconds. "Did you say *murdered*?"

"Yes. And I believe her killer came after the quilt, among other things."

"This is devastating news. I so hoped . . . Please let me know if anything changes, Mrs. Rose."

I promised to contact Dr. Hunter the moment I located the quilt.

I began to connect the dots. The items missing from Harriet's house suggested the killer wasn't interested in Native American baskets or folk crafts— no matter how valuable. He wanted certain Early Americana. The first-edition books by the Founding Fathers and the quilt with the signatures would be the crown of anyone's collection.

I still couldn't fit the missing jewelry into the whole puzzle. I needed to find out how Isabel got Harriet's ring and if she had any more of her things. I also needed to figure out how to examine the bracelet Paulina wore today. Was it Harriet's? Did one of those women kill Harriet and steal her property? Could the slender Isabel or the short Paulina have overpowered Harriet and strangled her?

The phone rang while I washed out my teacup. I turned off the faucet and dried my hands on a red-and-white-striped dish towel. The voice on the other end wheezed.

"This is Detective Farkas. We'll be through with the Oliver house by Wednesday."

"Thanks for the heads-up. Listen, Detective, I need to check Harriet's financials. Can you recommend a good forensic accountant?"

"If you're thinking about investigating your friend's murder, forget it. Don't start going all *Rizzoli & Isles* on me."

"No way, Detective." *Rizzoli carries a gun.*

He exhaled noisily. "Yeah, I know someone. A young guy used to work for the DA. He opened his own offices in Westwood, and I hear he's doing real well. He's testified in some big cases—the corruption scandal with the City of Bell and the federal beef with Morgan Stanley. Name's Julian Kessler. Tell him Gabe Farkas sent you."

I wrote down Kessler's phone number and called his office.

He spoke rapidly. "Farkas referred you? Cool. Tomorrow at three. Don't be late. I don't like it when people are late."

The next morning I drove to Birdie's house for quilty Tuesday and pushed open the front door. The aroma of cinnamon and cardamom circled in the air. "I smell applesauce cake."

Birdie smiled and hugged me. "I figured you deserved a special treat after yesterday, so I baked your favorite."

"How're you doing, girlfriend?" Lucy glanced up from her sewing. She dressed all girly today in her pink denim jeans and a pink angora sweater. Little flowers carved out of rose quartz decorated her earlobes.

I sat in the green chenille easy chair. "Yesterday was rough." I stretched my Jacob's Ladder over my wooden hoop. I always started sewing in the middle of the quilt, working my way toward the edges and smoothing the fabric as I went. Stitching this way avoided sewing puckers into the backing and produced a perfectly square and flat quilt. I threaded a size eleven "between," a one-inch-long needle perfect for making tiny stitches, and took a deep breath. "Don't know what I would've done without your help."

Birdie, still in her trademark denim overalls, wore a blue hand-knit cardigan against the chill. She waved her hand in a circle. "All for one, and one for all."

The three of us helped each other through some pretty rough times over the years, creating strong bonds of friendship. We could always count on each other.

"I spoke with Dr. Hunter at the Smithsonian yesterday." I told them all about the Declaration Quilt.

"Heavens, how exciting!" Birdie clasped her hands. "I've never heard of it, have you?"

I shook my head. "No, but apparently certain historians knew about it. They assumed the quilt no longer existed—that is, until Harriet contacted the International Quilt Study Center."

Lucy gathered two more pieces to join together. "A two-million-dollar historical quilt? Just think. We'll be national heroes when we find it."

"Don't get your hopes up, Lucy."

She held up her hand. "I've got one of my feelings. The quilt is definitely in Harriet's house."

From long experience, I understood the futility of arguing with one of Lucy's *feelings*. "I hope you're right. Detective Farkas says we can go back inside tomorrow."

"Paulina the psychic came across as quite a

character in her purple cape yesterday," Birdie chuckled. "Why did Harriet fire her?"

"Harriet stopped seeing her when Nathan showed up in the middle of their last session."

"What do you mean 'showed up'?" Lucy sat forward.

"Paulina channeled him during a séance. Harriet got so frightened she broke off all contact with the psychic."

Birdie grabbed the end of her braid and frowned. "You can certainly understand her reaction, given the abuse she suffered during their marriage."

"You're right. I suspect if Harriet thought Nathan could talk to her from the dead, he might still be able to hurt her. Of course I don't believe Harriet actually talked to any ghosts. I think Paulina decided to spice things up a bit by pretending to be a new so-called spirit."

Lucy sat up a little straighter and stopped stitching. "Well, I for one believe there are things we can't explain by science or the rational mind. Many of my premonitions have come true, and you know it. Remember Claire Terry's murder last spring?"

Lucy referred to the time we discovered the body of a dead quilter. She warned me bad things were about to happen and they did. But did she really have ESP, or was she just expressing her own fears and apprehensions?

Lucy picked up her needle again and resumed stitching two triangles together. She didn't like to use the sewing machine to piece the tops of her quilts. Instead, she preferred to take her time and make the seams the old-fashioned way. "You've got to keep an open mind, Martha." Without dropping her needle, she curled her fingers in an air quote.

"Nathan Oliver certainly was a mean *ess oh bee*. How can you be so sure he didn't possess the power to come back from the dead?"

Is she kidding? "Because Harriet struggled with someone strong enough to break her wrist and strangle her. No ghost could do that."

Birdie handed us thick slices of spicy, warm applesauce cake with plenty of plump, sweet raisins. "Martha dear, to find poor Harriet's killer, you should examine his motive. What's your best guess?"

"Theft is at the top of my list. Someone wanted Harriet's priceless items of Early Americana."

Birdie nodded. "Okay, who in her life knew what she owned?"

"Her attorney, Abernathy; Emmet Wish, her insurance agent; her friend Isabel; Paulina; Estella Oliver and her brother, Henry; people at the International Quilt Study Center; and people at the Smithsonian—even the philanthropist who's willing to pay two million dollars for the quilt. Maybe the fund-raiser from Children's Hospital and whoever else came into her house. Harriet didn't exactly hide her things."

Lucy ended her thread with a knot and cut a new strand from the spool. "So, what you're saying is there's no shortage of people who could've stolen the books, the quilt, and the jewelry."

"Pretty much." I took a stitch, pulled the thread through the top layer of my quilt, and hid the knot in the batting. Then I started a new line of stitches. "I've seen some of Harriet's missing jewelry, though."

Lucy spoke through a mouthful of cake. "Where, for heaven's sake?"

I told them about Harriet's ring sitting on Isabel's finger and possibly Harriet's bracelet on Paulina's wrist at the funeral.

"Oh dear," said Birdie. "Do you think one of them is the murderer?"

I shrugged. "Who knows?"

"This doesn't get us any closer to identifying the killer." Lucy began a new seam.

"Not yet, but I have an appointment this afternoon with a forensic accountant. I'm going to ask him to examine all of the financial records prepared by Abernathy's office. Bunny Friedman, the fund-raiser he brought to the funeral, seemed awfully anxious to get her hands on Harriet's money."

Birdie brushed a wisp of white hair from her face. "Do you suspect something?"

"I want the accountant to look closely at the financial activity during the ten months Harriet lay dead in her house. Did Abernathy authorize transfers of money, gifts, or donations? If we uncover any fraud or embezzlement, we might find the motive for Harriet's murder."

Birdie said, "At which point you'll hand the information over to the police and let them go after the murderer. Right?"

"Right."

Lucy put down her sewing and narrowed her eyes. "Why do I only half believe you?" She shifted uncomfortably in her seat. "Be careful, girlfriend. I'm getting one of my strong feelings."

With every unanswered question about Harriet, I also developed some strong feelings.

On the drive back to my house I realized I'd completely forgotten about another person who'd been familiar with every item in Harriet's place—a person who might have carried a grudge for being fired. Abernathy said he'd e-mail me her contact information, but I hadn't checked my computer in days. Maybe Harriet's housekeeper could shed some light on the mystery.

CHAPTER 14

I arrived home from Birdie's house at two and rushed inside because my phone was ringing.

"Martha?"

Oh my God. Arlo Beavers, my ex-boyfriend. I hadn't heard from him since he dumped me four months ago and had a fling with his dog Arthur's pretty blond veterinarian. A little later Beavers wanted to get back together again, but I could no longer trust him. Then he got angry when he found out that during his fling with the vet I had my own amazing encounter with Crusher. It was complicated.

"Hello, Arlo." I could barely keep my voice even. "How are you?"

"Fine. And you?" *This is awkward.* "How's Arthur?"

He let out a breath. "Actually, Artie's my reason for calling."

"Oh my God, he's okay, isn't he?" Four months ago the dog ended up in the hospital because of me. I never got over the guilt.

"Yeah. He's fine, but I'm leaving town for ten days and my dog sitter bailed out at the last minute.

I hate to leave him in a kennel. He'd be more comfortable with someone he knows and likes. Do you think you could you take him?"

First he dumps me, now he's dumping his dog on me?

My gut wanted me to tell him to go take a flying leap, but I opted to say yes for a couple of reasons. First, I loved the dog and owed him a huge favor for saving my life. Second, I'd show Beavers I no longer cared about him. I could take care of Arthur and not think twice about his owner. "Sure. When are you leaving?"

"Tonight. I'll bring him over around five if that's okay with you."

"No problem. Looking forward to it." *Not!*

"Good. See you then. And thanks for the favor."

"Where Arthur's concerned? Anytime."

I traded my jeans for black wool trousers and added a soft aqua turtleneck sweater that was nicely filled out by my ample bosom. A square turquoise pendant hung from a long silver chain and nestled between the girls. I grabbed the accordion file with all of Harriet's papers and headed toward Westwood and the forensic accountant's office. Leaving at two-fifteen left little room for error. If the traffic slowed me down, I'd be late. Kessler had said he hated when people were late.

Fortunately, the traffic fairy smiled on me and I arrived at Kessler's building with fifteen minutes to spare. Julian Kessler Associates was on the twelfth floor, two floors above Abernathy, Porter & Salinger. I made a mental note to ask for a validation for the twenty-dollar-an-hour parking at the end of our appointment.

The small gray reception area offered Spartan

seating for four people at most. Black and white photos of LA City Hall, the Capitol Building in DC, and the Eiffel Tower decorated the walls. A sliding window closed off a reception desk on the wall opposite the main door. Unlike the luxurious ambiance in Abernathy's office, the message here implied "all business." If someone was hiding something, Julian Kessler would find it.

I pushed the buzzer and the window at the end of the room slid open to reveal the friendly face of a young woman with dyed black hair cut in asymmetrical spikes with multiple piercings in her ears and another in her nose.

"May I help you?" She smiled. A small silver knob twinkled on her tongue.

What's the deal with tongue balls? "Martha Rose to see Julian Kessler."

"Awesome. You're a bit early. He'll like that."

She handed me an iPad in a blue cover. "Please fill out our New Client form."

I swiped pages, typed with one finger, and filled out the electronic form in under five minutes.

I handed the iPad back to her.

"Finished already?"

I nodded.

"Awesome. Please come through."

A buzzing sounded at the door next to her window, and I walked into a large, well-lit interior space painted butter yellow in startling contrast to the gray waiting room. Not so many years ago, employees of an accounting firm wore suits and sat in austere cubicles. Today, however, a dozen young techies in T-shirts and jeans sat at desks in an open area with computers and thirty-two-inch monitors.

Two of the guys played catch with a ball of wadded paper. One of them wore a black T-shirt that said, "ATOMS MAKE STUFF UP." In the far corner a young woman ran on a treadmill.

We walked toward a glass-walled office in the back, passing a pristine room filled with electronics stacked on shelves and connected to each other by yards of cable.

"Here you go." Pierced Girl walked away, leaving me standing in the open doorway of the office.

A gawky thirty-something guy stood behind his desk. His eyes dropped below my chin. He must've really liked my turquoise pendant. He finally tore his eyes away and hastily gestured toward a chair. "Nice. Take a seat. You're early."

I looked at my watch. *Two minutes before three counts as early?*

Julian Kessler started to sit back down again, hesitated, and came around his desk to sit in the chair opposite mine. His dark-rimmed glasses suggested brilliant geek, but the stray piece of brown hair tickling his forehead made him seem twelve. He dressed slightly more formal than his associates, wearing khaki Dockers and a blue plaid shirt. Kessler nervously tapped his fingers together as he talked.

"Farkas referred you. What do you need?" His eyes slid down to my pendant again and his finger dance sped up.

"I need someone to examine my friend's financial records to make sure she hasn't been ripped off."

He adjusted his glasses. "Why doesn't she come in herself?"

I told him all about Harriet and the missing items from her house. "Right now I don't trust anyone. Her attorney has been handling her financial affairs. He'll have all her records."

"Who's the attorney?" Now he jiggled his right knee.

"Deacon Abernathy."

The tapping and bouncing stopped. "The guy in this building?"

"Yes. Will that be a problem?"

He sat back, frowned, and tapped his fingers again. "Nope. When I worked with the DA, we took a look at his firm."

Crap. This didn't bode well. "For what reason?"

"No charges were ever filed. I can't tell you any more."

My heart sank. If Abernathy's office stole from Harriet, settling the rest of her estate would be an endless nightmare. "We need to look closely at the financial activity, especially during the months Harriet lay dead in her house. Will you help me?"

His eyes darted southward again. "Sure. First, you need to sign this. It gives me the power to access all your friend's records. Did you bring any papers with you?"

I signed the release and handed him the accordion file. "You can make copies of these."

He picked up his phone and sent a quick text. Two minutes later Pierced Girl showed up in the doorway.

Kessler handed her the accordion file and pointed to me. "Isis, I need you to make some copies before she goes."

When Isis disappeared, he turned to me. "Phone Abernathy's office right now. Tell him we'll pick up all the paperwork tomorrow morning at ten."

I fished my cell phone out of my purse. Abernathy

wasn't in, so I spoke to his assistant, Nina, and put her on speaker.

"*All* the paperwork?"

"Yes. Going back to the beginning."

"We'll need some time, Mrs. Rose."

"Then I'll fax you a release form right now so you can get started. Kessler Associates will be in your office at ten sharp tomorrow morning. Please have everything ready by then."

I ended the call and Kessler grinned at me.

"What?"

"Can I call you Martha? Call me Julian. I'd like that."

"Okay."

He spoke briskly. "You handled her great. You're smart. You get things done. I like that."

"Well, thanks, Julian." I took a pen and notepad from my purse and changed the subject. "I'm going to need a high-end estate manager to help me dispose of Harriet's possessions. A lot of stuff needs to be appraised before it's sold, but there's too much for me to handle alone. I need a professional. Can you recommend anyone?"

"Yeah. There's this woman, Susan something. I've never met her, but she's done work for my clients. I'll have Isis look it up for you." He picked up the phone and sent another text. I placed the pen and notepad back in my purse.

Kessler's knee jiggled again and he cleared his throat. "So, are you married or what?"

This kid's social graces could use some polishing. "No."

"Boyfriend?"

He's flirting with me? Thankfully, Isis walked in with my accordion file and a slip of paper with the name Susan Daniels and a phone number. I thanked her as she left the office, and gathered my things.

"Wait," said Kessler. "Will you go out with me?"

My jaw dropped open. "You mean like on a *date*?"

He nodded, his Adam's apple bouncing this time.

"How old are you, Julian?"

He sat up straighter. "I know I look young, but I'm thirty-six."

I stood to leave. "I've got slippers older than you."

Kessler stood also. "I like mature women."

So it wasn't the turquoise pendant that fascinated him.

His Adam's apple bobbed faster. "You're hot."

Dear God.

I hugged the accordion file to my chest. "Well, I'm flattered, Julian, but dating is strictly off the table. I understand you're the best forensic accountant in the country, and I'm glad you're going to help me. I have a rule. I never date the people I do business with."

Kessler put his hands in his back pockets and looked at the floor. "Is that a firm rule?"

"Hard and fast."

Kessler's head jerked up. By the expression on his face, I immediately regretted my choice of words.

He cleared his throat. "So, I'll call you if I come up with anything on the case."

"Of course." I offered my hand, which he grasped with a sweaty palm. I felt sorry for Kessler. A genius with numbers and computers, social situations clearly baffled him. I hurried so fast to get out of there, I forgot to ask for parking validation.

By the time I drove onto the northbound 405 Freeway, I hit rush hour at four. I didn't pull into my driveway until five, just as Beavers arrived. A ninety-pound German shepherd jumped out of Beavers's silver Camry and bounded toward me. I crouched down and hugged the dog for the first time in four months. Beavers hadn't allowed me to see Arthur after his injury. Arthur licked my face and wagged his tail. Obviously dogs were more forgiving than certain people.

Beavers stood on the porch with a thirty-pound bag of kibble, dog bowls, a hairy dog bed, a pooper scooper, and a leash. He wore jeans, cowboy boots, and a Western shirt with pearl snaps. I stood and his woodsy cologne brought back memories of happier days together. His mustache tickled as he gave me a quick peck on my cheek. "I'll take these inside for you if you'll open your door."

Before I could get the key in the lock, a woman's voice commanded, "Hurry up, honey. We don't want to be late for our flight to Hawaii."

I froze and looked over at his car parked on the street. A pretty woman with a perky blond ponytail sat smirking. Kerry Andreason, Arthur's veterinarian and the woman Beavers cheated with four months ago. My hand started shaking as I shoved the key into the door. "So, you're back together? Or were you ever apart?"

Beavers cleared his throat and looked away. "Look. I really appreciate your taking care of Artie for me."

"I guess this means you're no longer afraid I'll get him hurt or killed?"

His eyes pleaded with me. "Come on, Martha. Let's not do this."

The muscles in my neck tightened. Beavers had moved on from our relationship. He was showing me, not the other way around. Paulina the psychic predicted he'd want to come back into my life. But only to use me as a dog sitter. I tried to hide the tremble in my voice. "You're right. Just dump the kibble in the kitchen and I'll take care of the rest. You don't want to miss your flight."

As soon as he crossed my doorway into the house, the Camry horn started honking. He placed the bag near the washing machine and ruffled the dog's ears. "Gotta run."

I closed the door behind him. The pain from my neck reached across my shoulders. I unrolled my yoga mat. Maybe some stretches would help. I sat down on the floor and Arthur sat next to me. The next thing I knew, I threw my arms around the dog and wept into his fur. He sat there patiently, slowly thumping his tail against the floor.

I finally stopped crying and stroked his fur. "You're so much better than he is, Arthur." A meow sounded and the shepherd's tail thumped rapidly. When Beavers and I were an item, our animals became best friends.

Bumper walked over to the dog and they touched noses, which meant "nice to see you again" in cat language. Bumper turned around and Arthur stuck his wet nose in the cat's butt, which meant "like-wise" in dog language. The cat looked over his shoulder and the dog bowed in the downward facing Arthur position. Then they both ran to the back door for outside play time. Thankfully, some relationships never changed.

The crying jag released my stress and tension, but I still felt heavyhearted and sad. I stood, rolled up my mat, and there was a knocking on the door.

Crusher stood in his leather jacket and a brown bandana.

I stepped back and opened the door wider. "Come in."

He bent to kiss me, but I turned away. I had already rejected one man today and was rejected by another. All the drama had exhausted me.

"Babe. What's the matter?"

I puffed out my breath and shook my head.

His voice softened. "The funeral yesterday, right?"

I nodded and avoided his eyes. I didn't want to tell him the real reason for my mood. I had just seen Beavers with *that woman.* Thankfully, I didn't have to explain Arthur's presence since he was out of sight in the backyard.

Crusher shrugged off his leather jacket, gathered me in his arms, and pulled me into his massive chest. His heart thumped underneath his T-shirt. He must have just come from his shop because he smelled faintly like gasoline.

With my ear pressed to his body, his voice rumbled in his chest. "I can see you've been crying. Let me be a part of it. Wherever you want to go, let me take you there."

I pulled away and looked up at him. "Thanks, Yossi, but I'm mentally exhausted right now. I really just want to be alone."

He bent to kiss me softly on my forehead. "I'll be back tomorrow, babe. I talked to your uncle. You and I have something serious to discuss."

"Oh my God, is he all right?" I lived in fear of the day when something happened to Uncle Isaac. I knew his mind was still top-notch. What about his health? Why would he confide in Crusher and not me?

He smiled. "Don't worry. It's not anything bad. I just needed to ask his advice about something." He put on his jacket. "Get some rest. I'll see you tomorrow night."

I closed the door behind him and slumped against it. Thank God he hadn't seen Arthur. I opened the back door and let the boys come inside while I filled their dinner bowls.

What kind of advice did Crusher need from Uncle Isaac? I didn't even want to think about the possibilities.

CHAPTER 15

Arthur woke me up Wednesday morning at eight. I slowly eased my aching and stiff body out of bed and swallowed a Soma, my go-to medication. Then I stepped into a clean pair of size-sixteen stretch denim jeans and a long-sleeved pink T-shirt. While I waited for the coffee to finish brewing, Farkas called.

"I hope I didn't wake you."

"Not at all." I poured a dollop of milk into my coffee. "We never got to talk about the funeral, Detective. What did you think?"

"Nice ceremony."

"No, I mean suspects. Did you notice anyone shady?"

"Only Sybill Trelawney in the purple cape."

I laughed. "You read *Harry Potter*?"

"Negative. But I sit through the movies every weekend. Got my kids the set of eight DVDs." He cleared his throat. "I called to inform you we've finished with the Oliver house. I can meet you in Brentwood this morning to hand over the key."

"Did forensics uncover anything? I seriously doubt they found any useful evidence after so many months."

"Probably not, but they've taken samples back to the lab. Including the vacuum cleaner with all your dead flies."

"You're actually going to examine a million flies?"

"We're looking for other trace evidence you may've picked up. Normally SID does the vacuuming, but you saved them the trouble."

"What's SID?"

"Scientific Investigation Division."

"Is that the same as CSI?"

"Exactly the same. We'll need a set of everyone's fingerprints for elimination purposes."

"My, Lucy's, and Birdle's prints are already on file in the West Valley Division."

Farkas wheezed heavily in what might have been a chuckle. "Funny, you don't look like a gang of desperados."

"We stumbled on a crime scene last spring. They took our prints then for the same reason."

"I'll check it out. The guys you hired to guard the house are already in the system. Interesting choice of friends you have."

"To me they're just a group of regular guys getting together to ride motorcycles."

"Right." Papers shuffled in the background. "Do you know something about a watch collection?"

"The collection is worth a quarter of a million, according to the insurance rider."

"We found a display case in a drawer upstairs. One of the watches is missing. Has anything else disappeared from the house?"

"Not sure. I haven't finished exploring Harriet's

house or compiling an inventory of her possessions. Once we go back inside, I'll have a better idea."

"Keep me informed. Robbery gives us a clear motive for the homicide."

I'm way ahead of you, Detective.

I checked the clock on the microwave. "Can I meet you at Harriet's house at ten?"

"You have my number. Call me when you get there. I'm ten minutes away."

I called Lucy. "Farkas says he'll give back Harriet's key today. Want to come with me?"

"You know I do. I'll bring Birdie. What time shall I pick you up?"

"Before nine-thirty. I promised him I'd be in Brentwood by ten. Oh, and, Lucy, I'll have Arthur with me."

"Who?"

"Arlo's dog."

"Are you serious? What are you doing with his dog?"

"Arlo called yesterday. He planned to leave town on vacation. When Arthur's dog sitter dropped out at the last minute, he asked for a favor. I said yes."

"Why, for heaven's sake?"

"Because I owe Arthur big time for saving my life. Turns out Arlo's in Hawaii with his skinny blond vet."

"NO! And you took the animal anyway?"

"Of course I did. Arthur can't help it if his owner's a jerk."

Twenty minutes later Lucy showed up dressed in fifty shades of orange. From her brassy dyed curls to her tangerine canvas shoes, she shone like the sunset over a Moroccan brothel. In contrast, Birdie wore a hand-knit fisherman's sweater over her denim overalls and had bundled her feet in gray woolen socks and Birkenstocks.

The dog sat with me in the backseat of Lucy's Caddy, smearing his window with nose slime and fogging it up with his breath. We took the Sunset Boulevard off-ramp at ten-fifteen, and I called to inform Farkas we were almost at Harriet's.

Malo jumped out of his maroon SUV and opened the Caddy doors for us. *"Buenos días,* ladies." When he smiled, the vertical lines tattooed on his cheeks stretched wider.

I grabbed Arthur's leash and got out of the car. "Thanks for braving the cold for the last few nights. You're really earning your money."

Malo briefly thrust his chin forward. "You pay me good."

Farkas pulled up behind Lucy's car and rolled down his window but didn't get out. "I got a call. Fresh homicide. Take this." He put his arm outside and handed me two keys.

"Thanks."

He rolled up his window and drove away.

The dog walked over to Malo and sniffed his hand.

The biker squatted down and scratched him behind the ears. *"Chucho."*

"Malo, what happened when the police were here?"

He stood. "They were in the house day and night. Carried out a lot of plastic bags and a vacuum cleaner. Finally finished about one this morning." He spat on the ground. "Those *pendejos* wouldn't let me go inside. They said I'd have to wait for the all clear from the cops."

I tried to hand him one of the keys, but he waved

me off. The roar of a high-test engine filled the air. "Nah. Carl's here. Give the key to him."

Carl parked his yellow Corvette behind Lucy's Caddy. A lock of his sandy hair slid down his forehead as he bent down to give Birdie a hug.

She patted the arm of his black leather jacket. "Oh, such a pretty car, dear."

He stuck out his chest a little. "Thanks. Since the house is off-limits, I had to work from somewhere, so I brought my wheels."

Arthur trotted over and licked Carl's hand. Carl helped me save the dog's life four months ago when a lowlife stabbed him in the shoulder. He pointed to Arthur. "Is this . . . ?

"Yeah. He remembers you."

Carl bent over and ruffled the dog's fur and got a funny expression on his face. "Doesn't he belong to that cop friend of yours?"

Malo tensed and frowned at me.

"Not this week. For the next eight days, he belongs to me while his owner is on vacation"—I winked at the biker—"with his *girlfriend*."

Malo relaxed and did the fist dance with Carl before he drove away.

I opened the house, not knowing what we'd find inside. Nothing much seemed to have changed. The pictures still hung on the walls and the books still sat on the shelves. But gray and white fingerprinting dust covered almost every surface.

I unhooked Arthur from his leash and he immediately began to explore. He started in the foyer, sniffing his way in a circle around the baseboards. We walked to the library and found, to our relief, Lucy's inventory equipment on the table hadn't been disturbed by the LAPD. Carl sat down, opened his laptop, and scrubbed Arthur's belly.

Birdie leaned heavily on Lucy's arm as we slowly climbed the stairs.

"Take your time," said Lucy.

Birdie winced. "Rain is coming soon. My knees are barking."

When we reached the top, I said, "Let's start in the linen closet at the end of the hall."

The long and narrow space only accommodated two of us.

"You wait here, Birdie." I brought her a chair from the guest room so she wouldn't have to stand in the hallway with her bad knees.

The ironed sheets, neatly stacked before the forensics team arrived, now sat slightly askew. We opened the cupboards one by one and removed and unfolded every blanket, sheet, and towel. We didn't find the quilt.

Lucy pulled the shelves and pushed on the wall, trying to detect a secret compartment.

I rolled my eyes. "Oh, for the love of God. Are you still looking for a hidey-hole?"

"Yes. My gut is telling me I'm right about a secret hiding place."

A search of the guest suite yielded nothing. We stripped the bed and lifted the mattress and emptied the drawers and the closet.

Lucy poked and knocked and jiggled every surface. Finally, she pronounced, "Nada. Nothing here."

Birdie pressed her fingers against her lips and tears filled her eyes when we entered Jonah's room. "Why, I bet this room's been preserved exactly since the day the little boy died."

I picked up a small frame with a photo of a smiling

fair-haired child. He reflected Harriet's soft eyes and generous smile. "You're probably right, Birdie. I don't think Harriet could bear to part with anything belonging to him." I put the photo back down next to a pile of perfectly folded little T-shirts and tiny clean socks divided into pairs.

Lucy picked up a hairbrush. "Look, there are fine strands of hair still in the bristles."

We searched Jonah's room in silence, handling every item with special care. After stripping the bed, moving the furniture, and emptying the drawers and closets, the only things we discovered were dust bunnies and a few dead flies. Lucy knocked on the last section of wall and reluctantly declared the room solid.

Finally, the time had come to search Harriet's suite. I peered at Birdie, remembering how she turned green in the closet where Harriet's body had lain. "Are you up for this?"

She nodded.

"Let's do this." Lucy peeled off her peach sweater. She threw open a window. "How about letting some fresh air in here?"

We investigated the room methodically, first searching through the covers and under the mattress. Despite my best efforts to vacuum the week before, more dead flies fell out of the folds of the bedding and the drapes.

Next, we pulled out all the drawers from the dressers and side tables and emptied their contents one at a time on Harriet's bed. We didn't discover the quilt or any jewelry, but we did find the pocket watch collection Farkas mentioned earlier.

White satin lined a black leather case. Nine of the ten pocket watches, each in a separate niche, sat in two rows. The seventh timepiece was missing. I checked the photos from the flash drive. Number seven, the heavily engraved gold case with a ruby on top of the stem, had belonged to Benjamin Franklin.

Another valuable piece of Early Americana. Gone.

Clothes in neutral black, beige, and navy blue filled Harriet's closet. Where were the bright colors she loved as a girl? Where were the leg warmers and torn jeans?

"We should go through every pocket and purse to see if maybe Harriet stashed any of her jewelry."

Arthur barked once, his signal for needing a potty break. I headed toward the stairs. "Go ahead and start without me. I'll be right back."

Arthur's toenails clicked on the hardwood floor as he ran from the library at the opposite end of the house toward my voice in the family room. I opened the French doors leading to the backyard. "Okay, boy. Go do your thing." I left the door open so he could come inside when he finished, and rejoined my friends in Harriet's closet upstairs.

Lucy made her way along one wall, dipping her hands into the pockets of outerwear lined neatly in a row. She pulled her hand out of a brown tweed jacket and held up a gold locket. Two pictures sat inside. The first showed a dark-haired boy around nine. Harriet's twin brother, David. The second held a photo of the fair-haired Jonah. "Is this on the list of missing jewelry?" Lucy handed me the golden keepsake.

"No, she didn't insure this piece. I guess it mainly held a sentimental value." I walked to the built-in dresser sitting in the middle of the closet and placed the locket next to a gold charm bracelet in the top drawer.

In one of her letters from Brown University, Harriet wrote she had discovered Coach handbags. "One day I'm going to own one of these," she'd declared. Now several sat in her closet. However, despite being able to afford couture, Harriet seemed to have retained her middle-class tastes. Nothing in her closet screamed money.

"Look!" Birdie fished a plain white envelope from inside a navy blue Coach purse. "There's no writing on it, but something's inside."

My heart sped up a little as I opened the envelope and gazed at a photo of a quilt spread on top of a bed. A blue medallion with thirteen white stars appliquéd in a circle occupied the center. Faint writing appeared on white snowball blocks with red triangles in the corners. Red borders finished the edges. "Oh my God! This is the Declaration Quilt." I held it out for Birdie and Lucy to see.

Birdie drew the picture closer to her face. "We've just got to find it, Martha."

"Tell me about it."

I gradually became aware of Arthur barking outside. I strode to the open bedroom window overlooking the backyard. "Be quiet, Arthur! You'll disturb the neighbors."

He turned toward my voice and barked once in answer. Then he whined, lowered his head, and pawed at the soil in a bed of white chrysanthemums, purple bleeding hearts, and lots of weeds.

Oh, great. "Stop it!" I shouted. If he ruined the flower bed, I'd have yet another thing to fix before I could sell the house.

I returned to the closet, and after ten minutes,

the barking started again. "Oh, for heaven's sake."
I threw a blouse on the built-in dresser. "What is
bothering that dog?"

From the upstairs window I could tell he'd dug
about a foot down. "No! Bad dog."

He abruptly ran into the house and bounded up
the stairs and into Harriet's bedroom. He sniffed
the air and made a beeline for the closet, whining
and snuffling for more than a minute at the hole
in the carpet where her corpse had lain for ten
months. Satisfied, he barked and sat at attention.

I shooed him out of the room. "Leave. You're in
the way."

He returned to the yard and after five minutes
raised the alarm again. Back at the window, I observed him digging in the same spot.

Wait. Arthur was a retired police dog. He'd been
trained to sniff out and locate . . . what?

"Oh my God! Arthur's found something in the
backyard."

The three of us rushed downstairs and joined
the dog near a gaping hole about two feet deep.
Arthur looked at me, whined, and then turned
toward his handiwork, ears pointed forward. I got
down on my knees and examined the hole. Barely
exposed at the bottom were the bones of a human
hand.

I looked up at my friends. "There's a skeleton
hand down there!"

"Get out!" said Lucy.

Birdie covered her heart with her right hand.
"Oh, Martha, not again."

I backed away from the hole. "Look for yourself."

Lucy squatted down, peered inside, and made

the sign of the cross. "Holy mother of God! Is there any more of him?"

"How should I know?"

Lucy stood. "Dig around a little. Maybe you'll find more bones."

She can't be serious. "Me dig? Why don't you dig?"

"You found him first!"

"I don't touch dead bodies."

"No, Martha dear," Birdie piped up, "you only find them."

I ignored her remark about my knack this year for finding murder victims. After all, Arthur discovered this body, not me.

Lucy said, "Tell the dog to dig some more."

I put my hands on my hips. "Just how do you say that in dog language?"

Lucy pointed to the hole and used a commanding voice. "Arthur. Dig!"

Arthur looked at Lucy, tilted his head, and barked once.

"Good boy, Arthur." I patted his head as he sat at attention.

Birdie bent over at the waist and looked into the hole. "Do I see something shiny down there? Maybe you should take it out."

Lucy took one step backward. "Don't look at me."

I knelt again at the edge of the hole and bent forward. Birdie was right. A shiny gold object circled the third finger. With shaking hands I brushed dirt away from the bones and slid the ring off, careful not to disturb the position of the digits.

Carl walked into the backyard. "What's all the noise about?"

I stood. "Arthur dug up a body."

The young man's eyes widened. "No way."

Birdie pointed to the hole. "Take a look for yourself, dear."

Carl bent down and whistled softly. "Better call the cops again."

I inspected the ring and discovered some engraving on the inside, but soil obscured the letters. "There's some writing on this, but it's too dirty to read."

We hurried to the kitchen sink where I found a scrub brush and cleaned the grooves. I pushed my glasses up my nose and squinted to read the words written inside. At first the letters were upside down, so I turned the ring around. "No way!"

Everyone said, "What?"

"I think Arthur's just found the missing Nathan Oliver."

CHAPTER 16

The squad cars came first. Three of them. Uniformed officers taped off the backyard and shooed us inside the house.

A half hour later I watched from inside the family room as Farkas showed up to examine the grave.

Then he ambled through the French doors. "How'd I get so lucky? Two homicides in one day." He gestured toward the yard. "Did you touch anything out there?"

I showed him the ring. "I removed this from the third finger of the left hand."

"I don't believe it," he growled. "You know you've broken the chain of evidence, right?"

I shrugged. "I didn't think it would matter. You need more than just a ring to identify a body, don't you?"

"This is exactly why we ban people from crime scenes. I thought someone as smart as you wouldn't need to be told."

"Sorry."

He gave his head one hard shake as he put on

blue latex gloves. Then he took the ring from my hand and read the inscription out loud: *"Nathan and Harriet June 15, 1980."* The gold band went inside an evidence bag. "We gotta wait for the coroner's positive ID, of course, but it appears you finally found the missing Nathan Oliver. How'd you discover the corpse, anyway?"

The dog yawned and I patted him on the head. "You're looking at a retired police K-9. He located the grave."

Farkas narrowed his eyes. "Don't tell me. You were using a police dog to investigate your friend's murder?"

"It wasn't like that."

"Where'd you get him? These dogs usually retire with their police handlers. The big dude I saw in your kitchen, he's a cop?"

Like I'm a runway model. "No, Arthur's just visiting. His real owner's on vacation."

"It's lucky you brought him. Otherwise the body could've lain there forever."

I brushed a curl away from my eye. "How soon do you think you can get an ID?"

He shrugged. "Depends."

Birdie twirled the end of her white braid around her finger. I could tell she itched to jump into the conversation. An avid fan of *CSI,* she knew a thing or two about police procedure—at least according to the script writers. "Well, if you need a DNA comparison, you'll find hairs belonging to Nathan's son in the boy's hairbrush upstairs. Lucy spotted them earlier today."

Lucy nodded in agreement.

Farkas looked at them. "Is the brush still there?"

"On the dresser in his bedroom."

He motioned to a uniform standing in the doorway. "Go upstairs to the kid's room and bag the hairbrush."

Carl stepped over to Birdie and hugged her shoulder with a supportive arm. "You sure know your stuff."

I peeked outside. A tech had set up a square sifting box and screened the dirt Arthur dug up for pieces of evidence. Other workers were on their hands and knees, carefully removing the earth covering the corpse with small hand shovels and brushes. They were meticulous, but slow. "How long will this take?"

"The grave's not very deep. It's Wednesday today? They'll work around the clock and probably be out of here before Friday. Meanwhile, you'll have to stay away from the house again."

I threw my hands up. "You're kidding! We're not finished yet. You've already searched the premises. Why can't we finish our work inside?"

"For one thing, we're required to secure the area against possible contamination of the crime scene. And since you seem to ignore the rules, you'll have to hand over the keys again until this is done." He stuck out his hand. "Sorry for the inconvenience."

I dug the key out of my purse and signaled Carl to hand over his copy. "Fine. Will you at least notify me with the ID and the results of the autopsy?"

Little beads of sweat sat on the detective's forehead, and he pulled out a handkerchief to dab them away. "You'll be notified. Right now, I want all of you to go to the West LA station to give statements." He gave us directions as we gathered our things to leave.

Lucy and I drove with the dog to the West LA Division on Butler Avenue. Carl and Birdie followed us in the yellow Vette.

"Well, obviously Nathan Oliver didn't *drown at sea* like the suicide note said." Lucy curled her fingers in an air quote. "How'd he end up buried in the backyard?"

"You're asking me? Like I know?"

Lucy made a left into the parking lot. "Do you think your friend Harriet killed him?"

"Absolutely not. Murder just wasn't in her makeup. "

Farkas met us at the door and we all walked in the station together. He took my statement in a small blue interview room. The walls and ceiling were covered with those acoustic tiles riddled with tiny holes. I wondered if somewhere in front of me, behind one of the openings, a camera lens recorded our session. I reached in my purse, put on some pink lipstick, and smiled at the wall.

The detective rested his iPhone on the table and pushed a button. "Okay, Mrs. Rose. I'm going to tape your testimony." He made a preliminary statement for the record and then began. "Please start with your arrival at the Oliver house."

I told him about our search for the missing Declaration Quilt and showed him the photo from Harriet's Coach bag.

"This quilt is worth two million dollars?"

"Now you get why we were anxious to go through every item in the house. We were searching Harriet's closet when Arthur barked for a potty break, so I let him outside. He sniffed out the burial site in the garden. I watched from an upstairs window as he dug in the dirt. I paused and smiled. "He wanted to give us a hand."

Farkas grunted. "Hilarious."

"Anyway, by the time I rushed outside, Arthur had stopped digging. I looked in the hole and saw the bones. I stuck my arm in, brushed away some dirt, and removed the ring. Then we called you."

Detective Avila walked in the room and nodded at me. He handed his partner a folder and left. After a minute, Farkas looked up. "We caught a break. This is the missing person's file on Nathan Oliver with his dental records. It'll make ID-ing the body much easier."

I slung my purse over my shoulder and stood. "Great. Do you have all you need from me?"

Farkas pointed to the chair and frowned. "No. Sit back down."

Whoa.

When I stiffened at his tone, he added, "Please."

From previous experience, I knew the police sometimes made you repeat your story to double-check details. I slumped back down in the chair. I hoped this wouldn't drag on forever.

"Anything else missing from the house?"

"Yes. We've almost concluded our inventory. Several things have vanished. First-edition books by the Founding Fathers, a watch belonging to Benjamin Franklin, the Declaration Quilt, and Harriet's fine jewelry."

Farkas shoved a pad of paper and pen across the table. "Write it all down. We find the stuff, we find Mrs. Oliver's killer."

"Maybe." I picked up the pen.

He squinted. "What do you mean, *maybe?*"

"Several rare and valuable things were left

behind." I described the baskets made by Dat So La Lee and Nellie Jameson Washington. "And you saw for yourself only one of the ten pocket watches is missing. I think the killer wanted specific items. Historically significant Early Americana."

Farkas scowled. "Really? Then how do you explain the missing jewelry?"

I screwed up my mouth and frowned. "I haven't worked that out yet."

"Do me a favor."

"What?"

"Don't try to *work it out*. Just tell me everything you've twigged so far and let me do the detecting. He pointed to the yellow lined pad in front of me. "Go ahead, put together a list of the missing items. And hand over the photo of the two-million-dollar quilt. I'll make a copy."

I clicked the top of the pen. "I'll do better. I'll provide you with photos and descriptions of everything."

I hadn't eaten since breakfast and my stomach growled. "I'm hungry."

He picked up his iPhone and consulted his watch. "Interview stopped at two-thirty."

"I'll have someone make a run to the nearby Subway."

"Fine. I want a six-inch turkey on jalapeno bread with extra cheese, avocado, and all the veggies. And chipotle mayo. You can also get me a couple oatmeal cookies and a Coke Zero."

He raised one eyebrow. "You said a *diet* Coke?"

He has an opinion? He should talk. I tugged my T-shirt over my hips. "Don't forget to feed my friends waiting for me out there."

Farkas got up, put his hand on the doorknob,

and turned back. "By the way, I heard from Kessler. He thanked me for referring you."

"Julian Kessler is . . . interesting."

Farkas scratched the side of his neck. "Give the guy some leeway. He's a little jiggy, but he's the best in the business. Kessler can afford to turn away potential clients if he doesn't like 'em. He made a point of telling me how much he liked you."

If you only knew.

Twenty minutes later the detective returned with my sandwich, two cookies, and a can of Coke Zero. He sat with his own can of regular cola, maneuvered his heavy bulk in the chair, and returned the photo of the Declaration Quilt. "Finished with the list?"

I handed him the legal pad and peeled the paper from around the sandwich. "Thanks for lunch. I couldn't remember every piece of missing jewelry, but I'll e-mail you the details when I get home." I took a bite. "Along with photos."

When I finished eating, he placed his iPhone in the middle of the table again. "Interview resumed at three-ten."

"How much longer will this take? I left Arthur with Lucy and the others. I hope someone thought to take him outside for a break."

"I appreciate your cooperation. We're almost done here." Farkas cleared his throat. "Assuming the corpse turns out to be Nathan Oliver, can you tell me who might've killed him and why?"

"Nathan Oliver was a bully. There are bound to be people he pissed off."

The detective tapped the can of soda with his pudgy fingers. "I'm going with the wife. Do you know if she had a reason to kill him? You said he bullied her?"

"I don't believe for one second Harriet murdered Nathan, but I understand why she could have. Two years after Jonah's death, Isabel Casco told Harriet the boy drowned because Nathan was too drunk and preoccupied to watch him. Even worse, Nathan didn't jump in the water to save his own son."

"Who's Isabel Casco?"

I told him about Harriet's college roommate and how she discovered the details of Jonah's death.

Farkas handed the pad back to me. "Write a list of everyone you've talked to so far."

As I recorded the names, he said, "Mrs. Oliver could have killed her husband in a rage. The timing coincides with his disappearance."

I put down the pen. "No! There has to be another explanation. Harriet would never commit murder. I won't let you ruin her good name just because you think she *might* have. What's more, ever since she was a teenager, she'd suffered a mild case of scoliosis. She couldn't participate in high-school sports and never did hard physical labor. She couldn't have dug Nathan's grave."

Farkas took a drink from his can of soda and studied me for several seconds. "The truth hurts sometimes."

My neck muscles tightened, a sure sign of stress. I stood. "You're wrong, Detective, and I'll prove it."

"Don't do anything reckless, Mrs. Rose. A killer is still out there."

"Well, of course, I won't. I'm not an idiot. My ultimate goal is to disburse Harriet's estate according to her wishes."

And find those books.
And the quilt.
And the Benjamin Franklin watch.
And the jewelry.

In the lobby, a uniform squatted down and scratched Arthur's belly. "Hey, buddy."

When the dog saw me, he jumped up and wagged his tail. Lucy handed me the leash and we walked toward the door.

"Where are the others?"

Lucy's keys jingled in her hand. "We finished our statements a long time ago. Carl took Birdie home, and Arthur and I waited here for you. He's been outside twice."

Huge black clouds covered the tops of the mountains to the east as we headed down Santa Monica Boulevard to the 405. Pinpoint specks of drizzle covered the windshield. Lucy turned a switch and the wipers thumped slowly across the glass, pausing between each stroke. "So, what happened in there with Detective Farkas?"

"He thinks Harriet killed Nathan." I stared at the drops of water getting bigger on the windshield. "I just don't believe the Harriet I knew could kill anyone, even an abusive husband. And another thing doesn't add up." I told her about Harriet's scoliosis. "She couldn't have moved his body and buried him."

Lucy clicked her tongue. "Let's say she didn't kill her husband. How did his body end up buried in the backyard? How could Harriet *not* know about that?"

Lucy had a point. How much did Harriet know about the grave in the flower bed? And who wrote the suicide note? Did Nathan's killer also kill Harriet?

I thought about the tarot card with the picture of people falling out of a tower. "Great danger," Paulina had warned. But all that stuff—tarot, tea leaves, auras—was nothing but quackery. Right?

CHAPTER 17

On the drive to the valley, Lucy sped up her windshield wipers against the heavy drizzle. Thunder clapped somewhere to the northeast over the San Gabriel Mountains. When we got to Encino, the storm hit in earnest. Arthur and I bolted for the house. While he and the cat ate their kibble, I checked my e-mail. Out of forty-four unopened messages, one was from Abernathy with contact information for Harriet's employees.

I called Delia Pitcher, the housekeeper, first.

"Yeah, I heard Miss Harriet died."

"Since you worked for her, Delia, I thought you might help me."

"Don't see how. I worked for Miss Oliver, but she let me go almost a year ago." Children argued in the background. Something made a loud pop and they exploded into gales of laughter. Delia muffled the phone. "Hush!"

"Maybe so, but Harriet left so many unanswered questions behind, I hoped you could fill in some of the blanks. She was murdered shortly after she let you go, but her body wasn't discovered until a few weeks ago."

Delia's voice rose two notches. "I heard, but I didn't kill nobody!"

"No one thinks you killed her. I just need to talk about the way she lived, who came to her house, things like that."

"I'm busy. Work all day for a family on the West Side; then I ride the bus back to Hargis Street to take care a my own. Don't have time for no chit chat."

"Are you home on the weekends? I could drive to your house. This is important."

"Yeah, I suppose, but I can't talk about it right now." She lowered her voice. "My kids will hear. But Miss Oliver, she had some strange ways."

"How?"

Delia whispered, "Ghosts."

"What do you mean?"

"Come on Saturday." She hung up the phone.

That was weird. Delia Pitcher seemed like a hard-working woman who was willing to talk. She didn't sound like the kind of person who had something to hide, but you never knew. Did she ever return the key to Harriet's house? Did the housekeeper take the missing items? Did she kill Harriet?

A pleasant baritone voice answered my call to the gardener. "Rudy."

I introduced myself. "I know you must be aware of what's been happening at Mrs. Oliver's house."

"Yes, ma'am. They found a body buried in back today," he said with a slight Spanish accent. "We showed up like always, but they wouldn't let us in. The police, they questioned me and my guys. We come here two times every week, but we didn't see nothing."

"Did you ever see the ground dug up before?"

"No. We work for Mrs. Harriet for over ten years and never saw nothing."

Rudy made sense. The killer dug the grave in 1997. Anyone hired after wouldn't have known the ground had been disturbed. What about the gardeners working at the time of the crime? Would Farkas bother to locate and question them?

I remembered how the flower bed looked unkempt and weedy compared to the rest of the well-groomed backyard. "The weeds in the flower bed seem so out of place in such a nice yard. Why didn't you take better care of that area?"

"Mrs. Harriet didn't like us to touch the flowers. When the weeds got too high, we used the weed whacker or sometimes Mrs. Delia pulled weeds by hand. But Mrs. Harriet told us not to dig. She said her dog is buried there."

Oh crap! For sure Harriet knew about Nathan's grave. Farkas must have already been aware of this when he questioned me today. But that didn't mean Harriet killed her husband. And because of her scoliosis, she certainly couldn't be the one who dug the grave.

"Did you ever notice anything disturbed around the house, like a window or door left open? Possibly someone wandering around you didn't recognize?"

"No."

I shifted the phone to my other ear. "How about visitors? An unfamiliar car in her driveway during the last ten months?"

"You mean after they said she died? A black Cadillac, a red SUV, and a yellow Corvette." He hummed. "Nice car."

I wished he'd tell me something new. Those cars belonged to Lucy and the two guys guarding the house. "Didn't you wonder why you didn't see Mrs. Oliver for ten months?"

"Like I told the police, Mrs. Harriet didn't come outside. If she wanted something, she send Mrs. Delia to talk to me."

How did someone not worry when they didn't encounter their employer for almost a year? "Who did you talk to after Delia left? Didn't you need approval to buy supplies or make repairs?"

"Uh-uh. I got checks every month from the lawyer. For extra charges, like fertilizer or sprinklers, I send the bill and they pay."

This inquiry seemed to be leading to a dead end. I tried once more. "Okay, I understand why you might not have suspected something was wrong if you never saw Mrs. Oliver, but after you stopped seeing Delia around, weren't you curious?"

"Not really. Mrs. Harriet, she hired many housekeepers. I figure Mrs. Delia leave like the others."

I sighed. "Thank you for your time, Rudy."

"You still want us to take care of the property?"

"Absolutely. Please come back next week. There'll be a lot of cleanup in the yard after the police leave. Of course you'll be paid extra. You can call me directly with any questions." I gave him my phone number and hung up.

A little later at six, Crusher knocked on the door. Arthur stood at attention.

Oh God. I'm going to have to explain why the dog's here. My stomach flipped.

I opened the door and Arthur barked once, tail wagging. He probably remembered Crusher as one of the good guys in the fight where he was severely wounded.

The rain came down in torrents.

Crusher dripped puddles on my oak floor. He stepped inside and immediately took the dripping bandana off his head and shed his wet boots and jacket. "If you bring me a towel, I'll clean this up."

I hurried to the laundry room and returned with a towel and several old cleaning rags. "Here, use these."

Crusher wiped the top of his head and studied Arthur through hooded eyes. "Is this Beavers's dog?" he frowned.

I nodded cautiously.

Arthur trotted over and sniffed the boots.

Crusher tossed the towel in the puddle. "Why?"

I took a deep breath. "Arlo called me at the last minute yesterday asking for a favor. His dog sitter backed out and he needed to catch a plane."

Crusher pushed the towel around with his stockinged foot, mopping up the water. "Why you?"

Reaching down, I stroked Arthur's head. "Because I love this dog and he saved my life."

"What about Beavers?"

My cheeks started to warm. I didn't like having to justify myself. After all, I didn't do anything wrong. "He's in Hawaii with his *girlfriend*."

Crusher hastily wiped off his boots and set them on the floor. He picked up another cloth and slowly wiped the drips from his leather jacket. Then he stopped moving and focused on my face. "So last night, were you upset because of the funeral or because you still have the hots for Beavers?"

I crossed my arms. What right did he have to question me? I hadn't made any commitments. "Think what you want, Yossi. Those are all the questions you get to ask. I'm done explaining myself to you or anyone else."

Crusher put the wet rags in the laundry room, then walked over to me, bent down, and kissed me hard. When he finally pulled away, I gasped for breath.

He took my hand and led me to the sofa, where we both sat. "Babe, you know how I feel about you."

My irritation softened. "So you say."

"I told you I talked to Isaac at the funeral." He held on to my hand, his face deadly serious.

"Now you're on a first-name basis with my uncle?"

The corner of his mouth turned up. "Yeah. We're friends."

A biker and an eighty-year-old retired tailor? "You mentioned last night you asked for his advice?"

He combed his short beard with the fingertips of his left hand. "Actually, several of us spent a long time on Monday discussing certain things having to do with me and you."

"Several of you?"

"Isaac, Morty, and the rest of the old guys from the *minyan*."

So now I understood what those smiles and winks were about. Crusher pleaded his case to the gang of *alte kakers*. "I'm on to you, Mr. Levy. You're trying to soften me up by going through my uncle. It's sweet and old-fashioned, but it won't work."

Suddenly he slid off the sofa and onto his knees in front of me. "I asked Isaac for permission to marry you. We talked mostly about my duties and responsibilities. When they were satisfied I would make a good husband, your uncle and those great old dudes gave me their blessing. So marry me already."

I smiled and wagged my head. "Just so you know? We're not in the second century where women are *given away* in marriage anymore. You can run to my uncle as much as you want, my friend, but I'll make up my mind when *I'm* good and ready."

Crusher nodded slowly and smirked as if making up his mind about something.

Oh, oh. Something's up. I stood. "What? What's so funny?"

"Babe. That's not the only advice they gave me."

He leaned forward and wrapped his arms around my legs. Then in one fluid motion, he stood and flopped me over his shoulder.

"Yossi! Put me down!"

He headed for the bedroom. "Those guys are old school. They said I should show you who's boss."

With my butt in the air and my head dangling, I battered his back with my fists. "Put. Me. Down!"

He dumped me on the bed and stood over me. "Me Ogg," he bellowed, slapping his chest with the palm of his hand and grinning like a meshugena giant caveman.

In spite of myself, giggles rose in my throat. My shoulders shook with silent laughter as I pressed my lips together. Why encourage him?

Arthur trotted in the bedroom, tilted his head, and perked his ears toward Crusher.

Crusher glared at Arlo Beavers's dog and pointed to me. "Mine!"

Arthur turned in submission and left the room.

Oy vey.

For the rest of the evening, I let Ogg believe he was in charge.

CHAPTER 18

Early Thursday morning after Crusher had left for the bike shop, I discovered he'd hung three pairs of jeans in my closet and put a stack of clothes on top of my dresser. Did he expect me to make a space for them in a drawer? We had never talked about his moving in, yet there sat a mound of clean white tube socks, underwear, and T-shirts. Wings of panic fluttered in my chest. Too much, too fast. I must slow him down.

I thought about the men in my life. Aaron, my withholding and manipulative ex-husband, left our marriage for the wife of a colleague. My romance with Beavers, a man basically rigid and set in his ways, started out well. But in the end, he, too, cheated on me.

Now I must decide what to do with Crusher. He embraced life with exuberance and humor. But he could also be fierce, like when he stabbed the lowlife who attacked me four months ago. Could I trust him? I buried my face in one of his fresh shirts and took a deep breath. The truth irritated. I was falling for Crusher—aka Yossi Levy, aka Ogg the caveman.

Gornisht helfen. It's hopeless.

I smoothed out the Grandmother's Fan quilt on my bed, changed into my loose yoga pants and a T-shirt, and carried my laundry into the utility room. Were those Crusher's wet socks and dirty shirt staring up at me from inside my clothes hamper? At least he picked up after himself. But a huge disappointment waited for him if expected me to wash his things

I turned on the television to catch the morning news while I ate a bowl of oatmeal. A veteran white-haired reporter stood in a street lined with big houses. I dropped my spoon when I recognized Harriet's place. Malo and several bikers wearing their Valley Eagles leathers protected the perimeter of the property. Malo must have called in reinforcements.

". . . body discovered yesterday buried in the backyard has been positively identified as Nathan Oliver, the homeowner reported missing over thirteen years ago."

The media attention didn't surprise me. A body buried in the backyard of a Brentwood home became headline news on any day.

"A suicide note found in the residence at the time of his disappearance indicated the victim intended to drown himself in the ocean. The police now believe the note was faked to cover up the murder."

Where do they find these genius reporters? Of course the note was faked, unless Nathan managed to kill and bury himself in his own grave.

"Just one month ago the police also found the

victim's wife, Harriet Oliver, murdered in this same house. She'd been dead for ten months."

The reporter stopped and adjusted her earpiece. "The police are about to give a statement."

The picture flashed to an exterior shot of the police station on Butler Avenue in West LA, then switched to an interior scene. Detective Gabe Farkas stepped up to a podium with several microphones attached and an LAPD seal on the front. He blinked several times as dozens of cameras clicked and flashed. Thanks to HDTV, every dot of sweat showed on his upper lip. He cleared his throat.

"The grave of missing person Nathan Oliver was discovered yesterday in the backyard of his home in Brentwood. The coroner estimates the time of death is consistent with Mr. Oliver's disappearance in 1997. The cause of death was blunt force trauma to the head. We have strong evidence pointing to the victim's wife, Mrs. Harriet Oliver, as his killer. Since Mrs. Oliver is now deceased, we consider the Nathan Oliver case closed."

Darn him! What proof does he have? Didn't he listen to a thing I told him yesterday?

Farkas removed a handkerchief from his pocket and mopped his face. "One month ago, the police entered the residence and found the body of Mrs. Harriet Oliver. The coroner estimated her death to be approximately ten months before the discovery of her remains. We have evidence Mrs. Oliver may have been surprised by a home invader who stole several valuable items. That investigation is still open."

Reporters shouted questions and the sound faded

out. Farkas's mouth still moved, but his fifteen seconds of fame ended with a commercial.

Of all the weasels in the world, Detective Farkas rose to the top of my list with his indictment of a poor woman not alive to defend herself. I'd prove Harriet innocent if it was the last thing I ever did.

Maybe a gentle workout would calm my agitation. I grabbed my keys and drove to my nine o'clock yoga class. The streets were still wet after last night's rain, and the cold air smelled like damp leaves. After checking into Sublime Yoga at eight forty-five, I rolled out my pink rubber mat on the bamboo floor of room two. A gray-haired man with a paunch leaned against the wall, listening to a group of women chatting. Dasha, the instructor, marched into the room like a dancer, curls bouncing around her face. She struck two small bells together. The room became silent as the notes faded in the air.

"Good morning, class. Today we're going to learn how to do *Uddiyana Bandha,* a position for massaging internal organs."

I didn't know a person could do that, even if she wanted to.

"Expel breath, put hands on thighs, and bend over at waist. Don't breathe. Pull belly toward spine and hold."

Bending over like this? Definitely not a good position for the girls.

After what seemed like an eternity, she said, "Come back to a standing position and breathe."

I gasped for air while my head floated slightly away from my body. I hoped my organs were happy.

Next we did something nobody should do in front of another human being. "Now we will add *agni sara* to pose. This time when bend over, pump belly fast. Pull in, flop down. Pull, release. Pull, release."

Agni. From a Sanskrit word meaning "fire." Other related words: igneous, ignite. Can we breathe now?

An hour later we finished on the floor with *Shavasana,* the corpse pose. I drove back home with a contented liver and joyful kidneys. But a fire still burned in my belly over Harriet being falsely accused. I hoped a little quilting would help me gather my thoughts.

When I was just a little girl, my bubbie taught me how to sew. Uncle Isaac brought home scraps of couture fabric from his tailor shop so I could make doll clothes. I complained about the needle poking my fingers as I pushed it through the cloth, so Bubbie showed me how to protect my hand by wearing a metal thimble on my middle finger. The dimples in the metal cradled the top of the needle and allowed me to quickly maneuver several stitches at once. Back then, the thimble felt bulky and awkward. Now I couldn't sew without one.

The needle bit through a red and yellow calico in a steady rhythm as I loaded the steel shaft with stitches and pushed it through the fabric. I tried to direct my thoughts in the same straight lines as my sewing. Who killed Nathan and buried him? According to Rudy, the gardener, Harriet must have known about the grave in the flower bed because she refused to let him dig there. I believed with all my heart she didn't kill her husband, but she did protect someone all those years. Who, and why?

I cut another length of red quilting thread from the spool and started a new row. Then there was the cocktail ring. *How did Isabel get it? She knows a lot more than she's saying. I've got to figure out a way to get her to open up.*

I paused to adjust my quilt in the hoop. Delia Pitcher, Harriet's housekeeper, mentioned ghosts. Was Delia referring to Paulina the ghost whisperer or the grave in the backyard?

Arthur barked around noon. I stood to let him outside for a break, but the dog stared at the front door. Did I have a visitor? I looked out the window. Detective Farkas heaved his girth from behind the steering wheel of his car. I opened the door and waited with my fists on my hips.

The short walk from the curb left him slightly winded. He reached in the pocket of his blue suit jacket and held out Harriet's keys. "You're free to go inside the Oliver house again."

I snatched them from his hand. "How could you say such a terrible thing about Harriet?"

"I have to follow the facts."

"What facts? You're only guessing."

Farkas rubbed his forehead. "Actually, after interviewing Isabel Casco, we're certain Mrs. Oliver had sufficient motive to kill her husband."

"Nathan abused Harriet, not the other way around. Blaming the victim is the lazy way out."

He puffed his breath through his lips. "You were supposed to e-mail me photos and a list of the items missing from the Oliver house."

"I got sidetracked last night before I could send them." *Ogg the caveman.*

"Since I'm already here . . ."

I stepped to the side and pointed to the living room. "Fine. Sit there."

The detective entered the house and lowered

himself in an easy chair while I sent copies of the photos from my computer to his iPhone. I photocopied my working version of the insurance rider. "The items I circled on this list are the missing ones."

"Thanks." He rifled briefly through the pages and stood to leave.

"Wait. You said on the news Nathan died of blunt force trauma and you're convinced Harriet did it. Did you ever consider self-defense?"

"I hate to burst your bubble, but if he was coming after Mrs. Oliver, the wound would have been on the front of his head. The death blow was administered to the back of Mr. Oliver's skull. That's murder, not self-defense."

I crossed my arms. "Well, who buried him, then?"

"I know you think she couldn't have done it. But I asked a doctor. Her autopsy photos show only a mild S-curve in her spine. Just because she had scoliosis doesn't mean she couldn't have dug the hole, dragged his body outside, and buried him. Adrenaline can give people more strength than they ordinarily have."

"Not that much strength, Detective. Why don't you find the gardeners who worked for the Olivers at the time Nathan disappeared? Ask them about the hole in the flower bed. Find the housekeeper and ask her what she knew."

He moved toward the door and grabbed the knob. "Thanks to the information supplied by Ms. Casco, the Nathan Oliver case is closed, Ms. Rose."

I thrust my head forward in disbelief. "Isabel? She told you Harriet killed Nathan?"

"Listen, I'm still investigating Mrs. Oliver's murder. Do you have any new information to share?"

"Yeah. As soon as I prove Harriet's innocence, I'm going to sue you for defaming her character."

He turned and walked toward his car, raising a parting hand. "Good luck with that."

CHAPTER 19

Shortly after detective Farkas left, Julian Kessler, my forensic accountant, called.

"This is Julian. I found something."

"Already? Good or bad?"

"It's big. Come to my office."

The clock read one. "I can be there by two."

I changed out of my yoga clothes into black trousers and a loose-fitting white blouse to hide my curves. I arrived in Kessler's waiting room early and knocked at the sliding glass window.

"Hello, Mrs. Rose." Isis, with the spiked hair and multiple piercings, smiled brightly. A small sapphire sparkled in her left nostril. "He's expecting you." She buzzed me through.

Kessler waited for me in his doorway, wearing jeans and a blue-and-white-striped dress shirt.

"Nice. You're early." His Adam's apple bounced.

Once again he sat in the chair directly facing me. He handed me a printout listing twenty monthly checks paid to WC Household Maintenance for $9,900 each—totaling nearly $200,000. "One of my guys got suspicious. He couldn't find invoices or a contract corresponding to the payments, so he shot this over to me. When I saw the amount of the disbursements, I knew exactly what happened." He sat back with a satisfied nod of his head.

"Okay, you have my full attention."

His fingers drummed on top of his thighs. "All the checks were under ten thousand dollars, the magic number triggering an IRS algorithm for reporting bank transactions. Someone greedy wanted to siphon off as much as possible and still stay under the radar."

"Who?"

"We haven't discovered who owns WC Household Maintenance yet, but all the checks were signed by Abernathy."

"Crap! Abernathy embezzled funds from Harriet?" I closed my eyes. This whole probate thing just blew up in my face. Visions of lawsuits and years of legal problems clawed at the right side of my head, and my neck muscles slowly tightened. Did Harriet know? Did she confront Abernathy and threaten to expose him? Did Abernathy kill Harriet to keep his secret? "What do we do now?"

"I spoke to Abernathy earlier. He swears he knew nothing about the theft. He claims he signs hundreds of checks every week without really looking at them."

"Do you believe him?"

Kessler hesitated. "At best, Abernathy got too lazy to properly oversee Mrs. Oliver's finances. Someone in accounting could have slipped bogus checks in with a large pile of legit ones, knowing he'd never look at the documentation. Abernathy's worried Mrs. Oliver's account isn't the only one they stole from. He wants to meet with me to 'make it right.'"

"Come on, Julian. Tell me the truth. Is this why the DA scrutinized Abernathy's office?"

"No."

I massaged my right temple. "I don't trust him anymore."

"But you can trust me. Let me handle Abernathy before you decide anything."

"At this point, what choice do I have? Did you find anything else?"

"Not so far. Most of my staff's working on the Oliver audit now."

I got up to leave. "I don't get it. Why couldn't you tell me this over the phone?"

Kessler also stood and looked at the floor and mumbled. "I don't care if you do have slippers older than me, I'd like to take you out for dinner tonight. . . ."

How could I discourage this guy without alienating him? I needed his help more than ever. "To tell you the truth, Julian"—I moved toward the door—"I'm already dating a younger man."

He looked up quickly. "So you're open to the possibility?"

I drove the short distance to Harriet's. Thankfully, the media circus was gone. One or two curious onlookers drove slowly past the house as I pulled into the driveway behind Carl's Corvette. He walked with me to the front door. I unlocked the entrance and handed him the spare key.

Carl headed toward the library. "I'm going to work on my computer."

I headed upstairs to Harriet's closet.

The wooden stairs creaked a little as I climbed to the second floor. Outside her bedroom window, the yard below appeared exhausted and ravaged by the digging and sifting. A gaping hole stood where the flower bed used to be, and mounds of soil formed hillocks on the lawn. I'd pay Rudy and his guys extra to erase the damage done by the SID field unit.

The discovery of Nathan's body raised a new question. Who would be responsible for his new burial? His only next of kin were Estella and the elusive Henry. Would they step up or would I have to arrange yet another funeral?

I flipped the switch in Harriet's closet. The light hurt my eyes—part of the migraine thing. Trying to ignore the pounding in my head, I searched through the pockets of all her pants, jackets, and coats. Aside from a used Kleenex and a creased twenty-dollar bill, I found nothing of interest—no jewelry, no correspondence, no clues. A set of blue canvas luggage stood on the top shelf, along with stacks of clear plastic bins containing more folded clothes, hats, and handbags.

Standing on my tiptoes, I could barely reach the bottom of the stack of luggage, so I grabbed a hanger and slipped the hook through the handle of the bottom suitcase. I pulled and jumped back as three pieces of luggage tumbled to the floor.

My head throbbed when I bent over to see if Harriet hid her good jewelry or the Declaration Quilt inside. I unzipped the carry-on first. Only an old shaving kit sat inside. The next two large pieces were empty, except for garment hangers and four plastic shoe bags.

Darn! Another dead end.

I rolled my head around my stiff neck and looked up. Whoa! There in the ceiling was a trap-door, previously hidden by the stack of luggage. Was this the entrance to Lucy's hidden room?

A thin rope hung down about two feet, too high for me to reach. I looked around for something to stand on and spied a round tuffet upholstered in the same rose velvet covering as the bed and windows in Harriet's bedroom. I dragged the fancy stool underneath the rope and climbed on it.

With a short tug on the rope, the trapdoor opened and a ladder descended at an angle, forming a slanted staircase. I climbed the ladder far enough to poke my head and shoulders into the attic. It smelled dusty and dry. Afternoon daylight crept in through the dormer windows, creating a gray gloom. The heating and air-conditioning equipment hummed in the middle of the large space. Otherwise, the room appeared empty. I climbed back down.

Looking through Harriet's closet completed my search of her house. Despite Lucy's pounding every wall and searching every nook and cupboard, she'd found no secret hiding place. I reluctantly accepted the inevitable truth. A fortune had been stolen from Harriet Oliver's house. My watch read three-thirty, and I was slightly nauseated. Time to go home.

The pounding in my brain increased on the ride to Encino. As soon as I opened my front door, Arthur greeted me with an eager tail, and Bumper rubbed against my ankles. I fed them early and took my headache meds. Then I made a cup of strong black coffee and rested. Often called an aura, a jagged arc of light—or scotoma—appeared in my visual field growing larger and larger until it disappeared. Twenty minutes later the throbbing ebbed to a dull, foggy ache.

I felt well enough to make dinner at five. Arthur and Bumper watched my every move as I took a chicken out of the refrigerator and rubbed the skin with olive oil, salt, and spices. Drool dripped from the corner of Arthur's mouth as I popped the pan in a hot oven. After fifteen minutes the kitchen smelled like garlic, rosemary, and cumin. The phone rang while I washed the skin of five white rose potatoes.

Uncle Isaac's voice wheedled, "So? Do you have any good news for me?"

I dreaded this conversation. "Not really. We found the body of Harriet's husband buried in their backyard. And I just learned someone embezzled money from her account. Also, several valuable items are officially missing from her house."

"*Oy gavalt!* You found another body? Martha Rivka Harris Rose, stop this *mishugas!*"

"I don't go out looking for bodies, Uncle. They just seem to pop up around me."

"Someone has given you the evil eye. Are you wearing your *hamsa*?" He alluded to a gold charm symbolizing the protective hand of God.

"I'm fine, Uncle. Don't worry so much."

"You shouldn't be alone." He waited a beat. "Sooo, maybe you've seen Yossi Levy lately?"

Here we go. "Yes, I saw him last night."

"*Nu?* What did you talk about?"

I could just imagine him rubbing his hands together in anticipation. "I think you know, Uncle."

He chuckled with delight. "Did he pop the question?"

I rolled my eyes at this archaic expression. "Yes."

"So tell me already. When are we going to have a wedding?"

"I told Yossi he can run to you and Morty all he wants, but I won't decide until I'm ready, and I'm not ready. So please butt out."

He clicked his tongue. "I hate to say this, *faigela*, but you're not getting any younger."

The headache that started at Kessler's office began to throb again. How could I deflect this conversation? "Speaking of not getting any younger, how's Morty? I'm worried about him. He left your house with Paulina right after the funeral."

"Who's Paulina?"

"The young woman with a scarf wrapped around her head, wearing a purple cape."

Uncle Isaac laughed. "The little zaftig one? I should've known. Morty likes a substantial woman."

"Oh my God! He's over eighty-eight years old and she's nothing but a young con artist. You've got to warn him, Uncle."

"Maybe you should warn the young lady instead. Morty's latest girlfriend, Marilyn Teitelbaum from the mahjong group, can't keep up with him and she's only seventy. The one before her died of a heart attack."

Unwelcomed pictures began forming in my head. "I'll call you later, Uncle. I've got a bird in the oven."

Ten minutes passed and the phone rang again. This time my daughter, Quincy, called from Boston.

"Hi, Mom. I just got off the phone with Uncle Isaac. He wants me to talk you into getting married to someone named Yossi Levy. Isn't he the big biker guy I met on my visit to LA four months ago? I thought you barely knew him."

Darn Isaac. "Quincy, honey, I would never do anything so important without talking to you first. Honestly, I don't know why Uncle Isaac's so anxious to marry me off."

"So, what's the deal? Are you dating that guy? You aren't sleeping with him, are you? I mean, aren't you a little *old*?"

"Oh, for heaven's sake. Don't be so judgy. When there's something to tell, you'll be the first to get the news, okay?"

She laughed. "Well, if Dad can get married so many times, I guess it's only fair you get some too."

I hung up the phone and a key scraped in the front door lock. *What the heck?* No one had a key but me, Quincy, and Lucy. Lucy would never barge in. She always called before coming over. My pulse hammered in my throat as I scanned the kitchen for a weapon. I grasped a cantaloupe from the marble counter so tightly my knuckles turned white. *Where's Arthur?*

The door swung slowly inward and I braced myself to hurl the melon. As soon as I saw the size-sixteen boot, I let out my breath and loosened my grip. "You scared me half to death!"

Crusher smiled at me. "Honey, I'm home."

"Very funny. How'd you get a key to my house?"

He pointed to the dish on the hall table. "I found a spare sitting there."

Beavers had tossed the key there four months ago when he broke up with me.

"Darn it, Yossi, you're pushing too hard. This morning I discovered your clean clothes in my closet and your dirty clothes in the hamper. I'm not washing those things and you're not moving in!"

"Babe." Crusher took a step closer.

"You shouldn't have gone to Uncle Isaac. He called me tonight to put the pressure on me to get married. He said I'm not getting any younger."

"None of us are and I'm getting older by the minute waiting for you to make up your mind."

I ignored him and held out my hand for the key. "Now I find out you snatched my house key."

He looked puzzled. "How else can I unlock the door?"

"Really? Have you been listening to me?"

"Okay, you're right. I should have asked about the key before I took it." He handed it to me. "We'll go slow from here on out, I promise."

"Don't be so sure of yourself, Yossi Levy. Someone else asked me to dinner twice this week already."

Alarm sparked his eyes. "Who? You're not going out with him, are you?"

I tossed the key back in the dish. "You can conspire with my uncle until the Messiah comes, but I'm still in charge of my life."

After dinner, Crusher massaged the stiffness out of my neck and shoulders and proved Quincy wrong about my being too old for certain things.

CHAPTER 20

Friday morning I put a small brisket with carrots and potatoes in the slow cooker for Shabbat dinner. Then I picked up the phone. Time to confront Isabel Casco and demand to know how she got Harriet's cocktail ring. When she didn't answer her phone, I called again, just to make sure I'd punched in the right number. After the tenth ring, I gave up in frustration.

Maybe I'd get luckier with Paulina and find her at home seeing clients. I jumped in the car and headed for the West Side, determined to find out if the diamond bracelet Paulina wore to the funeral belonged to Harriet. If so, I'd make Paulina tell me how she got hold of it. I'd also confront her about preying on poor old Morty.

I took the Venice Boulevard exit from the 405 and drove west. Paulina's black BMW sat parked in her driveway right beside Morty's gold Buick Regal, in flagrante delicto.

I fumed as I marched up the porch stairs, past the dying hibiscus, and knocked sharply on her front door. Whatever was going on in there would stop right now.

Paulina did a double take as she opened the front door. Her long black hair cascaded over her shoulders in sensual waves. "Martha? You shoulda called first. I'm busy with a client. Come back later."

I pushed past her into the darkened, terra-cotta–colored room. Purple candles flickered in the dimness, the air heavy with frankincense. A movement caught the corner of my eye, and I turned. Morty was seated at the round table with the shiny purple cloth.

"Martha?"

"Morty! What are you thinking? She's young enough to be your granddaughter. Nothing good can come of this. You need to leave now, and I'm not moving 'til you do." I crossed my arms.

Morty opened his mouth to speak, but Paulina got there first. "What're you. His mother? Morty's a big boy. He can do what he wants."

Morty finally found his voice. "I don't get it, doll. Why are you here?"

"To save you from this, this gold digger!" I pointed my finger at Paulina.

"Just a minute!" Paulina snarled.

I strode over to Morty and grabbed his elbow. "You're coming with me."

A soft, unfamiliar voice spoke from behind me. "And who are you?"

I whirled around.

A plump, white-haired woman emerged from the hallway. "What did I miss while I was in the powder room?" She frowned. Morty stood and patted the woman's arm. "Martha Rose, meet Marilyn Teitelbaum."

I stared at her dumbly. "From the mahjong group?"

The woman smiled cautiously. "Why yes, how did you know?"

"M-Morty talks about you." I snuck a glance at Paulina, who bit the inside of her cheek.

Marilyn put her hand through Morty's scrawny arm and pulled him toward her ample breast. "Well, my sweetie brought me to this nice young lady to get some special herbal tea." She lowered her voice. "I'm way past menopause, if you know what I mean."

I covered my eyes and shook my head. *Please, no more unwanted pictures.*

I looked at Morty, then Paulina. "I'm sorry. I thought . . ."

Paulina snorted into laughter.

"I'm an idiot." I put my hand to my forehead.

"Times ten," Paulina cracked.

The confused but happy couple left a few minutes later, carrying a fifty-dollar brown bag of Paulina's Senior Love Goddess Tea and a complimentary purple candle. The psychic closed the door behind them. "Your aura's almost back to normal. When you shoved your way in here, it oozed dark brown."

"I still have some serious questions about you."

"Sit down." Paulina disappeared into the kitchen and banged around for a couple of minutes, emerging with two tuna sandwiches and a plastic tray of Oreos. "Tea's almost done."

I launched into the sandwich like a junkyard dog. The tuna crunched with chopped dill pickles, and the small baguette was fresh and crusty. Okay, so maybe I jumped to conclusions about Paulina and Morty.

She returned with two cups of tea. "So ask. Whatever has your panties in a twist, you won't be satisfied 'til you do."

I sipped a cup of herbal tea sweetened with honey. *She means to calm me down with food and it's working.* "The diamond bracelet you wore to the funeral. Can I see it?"

Paulina sighed and got up from the table again. She returned with a glittering cuff about an inch wide and paved with hundreds of cut stones. I reached in my purse and pulled out the pictures of Harriet's missing jewelry. The bracelet wasn't a match.

"Swarovski," said Paulina. "Four hundred bucks' worth of crystals. Satisfied?"

I handed the bracelet back to her. "Okay, but I had to know. If I can locate Harriet's missing jewelry, I might find her killer."

"Don't look at me." Paulina leaned forward. "I saw on the news you found Nathan's body. Did you touch him or anything on him?"

"Well, kind of." I shuddered at the memory. "I slipped a ring off his finger bones."

"No wonder your aura's tinged with brown."

"Aura schmaura. If you're as good as you say you are, how come you never sensed Nathan's grave right under your nose in Harriet's backyard?"

Paulina sat up straighter. "Harriet and I never went outside. You gotta be outside to discover graves."

Of course you do. "So Harriet never mentioned she buried her husband in the backyard?"

"No. But even if she did, I wouldn't tell anyone. That's confidential."

"There's no such thing as psychic/client confidentiality."

"There is in the *other* world." She finished her tea. "Be careful, Martha. Spirits attach themselves to anyone who touches their bodies. Lucky for you, I possess the gift of banishing unwelcome spirits."

"I don't think that's my problem." I rose to leave. "But thanks for lunch."

"Call for an appointment if you change your mind."

When I got in my car, I tried Isabel again on my cell phone. This time she answered. "Isabel, I'd like to come over and talk."

She took a drag on a cigarette. "It's been all over the news you discovered Nathan's body. How awful for you. I wish I could talk, but I'm out the door. Leaving for a long weekend in Palm Springs. We'll have a nice, long chat when I get back. I'll call you next week."

I couldn't let her go so easily. I wanted to question her in person, where I could gauge her reactions. "Any chance you can delay leaving for a bit? I'm close by. I can be there in ten minutes."

Isabel coughed. "I'd really like to, but my date's picking me up in five minutes. You know what that's like, right? I don't want to seem like an old cliché and keep the man waiting."

"This is really important, Isabel. Especially with the discovery of Nathan's body. Harriet must have known about the grave."

"Just give it up, Martha. What's done is done. If you want what's best for Harriet, you'll drop the whole thing. Now I really have to go." She hung up.

Darn! Isabel knows a lot more than she's telling me. As soon as she gets back in town, I'll be all over her like cream cheese on a bagel.

On the way back home, I stopped at Bea's Bakery to pick up a raisin challah and ten inches sliced off a long apple strudel for dessert. Crusher would be bringing Uncle Isaac over at six, allowing me plenty of time to make a salad and prepare the dinner table with a snow white cloth and my bubbie's silver candleholders. I had just put the last piece of good silverware on the table when the phone rang.

"Hello, Mrs. Rose? This is Henry Oliver."

"Nathan's brother?"

"Yes, I'm sorry I didn't call you back sooner. I was on my way out of the country when I received your message about Harriet's death. When I returned home to Rhode Island last night, I got a frantic phone call from my sister, Estella. She'd been contacted by the Los Angeles Police Department. They told her you found our brother's body buried in his backyard. Could you please tell me what's going on?"

I laid out the sequence of events: Harriet's murder, the discovery of her body, my being named executor, and the discovery of Nathan's grave. "I'm really sorry for these terrible losses to your family. I suppose you'll be making arrangements for Nathan's funeral?"

"Of course. Estella and I are his only family. I'm flying to Los Angeles next week. I wonder if we could meet and talk." His voice turned silky. "Several items in Harriet's possession were family heirlooms, and I should like to have them back."

Wow. Not a word about Harriet's death. Like his

sister, Estella, Henry Oliver didn't seem to care about poor Harriet.

"I'm certainly open to discussion, Mr. Oliver, but you have to realize Harriet made no provision for you in her will. She wanted everything she owned to be donated or sold for the purpose of financing the Jonah David Oliver wing of the Children's Hospital."

His voice tightened. "Not everything was hers. Several items have been in my family for generations."

"And you don't consider Harriet to be a part of your family?"

"The police say Harriet killed Nathan. She can't gain from his death. As his closest relative, Nathan's estate should come to me."

What about Estella? I'd ask Abernathy if Henry Oliver was right about the laws of inheritance. If he filed a legitimate claim to the estate, Bunny Friedman, the fund-raiser, could kiss the Jonah David Oliver wing of Children's Hospital good-bye. "I'll have to clarify this matter with Harriet's attorney before I can consider your request. I have a duty to fulfill Harriet's last wishes, and I intend to do so."

"I don't know who you are," he growled, "but you have no authority to dispose of items that are rightfully mine!"

"They may already have been *disposed of,* Mr. Oliver. I hate to break the news, but in preparing to liquidate Harriet's estate, I discovered several things have vanished, presumably stolen by her killer. I suspect some of the family heirlooms you're talking about are among those missing."

After a long silence, he said in a clipped voice, "If anything is missing, I'll hold you personally responsible. It's the executor's duty to protect the estate from theft. I'll sue you. I'll file a criminal complaint."

"And I don't know who you think you are, Mr. Oliver, but I don't take kindly to threats and I don't like bullies. I've been executor for less than two weeks. Those items went missing long before I came on the scene."

"Some of those things are worth millions. Others have great historical and personal significance. They didn't belong to Harriet."

"I'm going to give you the benefit of the doubt right now because you've just received some disturbing news, but don't think you can intimidate me. Now, I am not unsympathetic to your desire to keep the heirlooms in the family. So, if you can be civil, I'd be willing to discuss this again once I've talked to the attorney."

"I'll call you next week," he snapped, and hung up the phone.

What a jerk. Apparently the Oliver family spawned a generation of bullies. Yet, even though Henry Oliver insisted he owned those family heirlooms, why didn't he step forward to claim those items after Nathan was declared legally dead? Why had he waited until now?

CHAPTER 21

I changed into my Shabbat clothes: a long black skirt and a white silk blouse with long sleeves ending in extravagant tiers of lace. A strand of large white pearls cascaded down my chest. Uncle Isaac and Crusher arrived at six.

My uncle wore his black embroidered Bukharin skullcap and a fresh white dress shirt. "Good *Shabbos, faigela.*" He kissed me on the cheek.

A line of black grease smeared Crusher's forehead and the front of his blue bandana. He smelled like petroleum. "I drove straight from the shop to pick up your uncle." He turned on his heel and headed for the bedroom. "I need to shower and change."

So much for hiding our intimate relationship from my uncle.

Uncle Isaac watched Crusher disappear down the hall, then turned to me. "I guess this means you're practically married, anyway?"

"I don't know what this means. He still has his own place." I focused on squeezing lemon juice over a chopped cucumber and tomato salad. "Can we please not talk about this?"

"I only want you to be happy. Yossi Levy could make you happy, and you'd never be alone."

I lifted the top of the slow cooker. Drops of moisture hung from the inside of the glass lid. A cloud of savory steam fogged my glasses. "What's so terrible about being alone? You've managed to stay unmarried your whole life, and look at you. You're eighty, you do what you want, and you're happy." I stabbed the tender brisket with a fork and unplugged the cooker.

I barely heard his soft response. "Getting married was never in the cards for me, but that doesn't mean you have to miss out."

I always assumed my uncle could have married if he wanted to, but what if he didn't have a choice? What did he sacrifice to take care of my bubbie, my mother, and me? My heart squeezed with love for my uncle, and I hugged him. "Oh, Uncle Isaac, you gave up so much for us. I'm so grateful."

He patted my back. "I've got you and Quincy girl. I'm not alone."

Arthur appeared in the kitchen and stared at the slow cooker, wagging his tail.

"What's this?" Uncle Isaac patted the top of the dog's head.

"I'm babysitting Arlo's dog."

"I don't understand. I thought you and the detective were through."

"We are. But I love this dog. I don't mind taking care of him."

My uncle shook his head in confusion as we moved to the dining room. The sun had set over an hour ago, so I hurriedly recited the blessing over the candles, poured wine into a polished silver kiddush cup, and placed a white cloth over the loaf of challah.

A knock sounded on the front door.

Uncle Isaac looked at me. "Who else is coming?"

"Nobody," I shrugged. "Don't get up. I'll get the door."

Julian Kessler, wearing brown Dockers and a green plaid shirt, stood in front of me, shifting his weight from foot to foot. He looked at me, blinking rapidly behind the heavy black frames of his eyeglasses. A large, reusable plastic bag from a big box store jiggled in his left hand and a gray plastic portfolio waved in his right.

"Julian! What are you doing here?"

"I wanted to tell you in person what I found. It's huge."

I moved aside. He stepped into the house and took a quick look around the living room. "Nice place." He apparently didn't see Uncle Isaac seated at the dining room table, "You look nice."

I pointed to the portfolio. "More bad news?"

He sat on the sofa without being asked and bounced on the cushion a couple of times. "I like it. It's comfortable." He handed over the portfolio. "This time I've got good news."

I sat next to him and opened the gray plastic envelope. Inside were several invoices from Safe-T-Construction dated 2005. The first invoice listed an air-purifying HVAC system with HEPA filter and humidity controls installed at Harriet's address. The second listed two fire doors and fireproof insulation. Others cataloged various construction materials and archival lights, whatever those were.

"Just what am I looking at?"

He smiled and leaned forward. "In 2005, your friend Mrs. Oliver built a safe room at her house."

"Where? We searched every square foot of her place. We didn't find any safe room."

Kessler's knee jiggled. "Maybe. But according to the financial records, these invoices were paid upon completion of the work. Safe-T-Construction is closed for the weekend, but I left a message for the owner. I'll ask him for the job specs and blueprints on Monday. We'll find out where the room is."

Lucy would be thrilled to learn she was right after all. Harriet might have built an actual hidden room in her house. Did her killer know about it? "This is stunning news."

Kessler smiled and thrust the bulky sack from the big box store into my hands. "Here, I bought something really cool to celebrate."

"Oh, but I can't. . . ."

"Go ahead, open it."

Several boxes of electronics sat inside. "What are these?"

"It's the Sony PlayStation PS3!" Kessler's grin stretched across his face. "I got two DualShock 3 wireless controllers and two headsets. I also got the newest *Call of Duty Black Ops* game. You have HDMI, right?"

My jaw dropped. "You bought me video games?"

"Don't thank me." He looked down shyly. "I just think you're cool." He stared at my pearls. "And, uh, you look really hot tonight."

"Faigela?" Uncle Isaac, sounding mystified, had apparently listened quietly to our whole conversation from the dining room.

Kessler whipped his head toward the old man approaching us. "Oh, I thought we were alone."

"Julian Kessler, this is my uncle, Isaac Harris."

Kessler jumped up, swallowed, and shook hands. Uncle Isaac smiled. "Kessler? That's Jewish?"

Kessler nodded.

"You'll stay for *Shabbos* dinner?" Uncle Isaac's eyebrows were raised in two big question marks.

Oh no! What are you doing?

Kessler tapped the fingers of his left hand against the side of his leg. "Yeah. Okay. Smells good in here."

We stood, talking in the dining room, while I laid another place setting on the table. Crusher came out of the bedroom with a freshly combed beard, a white dress shirt, slacks, and a white crocheted skull cap. He approached us, a towering presence. He smelled all lemony and bent to kiss me on the mouth. "Shabbat shalom."

Kessler's face fell.

I said, "Julian Kessler, meet Yossi Levy."

Crusher shook Kessler's hand and gave him a hearty *potch* on the back. Kessler lurched forward a little.

I put my hand on Crusher's arm. "Julian is the forensic accountant who's auditing Harriet's estate. He kindly came in person this evening to show me something important. Uncle Isaac invited him to join us for dinner."

"Must be really important for you to make a special trip to see Martha." Crusher puffed out his chest a little and adjusted the waistband on his slacks.

"Julian found evidence indicating there's a hidden room somewhere in Harriet's house. If her killer didn't get there already, we might still find her missing items inside. We have to wait until Monday to learn the exact location of the room."

"What's all that?" Crusher pointed to the boxes of electronics piled on the sofa where I'd dumped them.

Kessler's Adam's apple jumped. He stepped a little closer to Uncle Isaac.

"Julian brought over a video thing." I looked at him. "Tell me the name again?"

"PS3."

Crusher nodded his approval. "What games you into, dude?"

"*Call of Duty.* I bought Martha the latest version. Black Ops."

"Sweet." Crusher lifted his thumb. "Let's take it for a ride after dinner."

Kessler's shoulders relaxed.

During the meal, Uncle Isaac and Crusher discussed the Torah portion for the week, the story of how the Jewish people were enslaved by the Egyptian Pharaoh and how Moses committed a violent act and became a fugitive.

"Normally," said Uncle Isaac, "we Jews are a nonviolent people."

"Yeah, that's how Hitler could kill so many of us. We weren't conditioned to fight back." Crusher made a fist. "Never again."

Uncle Isaac rubbed his chin. *"Has v'halilah!"* God forbid. "But we shouldn't become bullies ourselves. Otherwise, the good things which set us apart as a people will become lost. God forced Moses into exile so he could teach him to govern his violent behavior."

"But sometimes a situation calls for violent action in order to protect the innocent."

After finishing generous slices of apple strudel, Kessler and Crusher hooked up the PlayStation while Uncle Isaac and I cleared off the table and loaded the dishwasher. Mercifully, the sounds from the video game flowed only through the headsets, not the television speakers. I could see the TV screen from the kitchen. Guns blasted as soldiers ran through passageways and climbed steps. The only thing I heard coming from the living room were: "Urf!" "Dude." "He's toast."

Uncle Isaac wandered over to Crusher and watched his fingers fly rapidly over the keys of the controller. "So, *nu*? What's this?"

Crusher got up and gave Uncle Isaac the seat next to Kessler on the sofa. Then he put the earphones over my uncle's skullcap and handed him the DualShock 3 wireless controller. Kessler showed Uncle Isaac how to work the joystick and buttons. Soon the two of them were focused on the TV screen playing *Call of Duty*.

"*Oy!*" came from the living room as the enemy surrounded a lone soldier. Uncle Isaac pressed a button on his DualShock 3 and bright flashes leaped from the mouth of the soldier's rifle. "*Gevalt!*"

Crusher walked into the kitchen as I finished wiping off the countertop. He leaned over to kiss my neck and mumbled in my ear. "Why is this guy bringing you presents? And why couldn't he just call you with the big news about the safe room? Is this the dude who's been asking you out on dates?"

I didn't want Crusher to alienate Kessler or scare him off. "Listen, Yossi. Julian is doing a brilliant job. He's already uncovered embezzlement and now this. So what if he has a little crush on me? I'd appreciate it if you'd let me handle this in my own way."

"Okay, but you're keeping the PlayStation, right?"

I squinted my eyes. "I'm sending all the game stuff back home with Julian tonight."

"Yeah, you're right. No use encouraging the dude."

I reached under the sink and pulled out a clean white trash bag. "You're also going to pack all your clothes and take them home with you tonight. Including the dirty ones."

His forehead wrinkled. "But I thought . . ."

"I know what you thought, but until I decide what I want, you have to back off. I need to take a break for a couple of weeks."

"Babe, you're killin' me."

CHAPTER 22

Saturday morning I woke up glad to be alone in my bed. Well, almost alone. Bumper stood next to my head, willing me to open my eyes. I scratched him under his jaw while he purred. "Okay, I'm getting up." Twinges of stiffness grabbed at my back and shoulders as I stood. Even the bottoms of my feet hurt—a sure sign of rain.

I threw on a pair of jeans and a long-sleeved blue T-shirt and thick woolen socks. While the animals ate their breakfast, I brewed a pot of Italian roast coffee and called my best friend. "You were right, Lucy." I told her about Kessler's revelation last night. "There is a secret room in Harriet's house."

"I knew it! I told you I had one of my feelings. Too bad you have to wait until Monday for the blueprints. Did you get any clue from the file about where the room might be?"

"Not really."

"Well, her house has a tall, pointy roof, so there must be an attic. Maybe the room's up there."

"I already looked in the attic when I searched Harriet's closet. It's as empty as a politician's promise. But I've been thinking. When we searched the house, we didn't measure the actual dimensions of each room against the outside dimensions of the house. Maybe there's a pocket of space behind a wall somewhere."

"Well, what are we waiting for, girlfriend?" Lucy's voice rose with excitement. "We've got to go back one more time. Now we know what to look for."

"First, I've got to drive over the hill today to talk to Harriet's last housekeeper."

"I'd like to come along. We could go measure the house afterward. I'll bring the tape measure."

I smiled. Lucy could always be trusted to help me out. "Sure. I'll call you back as soon as I can set something up."

Delia Pitcher agreed to meet at her house at noon. "I'll have my husband take the kids to the park down the street so we can talk."

For the next couple of hours, I sat in my sewing room planning a new quilt top with pencil, paper, and calculator. Since my daughter announced she had a serious boyfriend, I should begin making her a wedding quilt—just in case. I chose the traditional Double Wedding Ring design, which required a pattern for all the curved pieces. Constructing a quilt top always involved a little engineering, a little math, and a sense of adventure.

The Double Wedding Ring looked like a complicated Olympic flag with rows of interlocking rings against a plain background. I especially loved this pattern because each ring contained dozens of small wedges of fabric, a perfect opportunity to use hundreds of different prints in the quilt top. I planned to make each ring out of a different color family: all green fabrics in one ring, all yellow fabrics in another, all blue—the possibilities were endless.

Piecing the rings together would be the easy part. Sewing them to the curvy background shapes would be more tricky. Rather than drafting templates of the background sections on my own, I found a commercial pattern online and bought it with one keystroke of the computer.

I left my house at eleven. Dark gray clouds hung in the overcast sky toward the west, indicating a rainstorm approaching from the Pacific. I buttoned my bulky, hand-knit fisherman's sweater and jumped in the car. Once I pulled up in front of Lucy's house, I tapped the horn. Today, Lucy's clothing theme was A Day in the Pasture: grass green jeans (where does anyone find denim that color?) and a matching green pullover sweater and green tote bag.

"Is Birdie coming?" I asked.

Lucy put her large bag in the backseat and buckled her seat belt. "She wanted to, but she's got a garden club meeting."

"It's probably just as well. If all three of us descend on Delia Pitcher, she might not talk freely."

On the way south through the Sepulveda Pass, I told Lucy about Henry Oliver's call. "He acted like such a bully."

"Do you think he's right about being entitled to inherit Harriet's estate?"

"I don't have a clue. I'm going to have to ask Abernathy, even though I'm royally ticked off at him right now. Someone in his office embezzled nearly two hundred thousand dollars from Harriet over a period of twenty months."

"Have you gone to the police?"

"Not yet. I still need Abernathy to help me figure out Henry Oliver's claim. Maybe after Harriet's estate is settled."

Lucy shifted in her seat to look at me. "Good grief. Every time you turn around, you run into another complication."

"Isn't that the naked truth!"

Harriet had allotted a $10,000 per month stipend for my efforts as executor. Did she anticipate just how much trouble settling her estate would turn out to be?

Lucy shifted in her seat. "So, what do you know about the housekeeper?"

"Shortly before she was killed, Harriet let Delia and Paulina go. I don't even know if Delia still has a key to Harriet's house."

We transitioned to the 10 Freeway heading east, got off at Robertson Boulevard, and headed north to Hargis Street. Delia Pitcher lived in an area a lot like the one where I grew up. Small, 1920s Spanish-style bungalows with red tile roofs lined the street. In front of her house, two boxwood bushes trimmed into neat squares flanked the front steps, and a small dog barked at the window. I rang the bell. A little peephole guarded by an iron grate slid open in the front door, and a pair of curious brown eyes stared at me.

"Hello, I'm Martha Rose, and this is my friend Lucy."

The dead bolt slid back and the door swung open. A woman in her forties with a large gold cross around her neck beckoned us inside. Rows of braids on her head were threaded with bright glass beads. "I'm Delia. Come on in."

The smell of cinnamon filled the air of Delia's small and comfortable living room. Three West African wooden animal masks hung in a group along one wall. Someone very short had taped a picture crookedly to the opposite wall. Scribbled smoke poured out of a red chimney on a brown house. Behind Delia's legs stood a small terrier mix yipping loudly. She picked him up, and he wiggled in her arms and licked the air.

I smiled. "Thank you so much for agreeing to see me, Mrs. Pitcher. I promise not to take up too much of your time."

She gestured toward the red leather sofa and smiled. "Go ahead, sit down."

Lucy and I sat on the sofa, sinking into the marshmallow texture of the seats.

"I won't be a minute." She put the terrier on the floor and disappeared through a small dining area.

The dog immediately came sniffing at my feet and legs, no doubt picking up trace scents of Arthur and Bumper.

Two minutes later Delia carried a tray with three mugs of steaming coffee and a plate of snicker doodles. She set the tray on top of a carved wooden stool and pulled over a Parsons chair from the dining area to sit on. The dog settled at her feet, eying the plate of cookies. "Now, how can I help you?"

"Well, first of all"—Lucy chewed—"you can give me the recipe for these cookies."

Delia smiled briefly and clutched her coffee

mug with both hands. "Please tell me about Miss Harriet."

I took a deep breath. "She died around the end of January, beginning of February this year and lay in the house for ten months before the police discovered her body. Several items are missing, so the police think it was a robbery gone wrong."

Delia reached up and grabbed the cross hanging from her neck. "Lord! The detective told me the same thing. Someone must have broke in. Miss Harriet would never open the door to no stranger. What did he take?"

So Farkas got here before me. I should have known. "Some valuable old books, an antique quilt, an old watch, and her good diamond jewelry. Do you remember where she kept those things?" Maybe Delia knew about the secret room.

Delia frowned and thought for a while. "She always wore a gold locket. Once she showed me pictures of two little boys inside. One was her dead brother, David, the other was her baby boy, Jonah. She kept a few other pieces of jewelry in a drawer in her closet. She also kept a show box with several watches inside. Is that what you mean?"

"Yes. Did you ever see any fancy jewelry, like a diamond ring or bracelet?"

"Miss Harriet wasn't fond of bling like some of the ladies I worked for. Plus, where would she wear it? She never left the house. If she owned anything like that, I never saw none of it." Delia frowned and sat up straighter. "Anybody say different?"

I raised a reassuring hand. "No, no. Not at all. What about the other things I mentioned? The books. The quilt. Did you ever see them?"

Delia relaxed a little and studied the ceiling.

"A year ago, maybe, I helped Miss Harriet take a picture of a raggedy old quilt. I remember there was a circle of stars in the middle."

My pulse sped up. Delia actually saw the Declaration Quilt. "Do you know where she kept it?"

"Uh-uh. The quilt appeared one day and disappeared the next. I just figured she tucked it away in a drawer somewhere."

"How long did you work for Harriet?"

"About three years. Five days a week unless one of my kids got sick. Miss Harriet, she lost her own baby, so she was very understanding."

"The death of her boy must have affected her deeply."

"Oh, yes. Poor Miss Harriet always looked so sad, and she got worse over the years. She didn't trust no one. And like I said, she hardly ever left the house. She spent a lot of time in her baby's room by herself. Sometimes I heard her talking and singing to him. Like he was still alive. You know?"

I pictured Harriet sitting in that blue room folding and unfolding Jonah's little socks and smoothing the blanket on his bed. Tears filled my eyes. "Did you ever go in that room?"

"Not often. Miss Harriet didn't want nothing disturbed. I had to be real careful when I dusted in there. She told me she fired her last housekeeper because she messed up her baby's things. She said, 'Delia, you're the only other person I trust in here besides myself.'"

"Did she ever have visitors?" I bit into a cookie and a small piece fell on the floor. The dog had been waiting for just such an opportunity and quickly scarfed it up.

"Not very many. Her lawyer, Mr. Abernathy. He'd

bring papers for her to sign. And sometimes he just came to check on her. He'd try to take her out to dinner, but Miss Harriet, she always made an excuse."

Harriet didn't want to spend time with Abernathy. Did she suspect him of embezzling her money? "What about other visitors?"

"Miss Friedman from the Children's Hospital came a few times with Mr. Abernathy. She always stuck her hand out for money."

There it was again. Abernathy the lawyer and Bunny Friedman the fund-raiser. Just how connected were they? Did Abernathy cultivate a friendship with Harriet just to get her money?

Delia counted on her fingers. "A neighbor lady visited occasionally, but she died. The insurance man stopped by a few times. Mr. Oliver's brother also called on Miss Harriet when he visited LA. And then there was Miss Isabel."

I pricked up my ears. "Tell me about her."

Delia's voice dripped with disgust. "When I first worked for Miss Harriet, that woman hung around all the time. I mean, *all* the time. One day, about two years ago, I heard them arguing and Miss Harriet told her, 'Just leave me alone, Isabel. Just go away.' Afterward, Miss Harriet told me to say she was sleeping whenever Miss Isabel called."

Two years ago. That was around the time Harriet named me executor of her will instead of Isabel. What caused their falling out?

I grabbed another cookie. The dog sat looking at me, waiting for the next crumb to fall. "What about other visitors?"

Delia's demeanor darkened. "Miss Harriet started seeing that Paulina woman right around the time she sent Miss Isabel away. Miss Paulina came by at least twice a week and they'd sit in the library. She gave me the willies. She always brought those picture cards and sacks of some kind of tea leaves. I'd have to brew a pot so she could read Miss Harriet's fortune."

"When I called you before, you mentioned something about ghosts."

"Yeah. Sometimes the two of them'd hold hands on top of the table and Miss Paulina would close her eyes." Delia lowered her voice. "She talked to ghosts."

Lucy perked up. Talking to ghosts was right up her ESP alley. She leaned toward Delia. "How do you know she talked to ghosts?"

"I pretended to dust the living room so I could listen in on them. I didn't want nobody to take advantage of poor Miss Harriet. Miss Paulina's voice changed from high to low, depending on which ghost was speaking. I tell you, the woman scared me!" She shivered and reached up to grasp the cross around her neck again.

I drank the last of my coffee. "I guess you heard about Nathan Oliver's grave in the backyard. Rudy, the gardener, told me Harriet sometimes asked you to weed the flower bed where the body turned out to be. Weeding seems like an odd thing to ask a housekeeper to do."

Delia stood, went to the kitchen, and brought back the coffeepot to refill our cups. "I didn't mind. I felt sorry for her. She told me she buried her baby's pet dog there and didn't want the gardeners to mess up the grave. A few times she asked me to use a hand shovel and pull up some of the uglier weeds. She said, 'Don't go too deep. I don't want to disturb the dog.' Then she'd stand right there and watch me 'til I was done."

Well, I could no longer deny Harriet knew about Nathan's grave. How could I ask the next question? "Harriet seemed to really trust you. Do you mind telling me why she let you go?"

"No, I don't mind. One day she sat with Miss Paulina in the library. I heard a awful scream and came running. Miss Harriet had turned white as a sheet. She shouted, 'Tell him to go back to hell! Tell him to leave me alone!'"

The day Paulina said she channeled Nathan's ghost.

"I helped Miss Harriet into the kitchen and sat her at the table while I put up some water for a cup of tea. Then I marched into the library and told that purple Paulina—did you know she always wore purple?—I told her to get out and leave Miss Harriet alone or I'd call the police."

Delia stopped for a moment and stared at the floor. An ice-cream truck rolled slowly down the street playing "Turkey in the Hay" over and over again.

"Miss Harriet shook so hard she could hardly hold her cup and drink her tea. She said, 'Nathan wants me dead. He wants to punish me. He wants everyone to know.' Then she got a funny look on her face, and asked me, 'How much did you hear in the library, Delia?' I told her I heard enough to know she shouldn't see Miss Paulina no more. Two days later she called me into the library and sat me down at the table. She hands me a check for three months' wages and a real nice letter of recommendation. I asked her if I did something wrong. She told me, 'It's got nothing to do with you, Delia. I just need to be alone.' I turned in my key and left. That's the last time I saw her."

Harriet must have been scared she'd revealed too much when she told Delia that Nathan wanted to punish her and wanted everyone to know. She probably thought she had no other choice. She had to let the housekeeper go to keep her from finding out the truth about Nathan's death and burial.

The terrier moved to sit at Lucy's feet and she reached down to pet the dog. "What's your opinion of Harriet now that her husband's body has been found?" she asked.

The little glass beads in Delia's braids clicked against each other as she wove her head from side to side. "I've worked for crazy, and I've worked for mean. But Miss Harriet was just sad. The poor woman couldn't kill no one. Lord only knows how her husband ended up in the backyard."

I placed my empty mug on the tray and stood to leave. "One more thing, Delia. You mentioned Henry, Nathan Oliver's brother, came for a visit. Did you ever hear any conversation?"

"They weren't friendly. On his visits I'd serve them coffee and go about my business. He never stayed very long."

So Delia went to work for Harriet four years ago. After two years, Harriet sent Isabel away and Paulina came into the picture. A year after that, Harriet got rid of both Paulina and Delia. Shortly afterward, Harriet died. I found Delia to be quite credible. I believed her when she said she gave her house key back to Harriet the day she was dismissed. Delia didn't kill Harriet nor did she steal anything from her. I handed her a piece of paper with my name and phone number. "Thank you for your time and the delicious cookies. If you can think of anything else, will you call me?"

"The fat detective said the same thing when he handed me his card. Which one of you am I supposed to call?"

"Call us both. Detective Farkas is trying to solve Harriet's murder. He thinks he's already solved Nathan's murder. As far as the detective's concerned, Harriet killed her husband, which means it's up to me to prove she didn't."

The beads clicked together again as Delia nodded. "I'll guess I'll call you first."

CHAPTER 23

After we left Delia's, Lucy and I picked up burgers and fries at In-N-Out Burger in Westwood. By the time we got to Harriet's house, the sun had disappeared behind dark gray clouds and the air smelled damp. Thunder rolled in the distance. Carl sat at his usual place in the library, working on his computer. A lamp with a green glass shade cast a warm light in the corner of the room. He smiled when I handed him a white bag with the red and yellow In-N-Out logo.

"Awesome. Thanks a lot."

I unwrapped my "protein-style" hamburger (lettuce leaves instead of a bun). "Anything interesting happen?"

Carl dipped a French fry in ketchup and shoved it in his mouth. "The gardeners came this morning and cleaned up the yard. The hole is gone and the backyard looks normal again. They want to know what kind of flowers to plant."

Selling a house where two murders had occurred might prove to be difficult. A flower bed would stand out from the rest of the yard as the obvious site of Nathan's grave. Better to extend the lawn over the area to make it disappear. "I'll call Rudy later."

When we finished eating, Lucy fished out a Stanley retractable tape measure from her green tote bag. "Time to measure the house." She dug inside again and pulled out a notepad and pencil, which she handed to me. "You can write."

Carl gathered the trash on the table. "What are you up to?"

I told him about the file from Safe-T-Construction indicating they built a safe room in 2005. "We're going to measure the outside proportions of the house and compare them to the dimensions of the inside. We hope to find a hidden pocket of space where the room could be."

Carl stood. "Cool. I'll come with you."

We circled the outside of the house. I recorded the numbers as Lucy and Carl stretched the fifty-foot yellow aluminum tape. When we got to the back of the house, where we'd discovered Nathan's grave, I was relieved to see a neat patch of bare soil ten feet by four feet where the flower bed used to be.

Harriet's Tudor-style home had a rectangular footprint with a bump out for the one-story garage, so calculating the outside dimensions took only ten minutes. Back inside, Lucy extracted two flashlights from her tote bag and handed them to Carl and me. Then she pulled out something that looked like a pair of binoculars attached to head gear and strapped it to her face.

"What in the world?" I stared as she telescoped the lenses about six inches in front of her eyes.

She swung her head toward me. "Night-vision

goggles. Ray wears them when he and the boys go to Wyoming to hunt." Lucy and her husband, Ray, grew up in Moorcroft, Wyoming. Ray returned every year with his five sons during deer season.

"What makes you think you'll need those?"

"To explore dark spaces."

"But it's still daylight."

She adjusted the focus on those protruding eyes. "Well, I know. But things look different with these on. Maybe I'll spot something not visible with the naked eye. And anyway, when we find the hidden door, who knows how dark it'll be on the other side?"

Who could argue with Lucy's logic?

Lucy waved her arm like the leader of a SWAT team. "Okay, let's roll." She strode toward the stairway in her matching green clothes and night-vision goggles, looking like a very tall praying mantis with bright orange hair.

Upstairs we measured every room, closet, bathroom, and hallway. I made a crude map of the second floor and added up the numbers. "I'm sorry, Lucy, but I just don't see any discrepancies between the inside and outside measurements. According to this, there's no hidden pocket of space.

Carl took the drawing and looked at it. "Yeah, I agree. While we were measuring, I kind of kept the numbers in my head. They didn't add up for me either."

Lucy removed the goggles and her shoulders slumped. "Dang it! I thought for sure we'd find something up here. What about the attic?"

"I already looked. Nothing up there except for the heater."

"Are you sure? Could there be a false wall up there?"

"Well, I did have a migraine when I looked before, so I didn't really spend much time. I just poked my head up there, took a quick survey, and left. We could always take a closer look."

We returned to Harriet's closet. Thunder boomed louder as the storm approached. "Up there." I pointed to the rope hanging from the ceiling.

Carl pulled on the rope, the hatch opened, and the ladder glided downward. He switched on his flashlight. "I'll go up first."

The wooden rungs squeaked and gave a little under his heavy brown work boots as he slowly climbed into the dark space above. I caught the occasional beam of his flashlight sweeping around. Then a switch clicked on above us and light spilled out of the opening. "You can come up now."

My adrenaline surged as I ascended the ladder. Would we finally find the Declaration Quilt up there? Did Harriet have to climb a ladder every time she wanted a piece of good jewelry? Why not just install an easily reachable wall safe? On the other hand, Delia claimed Harriet never wore bling, so maybe the inconvenience of retrieving her jewelry from the attic became an issue only on rare occasions.

My head cleared the opening and I looked around, my eyes even with the floor. Plywood covered the joists to make a crude deck. Above me, thick blankets of pink insulation covered the walls and sharply slanted ceiling. I climbed the rest of the way into the attic. Rain tapped against four dormer windows projecting from narrow alcoves on the front wall of the house.

In the middle of the large, unfinished space a chimney column rose two floors from the living room and penetrated the roof. Carl stood next to the only other objects in the room—two HVAC systems sitting twenty feet away. I walked toward the units. Pipes, wires, and ducting snaked out in several directions. Stacks of unused filters lay nearby.

Carl trained his flashlight on the structures and bent forward to examine them. "There are two separate environmental systems up here. One is large capacity. The other's considerably smaller."

Lucy scrambled up behind me and walked the perimeter of the space, thrusting her neck forward and adjusting the lenses on her night-vision goggles. There were no false walls to obscure the framing of the outer walls. After two minutes she gave up. "I don't get it. Where is everything?"

I walked toward Carl and sighed. "Obviously not here. This isn't a secret room. It's just a plain old attic housing plain old heating and air."

Lucy crossed her arms. "Well, that just takes the cake. If Harriet's secret room isn't in the attic, where can it be?"

"Maybe there is no secret room," said Carl.

A metal tag affixed to the smaller unit caught my eye. "Oh, there's a secret room, all right. Here's a label from Safe-T-Construction. The ducting leads downward to the lower part of the house. If only we could trace the lines attached to this unit, we'd find the room."

Lucy followed the aluminum tube, which led from the small HVAC to the studs in the back wall and disappeared downward through the insulation. "The room's gotta be in the part of the house facing the backyard."

Carl scratched the back of his head. "I've spent a lot of time on the first floor, and I'm pretty familiar with the spaces. I don't see where a room could be concealed."

I moved toward the ladder. "We should measure it, anyway. Don't forget the tape."

We started in the library. Lucy and Carl stretched the tape and called out the dimensions while I drew a map of the first floor. We ended up in the family room, where Carl worked the numbers several times on the calculator app of his iPhone. "I don't see any discrepancies. Every space seems to be accounted for."

As we headed back toward the library, I said, "We've got to be missing something." When we reached the foyer, I stopped. "The stairs! What about the space underneath the stairs?"

Carl looked at my drawing. "According to this, the stairway is four feet wide by twenty feet long. The area underneath is much smaller if you allow for the angle of the stairs and the framing of the walls. You probably won't find a room big enough to hold all those missing things. Especially not one with environmental controls."

I ran my fingers over the dark paneling on the wall on the stairwell. "It's the only place left to look."

The three of us poked and prodded and banged and pushed every inch of the foyer walls. We even tried turning the balusters on the staircase. Nothing moved. The wall remained as solid as a week-old bagel.

I folded up my drawing and shoved it in my pocket. "I'm stumped. There's nothing more we can do here today. We're just going to have to wait for those blueprints. We might as well go home." I wanted to be in my nice warm house, jump into my flannel jammies, and get cozy.

Thirty minutes later I dropped Lucy off at her house. Then I ran into Trader Joe's for some yogurt and a can of soup for dinner. Back home I changed clothes and sat on my sofa. Bumper jumped up on the blue and white quilt covering my lap and demanded to be scratched. Arthur rested his chin on my knee and gazed up at me. I looked into his brown eyes, so patient and intelligent, and wondered what humans ever did to deserve such devotion.

I relaxed into the cushions, closed my eyes, and practiced my yoga breathing. All the disruption and stress from disposing of Harriet's estate wouldn't last forever. A time would come when I could return to the comfortable rhythm of my life without all the extra worry. Simple and predictable. Breathe in, breathe out. No complications. No marriage.

I found the phone number of the estate agent Kessler recommended on a paper in my purse. I arranged to meet Susan Daniels at Harriet's house in the morning to discuss the sale of her property. Then I called my daughter. I missed my little girl and wanted to hear more about her new romance with the MIT professor. Hopefully some bright Jewish boy from a nice family. Maybe even another Mark Zuckerberg. Uncle Isaac would be pleased.

"Things are going great, Mom. He's brilliant and funny. We like a lot of the same things and we have the same sense of humor. Plus, he's incredibly hot. All his female students and half the female faculty are in love with him."

Alarms went off in my head. Would this gorgeous

man, desired by so many women, remain faithful to my Quincy? "With so many admirers, why do you think he chose you?"

She laughed. "Mom, he says he loves everything about me. But I think my red hair and freckles first attracted him. Red curly hair is a rare sight in his home country."

Home country? My stomach dropped.

People only say "home country" if it's an exotic location like Bhutan or Abu Dhabi—places where Jews aren't usually found. If they got married, where would they end up living? Would the children be raised Jewish? My heart sank as I imagined Quincy being swept away to a foreign land with no redheads, no freckles, and no bar mitzvahs. I swallowed my panic. "Where's he from? What's his name?"

"Naveen Sharma. He came from Mumbai to study theoretical physics at MIT. He never left. Now he's a US citizen and a full professor at twenty-nine. Pretty impressive, wouldn't you say?" India produced some of the most brilliant technological and mathematical minds of the modern age. One of the cofounders of Sun Microsystems came from India.

"Very impressive, honey." I swallowed. "Just how serious are you two?"

Quincy cleared her throat and remained silent just long enough for me to start hyperventilating. "We've decided to move in together."

Oh no!

"Naveen's parents are flying to Boston in six weeks to meet all of us—you and Dad and Uncle Isaac, if he can make the trip."

Quincy might marry a non-Jew. How was I going to break the news to Uncle Isaac? Marriage was hard enough. Successful cross-cultural marriages were even more challenging. Did Naveen Sharma's parents have the same misgivings I did? Was that why they weren't wasting any time checking out my daughter and her family?

I tried to keep my voice casual. "It sounds like you're contemplating more than just moving in together. Introducing the parents usually means everyone's going to be planning a wedding." I held my breath, waiting for her to answer.

"Don't be afraid, Mom. You'll love Naveen when you meet him."

I stared out the window at the rain, which now beat a hard staccato against my living-room window. I thought about the tablecloth my bubbie crocheted for Passover as a young bride and how pleased she'd be if one day Quincy covered her table with it for a family Seder. "Is he religious?"

"No, but he's very spiritual. I really like that about him."

Okay, so maybe he'll convert. "Of course I'll come to Boston to meet his parents. I just can't guarantee how Uncle Isaac will react. . . ."

"I know, Mom. So, I'm counting on you to smooth the way before his parents arrive."

Great. Quincy just handed me one more thing to fix. Could my life get any more complicated?

CHAPTER 24

I loaded the dog in the car Sunday morning and stopped for two lattes and a couple of fresh donuts on my way to Brentwood. The weather had cleared and Carl had parked his Harley in Harriet's driveway. He met us at the door and ruffled Arthur's fur. As I handed Carl one of the cups of coffee, the donut bag fell out of my hand and landed on the floor. A round glazed buttermilk rolled across the foyer and stopped next to the stairway. Arthur ran over and scarfed it down before I had a chance to stop him.

Carl snorted. "Once a cop, always a cop."

We sat in the library. I looked at the remaining donut wistfully, broke it in half, and virtuously handed a piece to Carl.

Motes of dust danced in a shaft of sunlight warming the top of the yellow oak table. A book sat facedown next to Carl's computer, *Zen and the Art of Motorcycle Maintenance.* By the fraying on the paperback cover, this book must have been a favorite of his. I pointed to the well-worn volume. "I've never read that."

"Every time I read this, I pick up something new." He scooted his chair closer to the table and opened the book to a dog-eared page. "Like this morning, I came across this passage:

> *"The truth knocks on the door and you say, 'Go away, I'm looking for the truth,' and so it goes away. Puzzling."*

"And that means . . . ?"

"Sometimes we're so sure we know what we're looking for, we become blind to new possibilities—and we miss out."

Carl had a point. I needed to be open to the unexpected to prove Harriet didn't kill her husband. Who else besides the people I'd already considered might have a motive for Nathan's murder? Since Abernathy helped Harriet get her husband declared legally dead, he probably knew a lot about their marriage.

I shifted in my seat and looked at the handsome young man sitting next to me. Carl Lindgren was a complex guy. He loved motorcycles and fast cars, yet he treated with tenderness Birdie, an arthritic woman in her seventies whom he'd adopted as his grandmother. He owned a successful software business, yet he volunteered to be a mere security guard to help me out. Because of his work, he probably had top security clearance with the government, yet he carried a gun and hung out with bikers.

Carl, a technological genius, earned a degree from Caltech, one of the top two science universities in the country. The other was MIT, where Quincy's boyfriend taught. Would Carl know of him?

"What do you know about theoretical physics?"

"What part? Quantum? Cosmology? String? Particles?"

"Never mind. I have no idea what you just said. Have you heard of a professor at MIT by the name of Naveen Sharma?"

"Yeah, Dr. Sharma's only the world's smartest string theorist. He made his chops early. PhD by twenty-two. I heard rumors he was up for a Nobel last year. Why do you ask?"

Okay, so at least I could tell Uncle Isaac they'd have really smart children. "He's a friend of my daughter, Quincy."

Carl whistled. "Awesome. I'd like to meet him sometime."

Harriet's doorbell rang at precisely ten.

Carl looked out the window. "You expecting someone?"

"An estate manager. She's going to give me an estimate on selling everything in the house."

"You mean like a garage sale?"

I laughed. "Yes. A very fancy one. I'll get the door." Carl followed me to the foyer.

Arthur snuffled around the floor, near the stairway. "Forget it, pal. Your owner would be upset if he knew I allowed you to eat a whole donut this morning."

I opened the front door to a very pretty young woman.

Susan Daniels parted her perfectly straight blond hair on the side, letting it hang over one eye. She offered me a dazzling smile and a slender hand with a French manicure. "I'm happy to meet you, Mrs. Rose."

I opened the door wider. "You came highly recommended by Julian Kessler. Please come in."

She stepped into the foyer on long, elegant legs and black stiletto heels. Carl cleared his throat behind me. I turned to look at him, and he gestured with his head toward the stunning young woman.

"Susan Daniels, this is Carl Lindgren. He's part of a private security team guarding this house."

"Hi." She smiled, then began to scan the house with an expert's gaze.

Carl darted his eyes back and forth, sending me a clear message. I'd screwed up.

"Of course Carl's just doing me a huge favor." I scrambled for words. "In real life he runs a successful company developing software for the SEC."

Carl nodded encouragement in the background.

"If in the coming days you see a yellow Corvette parked in front, you'll know Carl's here."

He ran his fingers through his sandy hair and smiled out of the corner of his mouth. "Pleasure to meet you. *Believe* me."

Susan looked down and her cheeks colored.

The dog still snuffled around the floor as if someone had smeared a pot roast there.

"Oh, for heaven's sake, Arthur." I clucked my tongue. "Give up. There are no more donuts." I turned to the others. "Let's sit in the living room and you can explain the process to me."

Susan sat on the green leather sofa and crossed her legs. Her slender skirt rode up her thigh. Carl switched to mouth breathing.

"Well, technically"—she folded her hands in her

lap—"an estate manager is like a chief of staff or head butler. I'm an Estate Liquidation Specialist. My company oversees the appraisal and sale of personal property, typically after the death of an individual."

Carl fixed his eyes on hers and flashed an engaging smile. "Fascinating."

At his point he'd find dust fascinating if she said she swept porches for a living. Susan smiled back.

I handed her a copy of the insurance rider. "Mrs. Oliver owned some very valuable items. They've already been appraised."

"Even if you have appraisals, we'll want to update them as these items may have increased in value." She scanned the list. "Why are some of them circled?"

Carl tented his fingers. "They were stolen."

Susan looked up sharply. "What did you say the name of this family was?"

"Oliver," he said.

Her forehead furrowed in concern. "Is this the house where they discovered the body buried in the backyard last week?"

"Yes." I let out my breath. "Does that make a difference?"

"It will probably make a big difference. Didn't they say the wife was also murdered recently? Is this her estate? I mean, are we safe to even be here?" Her eyes widened as she looked from Carl to me.

Carl puffed his chest out a little. "Don't worry. As long as I'm here, you'll be safe."

Oh, for pity's sake. "The circled items wouldn't be for sale, anyway. With the exception of a few specific objects, I'm anxious to liquidate everything else remaining in this house."

Susan let out her breath. "Okay. I'd like to do a

walkthrough and take pictures and notes as we go."
She took an iPhone out of her bag. "When we're through, I'll give you a rough estimate."

Carl insisted on accompanying us, lagging just behind.

After an hour, we ended up back in the living room.

Susan typed something on her iPhone. "The household furnishings can be tagged and sold at an estate sale. We probably won't gross more than a hundred thousand. My company takes thirty-five percent."

Did I hear her correctly? "Thirty-five thousand seems a little steep. The proceeds from the estate are going toward building a wing at Children's Hospital. Can't you give me a better price?"

Susan hesitated. "Thirty-five percent is the industry standard. We incur a lot of expense because of all the preparation, staffing, overhead, and insurance." She looked at the ceiling and bit her lip. "I can reduce the fee to twenty-five percent since the money's going to such a good cause." She smiled. "This is my own business, so I can be flexible."

"I really appreciate it." I liked her. Susan Daniels possessed a generous spirit to match her generous smile.

Susan consulted the insurance rider. "The really valuable things listed here should go to our auction house. Competitive bidding results in the best price. According to the last appraisals, they should bring in a minimum of over two million dollars. I'll give you the same break on the auction fee and only charge you fifteen percent, instead of our usual twenty."

"You're very generous, Susan. How soon can we get started?"

"I can bring a dozen packers back here tomorrow to start boxing everything. I estimate we'll be here two days. Meanwhile, I'll launch an advertising blitz. We'll be ready for the sale by this weekend."

She put her iPhone in her purse. "You should be aware, however, that because of the recent notoriety connected to this house, two things are bound to happen. First, serious buyers might stay away because of the murder. Second, hundreds of lookie-loos will probably show up out of morbid curiosity but not to buy. So I think it's best to relocate everything you want to sell to our warehouse showroom."

"Will the items still be insured once they're removed from the house?"

She waved a graceful hand. "Oh, yes, our insurance will cover everything, but I'll need you to sign off on each individual box."

I tapped my lips with my finger. "Okay. Before we get started, I need to clear up one more thing with the attorney."

"Fine, but if we don't proceed in the next day or two, we may have to push back the sale one week. I still need time to price each item."

We stood and shook hands. "I'll call you once the attorney gives me the go-ahead."

Carl escorted her to a cream-colored Escalade and returned with a business card and a grin on his face. "Dinner tomorrow."

"You work fast."

Arthur sniffed around the foyer again, nose to the floor. "Carl, remember what you said about looking for truth but being blind to possibilities?"

"Yeah."

I pointed to the dog. "What if he's not sniffing for donut crumbs? Remember how he discovered Nathan's grave? I think Arthur's sensing something hidden there. He's confirming what we already suspect. The stairway is the portal to the secret room."

Carl tapped his temple. "Smart dog. But we still have to find the way in."

I attached Arthur's leash and headed for the door. "We will when those blueprints turn up."

CHAPTER 25

When I arrived back home in Encino, I telephoned Abernathy. "Sorry to bother you on a Sunday, but I have several urgent things to discuss with you."

"Not at all. I'm anxious to explain the unfortunate business with Harriet's account. I guarantee I knew nothing about it. We're close to finding the culprit. And when we do, you can be sure we'll turn him over to the police."

"Well—"

"Furthermore, I'm working closely with Kessler to repair any damages done. My office is replacing the money in Harriet's account with interest. I sure am grateful for your understanding on this. If you have any concerns—any concerns at all—I want to put your mind at ease."

Plus, you don't want me to report you to the DA or the California State Bar. "You're right, Deke, I am concerned. What I do about the embezzlement will depend on the final audit of Harriet's estate. Right now, however, I need to talk to you about a couple of other things. We should talk in person." I wanted to gauge his reactions.

"Okay. I can meet you in my office this afternoon."

"I've already made one trip over the hill today and I don't want to make another. You'll have to come to my house." I figured Abernathy would do anything at this point to make me happy.

"How does four sound? I have your address."

I spent the rest of the afternoon with graph paper and colored pencils, working on the first step in engineering Quincy's Wedding Ring quilt. I plotted the placement of the different colored rings. I drew the yellow one in the middle of the quilt about two thirds of the way up. Yellow was the brightest color and immediately drew attention. Dividing the quilt into thirds created the *golden mean,* the point where the design reached a balance most pleasing to the eye. All the rings would be linked, and no ring of one color would touch another ring of the same color. How many rings I ultimately constructed would depend on the size of her bed—a detail I didn't yet care to think about.

Abernathy arrived at exactly four. We drank coffee in the living room and I told him about Henry Oliver's telephone call.

"Is he right? Can he nullify Harriet's will on the grounds the police think she killed her husband? Does he have any legal claim to family heirlooms or any of the property Harriet inherited from her husband?"

"Relax." Abernathy leaned back. "This is an easy one. It doesn't matter what the police think. Since Harriet was never *convicted* of her husband's murder, she inherits everything. Neither of Nathan's siblings have a right to any part of the estate. Even family heirlooms."

"What if they go to court and manage to convince a judge Harriet killed Nathan?"

Deke gave a short laugh. "You can't convict a dead person of murder. She has to be alive before you can potentially seek the death penalty on her."

"Well, what about wrongful death, like the O. J. Simpson case?"

"Same answer. You can't sue a dead person. Anyway, the Olivers don't have evidence to prove wrongful death. Just relax and continue on with what you're doing, Martha. No one can invalidate Harriet's inheritance. The relatives have no grounds to challenge her will."

"I'm still worried. Nathan's brother tried to bully me over the phone. When I told him most of the family heirlooms were missing, he threatened to sue me and file a criminal complaint. I don't look forward to telling him when he comes to LA next week that his only legitimate claim is for Nathan's remains, not his estate."

Abernathy swiped dismissively at the air. "You don't have to deal with him. You have me, remember? The guy's trying to do an end run around the will. Bring him to my office, and I'll take care of him. You can sit on the sidelines and watch from the bench."

I thought about Estella's request for the antique Spode china and the silver candelabras from Spain. "I'm actually considering letting the family keep some items. As I understand the terms of the will, I don't have the authority to give those things away, but I can sell them. Correct?"

"Yes."

"I plan to offer some of the family heirlooms to Estella for the price of one dollar. Will that satisfy the terms of the will?"

"No. The law is clear. You have to sell them at fair market value. Anyway, the whole question of heirlooms is moot since you say most of the items are missing."

"Maybe not. Did you know Harriet built a safe room in her house in 2005?" I watched his face closely.

Abernathy pulled his head back and stared at me. "No, I mean, I recall something about work being done, but I just assumed she remodeled her kitchen."

"I think the missing items could be inside that room. I'm pretty sure the entrance is under the stairway."

"Amazing. Let's hope Harriet's killer didn't get there first."

If Abernathy faked his surprise, I couldn't tell.

"There's one more thing, Deke. The police think Harriet killed Nathan. They're not going to investigate his murder."

"Yeah, I can understand why they came to that conclusion."

"According to Detective Farkas, they're basing their decision on something Harriet's friend Isabel told them."

Abernathy looked confused. "Do you know what she said?"

"No, but Isabel told me how Nathan abused Harriet."

Deke looked up sharply. "So you know about the abuse?"

"Yes. And I believe the police concluded Harriet reached a breaking point and attacked her abuser."

"I suppose . . ." Abernathy rubbed his jaw.

"Deke, you and I both know Harriet didn't have a murderous bone in her body. I want to know everything about Nathan. Who might have had a motive to kill him? Who were his enemies? Give me names."

The attorney pursed his lips. "Client privilege—"

"They're both dead! This is Harriet's reputation we're talking about."

Abernathy took a deep breath. "Nico Grimaldi is the name of the charter boat captain where Jonah died. Oliver refused to testify on Grimaldi's behalf at a hearing. As a result, Grimaldi was forced to sell his business to pay a huge fine. The captain swore he'd get even."

"Harriet kept the secret of Nathan's murder all those years. She knew his grave was in the backyard and made sure nobody else discovered it. She kept silent all those years to protect Nathan's killer. If Grimaldi killed Nathan, what would make her protect Grimaldi? He was a stranger."

Abernathy shrugged. "You knew Harriet. She might have felt sorry for the man and guilty for what her husband did to him."

"Anyone else you can think of Nathan screwed over?"

"Oliver was an SOB. Plenty of people hated the guy. But no one stands out at as a possible murderer."

"I want to talk to Grimaldi."

Abernathy did a double take. "He'll never talk to you."

"I'll pretend to offer him money. I'll say Harriet wrote in her will that she wanted to make restitution for an old injustice."

"Not very wise. He could be dangerous."

"Not if he thinks I'm only carrying out Harriet's last wishes."

Before he left, Abernathy promised to call me with Grimaldi's last known address.

I called Susan Daniels with the go-ahead for the sale. Tomorrow would be a very big day. Susan would clear out Harriet's house, and I'd finally get to see the blueprints. As for the secret room, I was almost there.

CHAPTER 26

Arthur and I pulled into Harriet's driveway at six forty-five Monday morning. Malo was stretched out in the living room asleep underneath a blanket on Harriet's green leather sofa.

"Some watchman you are!"

He snorted awake and jerked upright. "Hunh?"

I handed him a cup of Starbucks. "I said, 'Some watchman you are.' You were so dead asleep I could've walked off with the boots on your feet."

"Oh, man, I'm sorry. Usually I'm a light sleeper." He yawned and slid a very big handgun with a shiny steel barrel from under the sofa pillow and tucked it in his waistband.

I looked at my watch. "In about ten minutes, a lot of people are going to enter the front door with boxes and pack up everything in this house. I need you to walk around and keep an eye on things."

Malo stood. "Sure. What do you want me to do if I see someone boosting something?"

I looked at his gun. "Don't shoot."

A twenty six-foot-long moving truck pulled up in

front of the house. I put the dog in the fenced-in backyard to keep him from getting in the way or running out the front door. "If you find any more dead bodies, Arthur, just keep it to yourself." He walked over to the dirt covering Nathan's former grave, sniffed around, and squatted.

Malo followed as I opened the front door. Susan Daniels wore skinny leg jeans in what I guessed to be a size six. The black lace of her bra peeked out at her deep vee neckline. She jumped a tiny bit when she saw the vertical tattoos on Malo's cheeks. "Good morning." She eyed him curiously, then looked at me. "Is Carl here?"

"He's coming later." I stepped aside and gestured toward the foyer. "Susan Daniels, this is Hector Fuentes, nighttime security."

"Call me Malo." He grinned, flashing a gold incisor.

Susan nodded brightly. "Well, time to get to work." She waved out the door. A dozen workers carrying bundles of cardboard boxes, rolls of tape, bubble wrap, and huge bags of packing peanuts trooped behind her into the kitchen.

Malo sidled close to me, and whispered at the back of my head, "Damn."

I whispered back, "Carl already has first dibs. Dinner tonight."

"Now I know why that *vato* wanted me to take the last part of his shift today."

We strolled into the kitchen. Susan set up a coffee station for the workers, including gallon containers from Starbucks and two large flats from Western Donuts. "Please help yourselves." She smiled at Malo and me. Without hesitation, I reached for an apple fritter.

At nine, Carl arrived to begin his shift.

Malo bumped fists and left. "Later, dawg."

By eleven, everything in the kitchen had been divided into lots and packed. I inspected each numbered carton before the workers sealed them with tape, and initialed a pink manifest listing the contents. Then the boxes were loaded into the truck. With each departing container, my burden lifted a little.

The antique Spode china in the dining room and the silver candelabras were carefully packed in several shipping crates and set aside. Even though Estella didn't ask for them specifically, I also included a few more old silver pieces, probably family heirlooms.

Susan took several photos of the mahogany bowfront china cabinet with an elaborately carved lion pediment and claw feet. "This piece should fetch at least ten thousand at auction. Maybe double. I might have a couple of interested buyers."

A food truck showed up at noon and everyone took a lunch break. I brought the dog into the house. He sat next to me and thumped his tail loudly on the floor while I fed him half of my carne asada taco and called Kessler. He was unavailable, but Isis assured me she'd deliver the message. I wanted to know if he'd received the blueprints for the secret room from the owner of Safe-T-Construction.

Next I called Abernathy.

"It took him awhile, but my investigator finally

found Grimaldi's current address and phone number. I'm texting you the info."

I hung up and read the text. Nico Grimaldi, the captain of the boat who swore to get even with Nathan Oliver, lived in Santa Monica.

After lunch, half the workers moved into the library to empty the bookshelves. The other half followed Susan and me into the family room to pack the baskets and antique toys.

Susan removed her iPhone from her pocket. "I'll photograph each of these pieces in situ, then pack them separately. Because they're so valuable, they, along with the watch collection and the paintings, will be transported in an armored vehicle to our warehouse. Everything else in the house can go in the big truck."

The workers put on white cotton gloves, carefully lifted each basket from the shelf, and placed it on a nest of finely shredded excelsior in a reinforced cardboard container. Once I signed off, each box was sealed and carried to an armored truck sitting in the driveway.

As the gloved crew carefully enclosed the Early American toys in bubble wrap, I reached out for the wooden dreidel from Portugal, with the painted Hebrew letters, and put it in my pocket. Susan looked at me, her forehead wrinkled with a question.

"This stays with me." I gave no further explanation. According to Harriet's will, I could choose one of her possessions, even the most expensive item, for myself. The lovely little top, spun by so many generations of Jewish children, would be my keepsake.

At five, the movers cleaned up the coffee station in the kitchen, swept the floors, and left the premises.

Susan approached me to initial the manifest for the last of the boxes. "I'll see you again at seven in the morning. We made very good progress today. Packing the few things upstairs should be much easier tomorrow."

As soon as Carl and I were alone, I called Kessler again. "Did you get the information we wanted from the construction company?"

"Not yet. The owner's stuck in Dallas. All flights canceled. Ice storm. He gets back tomorrow."

Darn! Another day's delay. I walked slowly through the bare rooms on the first floor. Of all the furniture, only the oak library table and chairs remained. I asked Susan to leave them behind so we'd have a place to rest. Nail holes punctuated the walls in the cavernous living room where framed paintings once hung. In the foyer, the likeness of Jonah, which had dominated the wall, was on its way to Children's Hospital to one day hang in the wing bearing his name.

A few wooden crates packed with Oliver family heirlooms occupied one corner of the now-empty dining room. The cupboards and drawers in the kitchen were bare. Even the package brownies were gone. The boxes from the maid's room containing the hand-embroidered linens, the Passover dishes, and the Talmud were also gone.

My footsteps echoed in the lonely spaces where a family once lived—and died. The very air felt heavy with mourning and loss.

Time to call the insurance agent. I joined Carl

in the library and opened my purse. I found the business card Wish gave me at Harriet's funeral.

He picked up on the second ring. "Emmet Wish here."

I told him about the estate sale. "I wanted to let you know Harriet's insured items have been removed to the auction house and are now covered under their policy."

"Okay, but let's keep Harriet's policy intact until everything is sold. Just to be double sure." He cleared his throat. "In cleaning out the house, did you ever find any trace of the missing books, the quilt, or the jewelry?"

"Not yet."

"Very bad news, indeed. I sure hoped you'd have more luck." He sighed. "I guess there's no use delaying the inevitable. Time to prepare a claim for the stolen items."

"Hold off on filing that claim. Harriet built a secret room. We don't know the exact location yet. I'm just waiting to get the blueprints from the building contractor to find out how to get inside." I listened hard for a reaction.

"No kidding! A hidden room?" He sounded surprised. "Harriet never mentioned it. I might have been able to get her rates lowered if I'd known."

As I said good-bye to Wish, Malo walked in.

He clapped Carl on the back. "It's six, dawg. Time to go meet that fine . . ." Malo stopped when he saw me. "*Hola.* You still here?"

"Yes, *dawg*. Hope you got your beauty rest today because there are still some valuables left to guard in this house. Everyone's returning tomorrow morning at seven."

Malo scratched the back of his head and looked at the floor. "Tonight's my last night, boss. You'd better get a replacement if you still need someone."

I stood and grabbed Arthur's leash. "Thanks for letting me know, Malo. And thanks for all your help. If Susan and her crew clean out the rest of the house tomorrow, there'll be nothing to guard, anyway." I winked at Carl. "Have a nice time tonight." I loaded Arthur in my Corolla and drove to Encino.

When I got back home, I realized tomorrow fell on a Tuesday, and Tuesdays were sacred. My friends and I always quilted together, no matter what. I called Lucy. "I have to be at Harriet's house early. Can you and Birdie meet me there at ten? We can sew in the library while the workers pack the upstairs."

"What about the blueprints? Did you find the room? I want to be there when you go in."

"I don't have the blueprints yet." I explained about the bad weather in Dallas. "The guy is due back tomorrow. I'm certain the entrance is under the stairway, just like we thought. Arthur kept sniffing around there the same way he sniffed out Nathan's grave."

"See?" Lucy sounded relieved. "The Lord works in mysterious ways. Arlo dumping his dog on you turned out to be a good thing. Meet you *mañana*, and don't you dare go in that room without us."

I uncorked a bottle of my favorite Chianti and nuked a frozen lasagna from Trader Joe's for dinner. Something kept nagging at the edge of my mind, an important clue I kept overlooking. I thought about the quote from Carl's book, *Zen and the Art of Motorcycle Maintenance*. What part of the truth eluded me?

I grabbed a pad of paper and pen and began listing what I knew while I waited for the lasagna to cook. First, Nathan Oliver abused his wife and caused the death of their son. Two years later he had been murdered and buried in the backyard. How was Harriet involved? What about the boat captain, Grimaldi?

Abernathy brokered a huge donation to Children's Hospital and managed Harriet's financial affairs, but in the last twenty months someone in Abernathy's office ripped off nearly $200,000 from Harriet's account. Did she know about the embezzlement?

The microwave dinged. I removed the steaming pasta and grabbed a fork. I blew on the hot food and tucked into a bite. What about Isabel? Two years ago Harriet cut her off and changed her will, naming me executor.

Around the same time, Harriet started visiting Paulina the psychic. When Paulina channeled the ghost of Nathan Oliver one year later, Harriet fired both Paulina and Delia, the housekeeper, to guard the secret of Nathan's murder. Who was Harriet protecting?

I washed down the lasagna with a healthy sip of wine. Harriet said something to Delia about Nathan wanting people to know the truth about his death. Delia described Harriet as emotionally fragile. Did she reach her breaking point? Did the same person who killed Nathan kill Harriet to protect his secret?

As I considered these facts, I moved to the freezer and spooned some chocolate caramel swirl ice cream into a cereal bowl. Someone searched Harriet's house after her death. He found the Benjamin Franklin watch. Did he also have books from the Founding Fathers and the Declaration Quilt? How did the missing jewelry fit into the picture?

The key to the puzzle lay not only with what had been taken, but what he left behind. Somewhere in the sequence of events lay the identity of Harriet's killer. And the letter from Dr. Hunter, opened after Harriet's death, held an important clue.

CHAPTER 27

Tuesday morning at seven Susan Daniels returned with her crew and moving van. They set up their coffee station in the kitchen and trooped upstairs to remove the rest of Harriet's possessions.

From the way Susan smiled shyly, I guessed last night's dinner with Carl went well. I didn't feel comfortable asking her, but I'd get the truth out of Carl when he arrived later.

"What do you want me to do about the little boy's room?" she asked. "Do you want to set aside any items?"

"The things in his room held meaning only for his mother. We'll donate his stuff to a children's shelter. What's really important now is honoring Jonah Oliver's memory through a hospital wing named after him."

Susan tucked a wisp of hair behind her ear. "Shall I set aside anything in Mrs. Oliver's room for you? Pieces of jewelry?"

"All her personal photos should go to the hospital. I imagine they'll keep them in some sort of donor's archive. Everything else can be sold. Legally, I'm not allowed to keep anything. My job is to liquidate Mrs. Oliver's estate according to her wishes."

"I'm sorry." She shrugged. "I guess I assumed when you took the toy yesterday. . ."

"One thing. Harriet said I could have one thing."

Carl arrived at nine with a spring in his step and a big smile plastered on his face. I didn't need to ask after all. Things evidently went *really* well last night.

Malo shook my hand. "Take care of yourself, boss." He slugged Carl's shoulder as he left. *"Esay!"*

"So, how did the dinner go last night?" I ambled over to Carl.

"Where is she?" he grinned.

I tried hard to keep from smiling. "You're here to watch the house, remember?"

He rubbed the back of his neck. "Uh, yeah. Where is she?"

I pointed toward the ceiling. Carl took the stairs two at a time.

Lucy and Birdie arrived at ten, carrying their tote bags full of quilting. Lucy wore jeans with sharp creases down the legs, a red sweater with matching lipstick, and ruby studs in her ears.

Birdie stood in the foyer and looked around at the vacant rooms. "There's something so sad about an empty house and yet so promising, don't you think?"

"I know what you mean." Lucy followed her gaze. "Sad because something is ending, but promising because something new will take its place."

Susan came downstairs with three workers following behind carrying cardboard boxes. She handed me a clipboard holding the pink manifest. "I need you to sign off on these, please."

I inspected cartons 120 through 122 and initialed the paper. Harriet's clothes were neatly folded inside. The workers sealed the boxes and carried them to the truck.

Lucy gave me a not-so-subtle nudge and I introduced Susan to my friends. "We always get together on Tuesdays to quilt. Lucy and Birdie will be keeping me company in the library today."

Susan clasped her hands. "Oh, my *farmor* used to sew quilts. I come from Minnesota where you need lots of them during the cold winters. I always wanted to learn how to make one."

Birdie patted the young woman's arm. "*Farmor* is Swedish for grandmother, isn't it, dear?"

"Yes. And if I may say so, you remind me a lot of her. She had long white hair like yours, except she twisted her braid like a crown around her head."

Carl's boots clumped heavily down the stairs. "One more thing we have in common." He strode over to Birdie and gave her a one-arm hug. "Birdie's my *farmor* now."

Birdie beamed at him. Carl showed her far more affection than her husband, Russell, did.

Susan's eyes softened at the tender exchange. She smiled and gestured toward the kitchen. "Please help yourselves to donuts and coffee." She turned to go upstairs and Carl followed, with his fingertips touching the small of her back.

Birdie's mouth fell open. "When did that happen?" She twisted the end of her braid as I told them what little I knew about Susan. "They went out on a first date last night and I guess they really like each other."

"She does seem awfully sweet." Birdie sighed wistfully.

"Susan says she wants to learn how to quilt," said Lucy. "Not many young women are interested these days. Maybe you could teach her." Birdie's eyes sparkled. We cleared off the library table to help Lucy assemble a baby quilt. She unfurled a large fabric backing, a soft blue print with little white lambs. She attached it to the table with masking tape, wrong side up. On top of the bottom layer, she flattened a middle layer of cotton batting, smoothing out the lumps. The quilt top consisted of six-inch basket blocks pieced with triangles of blue and white for her infant grandson.

We stretched and smoothed and pinned everything in place to prevent puckers. Next we threaded long needles and spent half an hour sewing all three layers of the quilt sandwich together with big, temporary stitches. When we finished, Lucy removed the pins and tape, and held up the little blanket. The quilt hung in a perfect rectangle. "I should be able to finish quilting this in a couple of weeks."

The food truck showed up, and we took a taco break. After lunch Susan reappeared in the doorway. "Martha, you have to sign off on Mrs. Oliver's jewelry drawer. I've photographed everything in place, but I need a separate signature for each item."

"Be right back." I followed Susan upstairs to Harriet's closet. Two workers folded the last of her clothes and placed them into cardboard cartons.

I removed the pieces of everyday jewelry and handed them to Susan one at a time. She placed each one in a plastic baggie and marked the label.

I lifted the charm bracelet Harriet wore as a girl and fingered the tiny gold trinkets marking distinct milestones in her life. Among them was a pair of ballet slippers from the dancing lessons we took when we were seven, a Torah scroll for her bat mitzvah, and a little car she received after earning her driver's license.

A miniature gold book her parents gave her when she left home to attend Brown University also hung from the chain. Resentment briefly pushed at my chest. If Harriet had never attended Brown, she never would have met Nathan Oliver. And if she had never met him, maybe she'd be alive today.

I handed Susan the last item, a heavy necklace with round turquoise beads. The black velvet drawer lining slipped under my fingertips. While Susan filled out the label on the plastic baggie, I surreptitiously pushed the lining back from the front edge of the drawer. Two holes the size of a quarter were drilled into the front of the wooden bottom. I felt with my left hand underneath the drawer. No holes. About three inches of space separated my hands. The jewelry drawer carried a false bottom, and those were finger holes.

I replaced the velvet lining and put my hands in my pockets to hide the shaking. I didn't want any outsiders watching me lift the false bottom. I knew what would be hiding there.

I stayed until the workers removed the last of Harriet's wardrobe from the closet. I turned off the light and waited for everyone to leave the area. As Carl headed for the door, I called after him. "Stop. I need you to stay here and keep everyone away from the closet."

His eyebrows scrunched together.

"It's important. Nobody comes in here."

"Why?"

"I found something. I'll tell you after everyone leaves."

I left him standing in the bedroom while I joined Lucy and Birdie downstairs.

"What took you so long, dear?" Birdie sipped a cup of coffee and picked at a plain cake donut.

I looked over my shoulder to make certain no one observed me. Then I shook my wrists and did an excited little dance on my toes, not easy with size-sixteen hips. "Oh my God, oh my God." I tried to keep my voice down. "I think I just found the missing diamonds."

Birdie's hand flew to her mouth.

"Get out!" Lucy said. "Where?"

"The jewelry drawer in Harriet's closet has a false bottom."

Birdie whispered, "You *think* you found? Didn't you open it?"

"Not yet. I want to wait until we're alone. Carl's standing guard right now."

"What's the matter? Don't you trust Susan?" It was so like Birdie to jump to her defense.

"Of course. I've entrusted quite a few valuables to her care already. I just didn't want to open the drawer in front of so many strangers. First, I'll compare whatever we find against the list on the insurance rider and the photos. Then I'll hand them over to Susan to sell."

Lucy gathered the used pieces of masking tape into a sticky ball. "What about the blueprints? Weren't you going to get the blueprints for the secret room today?"

"You're right. I haven't heard from Julian yet." I grabbed my cell phone. "I'll call him now."

Kessler sounded busy. "Abernathy showed up this morning. He brought a check for the missing money. Plus interest."

"How much interest?

"Seven percent. More than remedial restitution. Prime has been a lot lower since the crash."

"Just as long as he doesn't think he's buying his way out with a few measly percentage points."

Kessler chuckled. "You're tough. I like that. Anyway, Abernathy tracked down the thief. WC Household Maintenance is a dummy corp set up by his accountant, Wendy Curtis. Turns out she siphoned off a couple million from various clients. Disappeared a month ago. Feds are after her."

"What about the blueprints? I thought you'd have called me by now."

"I finally heard from the owner of Safe-T-Construction. Records from 2005 are in a storage facility in Vernon. He'll send someone to retrieve them tomorrow. They should be in my hands by noon."

Maybe waiting yet another day for the blueprints wouldn't be such a bad thing. Susan and her crew would be gone for good in an hour or so. Like the false bottom in Harriet's jewelry drawer, I didn't want to open up the secret room with strangers around.

"Good work, Julian. Call me the minute you know anything more."

Susan asked me to do a final walk-through and sign off on the job. We started in the far end of the upstairs hall. The shelves and cupboards in the linen closet were bare. The bathrooms were completely stripped, except for the toilet paper in the holders. The only things left in the little boy's room were the blue walls. The guest room had been emptied of furniture, and the closets were stripped. We ended up in the master bedroom where Carl stood.

"You did a great job. Very soon I may have some more high-end items for you to auction off."

Carl raised his eyebrows in two question marks but said nothing.

"Fine. Just give me a call when you're ready." The young beauty put her hand over her mouth and yawned.

Must not have gotten much sleep last night.

She handed me several pages of carbons from the manifest. "This is a list of every item we removed from the house. I'll start pricing everything tomorrow." She looked at Carl. "Walk me to my car?"

I nodded. "Go ahead. I'll meet you back in the library."

Birdie stood at the front window, watching Carl and Susan in the driveway. "I do believe he's quite smitten. Look at the way he's mooning at her."

Lucy nodded. "And she's feeling it too. See how she's stroking his arm? I remember when Ray and I were young. We did the same thing. Couldn't keep our hands off each other. Couldn't wait to be alone." She turned to Birdie. "What about you and Russell?"

Bitterness sharpened the edge of Birdie's voice. "Russell was too uptight. He could never let go and just be happy. I thought I could change him, but I was naive. He was the same old poop back then as

he is now. What about you, Martha dear? Do you
feel the same way about your new beau?"

Good question. I had been so in love with my
ex-husband, Aaron Rose. I thought our marriage
would last forever. When he suddenly left me for
another woman, something switched off inside.
Then when I met Detective Arlo Beavers this year,
I thought I'd found love again. Until he also left
me for another woman. Crusher was my current
boyfriend. He was smart, sexy, and funny—and he
wasn't afraid of commitment. I was the one with
the problem. I'd lost the ability to trust. "No," I
sighed. "I don't believe I could ever feel the same
way again."

Susan drove off and Carl came back inside. I
locked the front door behind him, grabbed the
photos, and headed for the stairs. "Finally. Let's go."

Carl said, "What's the big mystery in the closet?"

Birdie and Lucy spoke at the same time. "Diamonds!"

CHAPTER 28

Carl helped Birdie climb the stairs as Lucy and I raced ahead to Harriet's now-empty bedroom and large walk-in closet. I placed the insurance rider and the photos of the jewelry on the built-in dresser, yanked open the top drawer, and pushed the black velvet cloth back a couple of inches. Finger holes, the size of a quarter, gaped in each corner.

Lucy touched my shoulder. "Go for it."

I curled a forefinger in each hole and lifted. The front edge of the false bottom came up smoothly. I pinched my thumbs for a better grasp, took a deep breath, and slid the piece all the way out.

"Mercy," Birdie's voice whispered next to me.

"Dang!" said Lucy.

Several fuzzy black boxes and smooth leather cases sat neatly in the drawer under the false bottom. I picked up the first ring-sized box and found a pair of two-carat diamond stud earrings sparkling inside.

Carl leaned in close. "Whoa."

Next I opened a large, flat case. A pendant with

a canary diamond the size of a thumbnail and surrounded by a starburst of clear baguette diamonds hung from a platinum chain. "This matches the cocktail ring I spotted on Isabel's finger."

Birdie adjusted her glasses and took the necklace from my hand to get a closer look. "Stunning."

Harriet's bracelet rested in a long, black leather box. Each diamond, individually set on a delicate underlay of platinum scrollwork, created the illusion of a sparkling lace cuff more than an inch wide. I draped it over my wrist. Every small movement produced darts of rainbow light. "This is appraised at one hundred thousand."

Carl whistled. "Even my new Vette isn't worth so much."

The rest of the small containers held pieces encrusted with exquisite diamonds and gems of various colors: indigo sapphires, dark green emeralds, blood red rubies, periwinkle tanzanite, and an opera-length strand of half-inch black pearls. Every insured item, except the cocktail ring, rested in the hidden drawer.

Lucy put her hands on her hips. "Well, this solves the mystery of the missing jewelry. If the killer were smart enough to search Harriet's closet a little more thoroughly, he would've found her stash."

"Don't forget about that." Birdie pointed to the hole in the carpet behind the dresser where Harriet's body decomposed for ten months. "He may not have been able to stomach being in here for long."

"Unless he wore a gas mask," said Lucy.

I recoiled at the image. Carl made a face.

Lucy threw her palms out. "I'm just saying . . ."

I began to pace. "I don't believe the killer wanted

the diamonds. Remember, he left tons of other valuable stuff behind. I'm convinced he came specifically for the books, the quilt, and the Benjamin Franklin watch."

Lucy slid a sapphire ring on her slender finger and twisted it in the light. "You may be right, girlfriend. Still, this is a lot of bling to pass up."

"What're you going to do with the jewelry now?" Carl blew into his palms.

"Since Malo's not coming back for the night shift, I'd like to give the whole lot to Susan for safekeeping until the auction." I stopped pacing and looked at Carl. "Can you call her?"

He removed his cell from his pocket and stepped out of the closet. After a few moments of muffled conversation, he returned and put Susan on speaker.

She shouted over the traffic noises in the background. "Hi, Martha. Carl said you found some jewelry under a false bottom in a drawer. You want me to sell them?"

"Yes. Can you keep them safe?"

"Sure, but the armored vehicle won't be available for transport until tomorrow."

"I can bring them over to you now." Carl leaned close to the phone.

There was a quiet pause.

"Will you be safe carrying all those diamonds?"

Carl pushed his shoulders back. "Of course. I'll be there in twenty minutes."

Susan giggled. "You'll take a little bit longer to get to Beverly Hills during rush hour. I'm still on the road. I'll meet you at the warehouse." She gave Carl the address and then hung up.

We found a clean trash bag under the kitchen

sink and I put the fuzzy boxes and small cases of jewelry inside. "Thanks for doing this, Carl. No one will suspect you're carrying a fortune in jewels in this trash bag. Aside from the few crates sitting in the dining room, the house is empty. Your job here is done."

Carl took the trash bag. "What about the missing stuff and the hidden room?"

"They'll remain safe without our help."

Carl removed Harriet's house key from his pocket and handed it to me.

"I can't thank you enough, Carl. Please be careful." He gave us each a hug and headed for Beverly Hills with a fortune in gems.

Lucy, Birdie, and I drove back to the valley in our separate cars. I stopped at Crazy Chicken takeout for some wings, thighs, and a side of coleslaw. Arthur and Bumper greeted me at my front door and herded me toward the kitchen and their empty dinner bowls. The cat purred and rubbed against my ankles as I filled his dish with star-shaped kibble. The dog thumped his tail, anxiously awaiting his turn.

Once the animals were settled, I called Emmet Wish. "We found the missing jewelry today, so you can forget about filing a claim."

"Remarkable. Where were they?"

"In a drawer."

"Did you find the books, quilt, and watch?"

"Still missing."

"What a darn shame. I have a client who'd jump to pay a fortune for those books if they ever came on the market. Oh well, just let me know when you're available to sign the insurance forms. We'll file a claim for mysterious disappearance."

Something Wish said set alarms off in my brain. Time to contact Farkas. I left a message on his voice mail. "Detective, I wanted to let you know we found the lost jewelry. Also, Julian Kessler uncovered evidence of a hidden room in Harriet's house. I'm convinced it's under the staircase, but we don't know how to get in. I'm hoping we'll find the other missing items inside. I should have the answer to-morrow."

I ought to tell him what I suspected, even though he probably wouldn't take me seriously. "In case you're interested, I also have an idea about who killed Harriet and why. You have my number."

I retrieved the mail from the hall table. While I ate dinner from a Styrofoam container, I sifted through the pile of mail, singled out a padded manila envelope, and tore it open. The paper pattern for Quincy's Double Wedding Ring quilt slid out. I unfolded the instructions.

Since the design called for hundreds of the wedge-shaped pieces to form the rings, I'd have to transfer the pattern to a sturdy substance that would stand up to repeated use. I planned to trace the paper patterns onto a sheet of Mylar and cut templates out of plastic.

I tossed the empty Crazy Chicken container and poured four ounces of Ruffino Chianti Classico into my favorite red Moroccan tea glass with the gold curlicues. I headed for my sewing room with the quilt pattern and glass of wine when the phone rang.

"Farkas here. Where'd you find the jewelry?"

"Under a drawer with a false bottom in Harriet's closet."

"I'm surprised the forensics guys didn't find it first. Anything missing?"

I could write a book about the ways in which the police mishandled Harriet's murder investigation. "I've accounted for every piece." I decided not to mention the cocktail ring until I found out why Isabel had it.

"You mentioned a hidden room under the stairs?"

"Correct. We haven't been able to find a way inside, so I'm assuming no one else has either. There's a good chance the other missing items are still safe in the house. We'll know for sure tomorrow. The contractor who built the room is sending over the blueprints."

Farkas grunted. "Interesting. You said you know who the killer is. Remind me again which one you are—Rizzoli or Isles?"

"Do you want to hear what I have to say or not?" Silence.

"Like I've been trying to tell you all along, I think the killer only targeted very specific items."

"How can you be so certain?"

"Harriet's house had been thoroughly searched by someone looking for something. A random thief looking for valuables to sell could've helped himself to plenty of loot sitting right out in the open. China. Silver. An Indian basket collection. Paintings. Antique toys. He even left behind the gold in the everyday jewelry. He only took a watch belonging to Benjamin Franklin and left all the other watches in the collection behind. Why?"

"I give up, why?"

"In addition to the watch, I believe Harriet's

killer knew about the rare books written by the Founding Fathers and the quilt. Harriet's killer targeted items specifically related to the Declaration of Independence."

"The Declaration of Independence, huh? Interesting." Farkas wheezed.

"Don't you see, Detective? The killer was either a collector or had a buyer already set up. He tried to get Harriet to tell him where she kept the things he wanted. When she refused to give up their location, he strangled her in a rage."

Farkas let out a breath. "At the risk of encouraging you, I gotta say your theory isn't without merit. You said you know the identity of the killer?"

"I'm getting there. When I looked at the people who might have known about the historical collectibles in the first place, I came up with a very long list. Too long. When I went over the sequence of events, something about the quilt jumped out at me. Only a few people knew about the quilt. Harriet, Delia the housekeeper, Henry and Estella Oliver, the quilt appraisers, Drs. Anne Smith and Naomi Hunter, and the anonymous philanthropist who pledged two million dollars to acquire it for the National Archives."

"How can you be certain Mrs. Oliver didn't discuss the quilt with anyone else?" Farkas sniffed.

"I couldn't be certain, of course. I just assumed nobody else knew since the quilt hadn't been mentioned in the will or insured. Then I remembered something from the timeline. The letter from Dr. Hunter arrived after Harriet's death, yet someone opened it. Whoever spent time searching the house for the books and the watch also read the letter and learned about the quilt.

"And that someone is Emmet Wish, the insurance agent. He kept asking me if I found the books, the quilt, and the jewelry—ostensibly to file a claim. How could he be aware of the quilt unless he opened the letter? And how could he have seen the letter unless he searched the house?"

Farkas broke his silence. "Your theory is full of holes, Rizzoli. Mrs. Oliver contacted the curators because she wanted the quilt appraised, correct? She could've given the agent a heads-up about adding the quilt to her policy."

Farkas had a point. "I know I'm right. Just before I called you tonight, I talked to Wish. He gave himself away. He told me about a client who'd be eager to buy some of the missing items if they ever came on the market. What if Wish decided to steal them from Harriet and sell them to the collector? Here's what I think happened. The insurance agent snuck in one night with the intent of stealing the books for one of his other clients. Harriet woke up and confronted Wish. He demanded she give him the books. When she refused, he strangled her.

"He later returned to the scene of the crime to look for the books. That's when he opened Dr. Hunter's letter and found out about the quilt. Unlucky for Wish and his client, he only managed to steal the one thing out in plain sight, the pocket watch belonging to Benjamin Franklin."

"Here's an idea, Mrs. Rose. You should enroll in the writer's program at UCLA. You'd ace the class on mystery fiction."

How could the man ignore the mountains of

proof I kept handing him? "That's all you have to say to me?"

"Not quite." Farkas switched from snarky to stern. "Hunting killers is my job. You've got a vivid imagination. Persist in this investigation, and you'll find yourself in some real trouble. Do everyone a big favor and go back to your knitting."

"Quilting!"

"Whatever. Have a nice evening, Mrs. Rose." He hung up.

Farkas refused to listen to me about Nathan's death. Now he refused to listen to the facts surrounding Harriet's murder. Clearly, I was on my own. If I didn't want Emmet Wish to get away with murder, I'd just have to rely on my friends to help lay a trap.

CHAPTER 29

Wednesday at noon, Lucy, Birdie, and I drove to Westwood. On the way I told them about Emmet Wish. "He killed Harriet. I'm sure of it. Since Farkas won't listen to me, I'm going to have to trap him myself."

Lucy's eyes got wide. "Tell me you're not serious."

I knew Crusher and his guys would help me. Four months ago I turned to them for protection. Once against a knife wielding psychopath and once in a homeless encampment. "Don't worry. I'll call Yossi."

Inside the accountant's office I made introductions. Kessler handed me photocopies of architectural drawings and a spiral-bound report. "These arrived about thirty minutes ago."

I grabbed the papers. "And?"

"I asked Jason Cho to decipher them. He's the engineer around here."

Kessler sent a text message and a minute later a tall Asian guy with a very square face walked in the office.

"Hi." He pointed to the drawings. "Those yours?"

I nodded and handed them to him.

"It's a very cool system." He opened the report. "Back in the day. There's an electromagnetic lock with digital keypad. Problem is, the system is grid dependent and won't work during a power outage. Today I'd use a retina scanner and install solar backup."

Lucy stepped forward. "Cut to the chase, hon. Where's the room, and how do we get in?"

Cho grinned at Lucy. "Yeah, okay. You sound like my moms. The room's located underneath the house."

I covered my forehead with the palm of my hand. "But that's impossible. We went over every inch of that house. There is no basement."

"The entrance to the stairway leading to the underground room is located behind a wall panel under the stairs in the foyer." He showed us on the drawing where to find the controls and how to open the panel.

"Clever." I pushed my lips together. "I never would have thought to look there."

"You have to enter a four-digit code on the keypad."

"Oh dear." Birdie pointed to the papers. "Do you have the code?"

Cho shook his head. "Nope."

"There are ten thousand possibilities," Lucy groaned. "How are we going to find the right one?"

"Relax. There's only one number it could be." I shoved the report in my purse. Everyone looked at me. "Think about what's hidden there and you'll figure it out."

Kessler, the brilliant numbers guy, tapped his fingers together furiously and stared at the ceiling.

Suddenly he stopped and looked at me. "Seventeen seventy-six."

"Bingo!"

"What if you're wrong about the code?" Lucy put her hands on her hips.

"Then we'll buy a hatchet and a blowtorch."

The ten-minute ride to Brentwood seemed like an eternity. Our long hunt for the secret room would soon be over. We pulled into Harriet's driveway, which seemed strangely deserted without one of Carl's vehicles. I gathered the spiral-bound report and drawings, and unlocked the front door. "Let's go see if I'm right."

Lucy ran over to the stairway and dumped her tote bag on the floor. "Which one?"

I turned the pages to one of the drawings and counted with my fingertip. "It's the fifth step up."

Lucy reached her arm through the balusters and ran her fingers under the front lip of the fifth stair tread. "I feel some kind of button." She pressed and the stair tread popped open with a *click*.

"Mercy!" Birdie pressed her fingers into her cheeks.

Lucy pushed the tread all the way up to reveal an electronic keypad in the hollow beneath. "We never would have found this in a million years on our own. Do you want to do the honors, hon?"

I reached over and keyed in 1-7-7-6 and hit Enter. Another *click* and part of the paneling near the back wall swung open to reveal a steel door. "That's the spot Arthur kept sniffing around. He knew all along something was there."

Lucy reached the door in two long steps. "I sure hope he didn't smell another dead body!" She pulled the handle, but the door wouldn't budge. "Oh no. What's wrong here?"

I consulted the report. "Another level of security. There's an override lock on the keypad."

"So you need a key?" Lucy threw up her hands. "Where are we going to find *that?*"

I opened my purse. "I think we've had it all along." I removed Harriet's key ring. The small key I'd found in the Dat So La Lee basket fit perfectly. The electromagnetic connection in the steel door gave way and opened the entrance to the secret room.

Cool, dry air pushed at our faces.

A dark, descending stairwell loomed on the other side of the door. Lucy rubbed her arms. "I've got goose bumps on my goose bumps." She removed her night-vision goggles from her tote bag, strapped them to her face, and handed flashlights to Birdie and me.

Lucy stepped into the darkness and swiveled her head. "Hey, these things really work. Everything's glowing green." She immediately found a switch at the top of the stairwell. Subdued lights flickered on and dimly illuminated the way.

Halfway down, another steel door blocked the landing. This one didn't have a lock. I stepped forward and pulled it open. Dim lights automatically blinked on below us. The rest of the stairway descended into a room about ten feet by twenty feet. I pointed to the vent in the ceiling. The air made a soft *whooshing* sound. A nearby cobweb hung down and swayed with the movement of air. "Maybe Arthur didn't smell anything unusual. Maybe he reacted to the hum of the machinery down here."

A library table and chairs, twins to the ones on

the first floor, stood in the middle of the room. A sheet of glass covered this table, and a basket with several pairs of white gloves sat on the end. A horizontal display case dominated one wall. All the antiseptic, hard surfaces served to discourage organisms from growing on the precious items stored here.

I walked to the display case and looked down. Carefully laid on their backs inside were fifteen volumes, fragile first editions of John Adams, Thomas Jefferson, and Benjamin Franklin. In this ultrasecure and climate-controlled room, Harriet could leave her masterpieces in the open air with no risk of harm. Did she come down here often to admire these treasures?

According to the insurance rider, none of the books was missing. "They're all here." A lump formed in my throat as I put on a pair of white gloves and lightly touched the top of Franklin's memoir. "Harriet didn't just collect these things, she preserved them."

"Oh my, I think I found it." Birdie's hushed voice came from behind me.

I turned to see her touching the lid of a gray archival paper box, about two feet by three feet, on another steel shelf. I carried the lightweight but sturdy box to the table. My fingers, awkward with anticipation, fumbled open the top. I pushed back the acid-free tissue paper covering the object inside. There sat a circle of thirteen fabric stars, yellowed with age, sewn with hundreds of tiny stitches on a faded blue field.

The three of us gasped.

Tears glistened in Birdie's eyes. "Martha dear, do

you think we can lay this out on the table for a closer look?"

With gloved hands, we lifted the nearly two-and-a-half-century-old quilt from its nest of tissue and carefully opened it flat on the glass tabletop. The fibers of the fabric had darkened and discolored along the original folds and the material had become friable.

Lucy and Birdie bent over the table with me to examine the smaller white blocks. Red triangles truncated the corners of each six-inch square. We read signatures penned with India ink and nib in old-fashioned cursive.

"Look."—Lucy pointed—"The guy who signed this block messed up." Over toward the red border were two black ink marks dripped on a block signed by Robert Treat Paine—just as Abigail Adams described in her letter to Sarah Franklin Bache.

I adjusted my glasses to get a closer look. "I imagine a lot of the signatures on the copies of the Declaration of Independence will also be found in this quilt."

Lucy gently picked up a corner. "Look at this signature," she whispered in awe. "Elizabeth Griscom Ross. Betsy."

"Yes, and here are Abigail Adams and Martha Jefferson." Birdie held two more corners.

I lifted the last one. "Sarah Franklin Bache over here."

History books were so often written about the exploits of men, as if the only events worth remembering were masculine endeavors. The lives of women were mostly relegated to a parallel world unworthy of comment. Yet, here in our hands, my friends and I held the legacy of four very remarkable women who possessed the foresight and skill to record the birth of the greatest democracy in the world. A story told not with sword and musket, but stitched with needle and thread.

"I think we're going to be national heroes, finding this stuff." Lucy gestured around the room.

Birdie smoothed the white cotton gloves against her fingers. "Yes, we're like archaeologists. First, we unearth a body, and now we find all these artifacts. Do you think we'll be on TV?"

"Are you kidding?" Lucy pulled in her chin and raised her eyebrows. "This is just what those daytime talk shows are looking for. They'll be begging to interview us. We might even get on *The Tonight Show*."

Birdie sighed. "I don't think I could stay up that late."

Lucy clucked her tongue. "Oh, for pity's sake, Birdie. They tape that show hours before they broadcast it."

"Well, I still wish Oprah hadn't quit. I liked her best of all."

While Lucy and Birdie planned their television careers, I stepped over to another shelf holding boxes of old documents carefully preserved in archival sleeves. The first sleeve I picked up contained seventeenth-century Dutch travel passes for Jacob José Oliveria and his wife, Estella. Like so many immigrants to America, they must have Anglicized their name.

I briefly sifted through the sleeves. "These are Oliver family papers dating back hundreds of years. I can just picture Harriet organizing these files the same way she kept her school notebook—neat and in order."

"Are you going to give those back to the Oliver family?" Birdie indicated the boxes.

"Neither Henry nor Estella mentioned the documents as something they want." I replaced the papers in the box. "I'll donate them to the Touro Synagogue or the National Library. These papers should be made available to historians and serious researchers."

Lucy looked at her wristwatch. "Holy cow. It's nearly two already. I've got to meet Ray in an hour. Our grandson, Little Tony, has a game this afternoon."

I walked back to the table. "Let's fold the quilt a different way. The fabric on the old fold lines is already stressed and may crumble if we continue to store it the same way." Instead of refolding in halves, we carefully brought the edges back to front and gently folded the quilt into thirds and replaced it inside the archival box.

We backed out of the room, turned off the lights, and closed everything up, hiding the treasures once again. Now, unless he knew where to look, Emmet Wish wouldn't have a clue to the location of the secret hiding place.

A phone message waited for me when I arrived home. "Babe, something came up. You won't be able to reach me for a while. I'll call you when I can."

First Malo, now Crusher. I sure hoped I'd find Carl around in case I needed his help. When I called his number, I heard, "I'm unavailable for the next few days. Leave a message." All three of them were off the grid? What was going on? Did this mean I'd be on my own if I went after Wish?

CHAPTER 30

I popped open a can of Coke Zero and called Dr. Naomi Hunter at the Smithsonian. "I think we found the Declaration Quilt today."

"Oh, Mrs. Rose, this is monumental! Simply unbelievable. What condition is it in?"

I described the fragile artifact to her, from the crumbling and discolored fold marks to the ink spots on the Robert Treat Paine block. "It looks genuine to me."

"How soon can I examine the quilt?"

"Anytime, really. It's tucked away safely in Harriet's house."

"I'll try to book a flight in the next couple of weeks."

I finished my cola, trying to figure out how to prove to Farkas that Emmet Wish killed Harriet. If only I could trick Wish into confessing. An idea started to form that was crazy enough to work.

The insurance agent picked up on the third ring.

"Mr. Wish, this is Martha Rose. I'm calling to

let you know I opened the secret room today. Thankfully, I found everything inside, except the Benjamin Franklin watch."

Wish took in a little sip of air. "Really. Everything's there?"

"Yes. The books are all in lovely condition for their age. They should bring millions to Harriet's estate. The Smithsonian has already offered seven figures for the quilt."

"This is very good news indeed. Did you have trouble getting inside?"

"Oh no. I was able to enter all by myself. Nobody else was there. You're the first person I thought to call because of the insurance thing. We don't have to file a claim for stolen property after all."

He cleared his throat. "I'd like to check out everything, just to make sure, but I'm really over-scheduled for the next few days. I do have some time this evening, though. I wonder, if I wouldn't be imposing, would you mind meeting me at Harriet's house tonight?"

Hah! If he only knew what I have planned for him. "Not at all."

"Good. And, Mrs. Rose? I think it's a good idea if you hold off on telling anyone else about your discovery. Let's just keep this to ourselves for now."

I used my stupid voice. "Okay, but why?"

"Harriet's killer is still on the loose. If he knows you found her things, you might be in danger. We don't want anything to happen to you too."

I agreed to meet him at nine, but I didn't plan to come alone.

Around dinnertime I made a peanut butter sandwich on challah and called Lucy. "How was the game?"

"The bleacher seats get harder every year, but Little Tony won, so it was worth a little discomfort."

I told her about my meeting with Emmet Wish later tonight at Harriet's. "I'm going to try to get him to confess to Harriet's murder."

"You've done some risky things in your life, Martha, but this is downright lunatic. Yossi Levy is going with you, right?"

"Not exactly. The Valley Eagles are suddenly unavailable for a few days. I don't know what's going on, but I'm not waiting for them."

Lucy exploded. "Are you crazy?"

"I'm taking Arthur with me. He's a great police dog. He won't let anything bad happen. And between you, me, and the dog, we can't fail."

"What do you mean you and *me*?" Lucy gasped.

"I kind of need another person if this is going to work. You and I will get there early and you'll stay out of sight. I'll take Wish into the secret room and get him to confess. You'll follow quietly and hide behind the door on the landing, where you can record the whole conversation. When we have what we need, you'll call Farkas to come and get him."

"In what universe would a man confess to murder and then wait quietly for the police? If he strangled Harriet, he could kill again. Remind me, how big is this guy?"

"Don't you remember him from the funeral? He's shortish and dapper and wears a ring with a ruby in it. We could overpower him if we have to." Lucy was inches taller than Wish, and I outweighed him by at least twenty pounds. Okay, maybe more, but that was between me and my Weight Watchers scale.

"What if he brings a gun?"

"You forgot about Arthur. He's ferocious. The dog's trained to take down an armed suspect. Once we subdue Wish, we tie him up with duct tape and wait for the police."

Silence. A good sign. "Ray would never let me go if he knew."

"So don't tell him."

More silence. "I'm bringing a gun."

Lucy and her husband, Ray, were gun owners and collectors. I once borrowed one of their weapons to defend myself against a killer, and it saved my life. I wholeheartedly supported the Second Amendment. "Okay, but I don't think you really need to. My idea is foolproof."

"You're the fool if you think so."

"So what does that make you?" I chuckled.

"A fool's best friend. Pick me up at seven-thirty."

An hour later the phone rang. I immediately jumped to the defensive when I heard the voice on the other line.

"This is Henry Oliver. I just checked in at the Four Seasons in Beverly Hills. I want to talk."

I bristled at the man's attitude and dreaded his reaction when he discovered he wasn't entitled to anything of Harriet's. I'd let Abernathy tell him. My palms began to sweat. "I think it's best if we meet in the attorney's office. I'll call him tomorrow for an appointment and get back to you."

"I demand an accounting for every family heirloom, including the ones you claim are missing."

I stared at the phone, seething. He had no right to demand anything. Henry Oliver reminded me of a pit bull on a bad day. "They were missing, but they've just turned up."

"Well, thank goodness. Have you sold them already?"

Could he be more insulting? A vein in my neck started to throb. "Of course not. Not yet."

Oliver's voice turned silky. "Look, perhaps I misspoke. Why do we need to involve an attorney, Mrs. Rose? Surely we can work this out on our own. My sister, Estella, informed me you'd consider letting the heirlooms stay in the family, correct?"

"Yes." *Before I knew what a jerk you were.* "However, I'm not prepared to discuss this now, Mr. Oliver. I'll contact you tomorrow."

I disconnected the phone. My fingers were shaking as I punched in Abernathy's number. I took a few deep yoga breaths while I waited for him to answer.

"Deke here."

I told him about Oliver's call. "He tried to bully me into a conversation, but I did what you suggested and told him I'd schedule an appointment with you tomorrow."

"Good girl. What did he say?"

Girl? Does he think he can treat me like an obedient child? Did he forget I can still report him to the police and the California State Bar for embezzlement? I swallowed my annoyance. "At first Henry Oliver was aggressive, but then he turned all friendly when I told him the heirlooms were safe inside a secret room. He tried to talk me out of meeting in your office, but I stood firm. I have a Yoga class in the morning. Can we meet after lunch?"

"No problem. Tell Oliver to be in my office at two. You don't really have to attend if you don't want to. I can tell him to stop bothering you and threaten him with a restraining order."

"No, I want to be there. To be honest, I haven't made my final decision about the heirlooms."

I could understand why Harriet didn't include either Henry or Estella in her will. They hardly seemed the loving family. However, I couldn't help wondering how I'd feel if someone took away the things important to me, like my bubbie's tablecloth or her silver Shabbat candleholders. Family history was important, and the Olivers were proud of theirs. They could trace their roots back to the 1600s. How many people were able to do that?

I never knew my father or his relatives. How much richer would my life have been without those gaps in my history? I rubbed my eyes. "As odious as Henry and Estella might be, I want to do the right thing."

Abernathy's voice softened. "You're being more than fair, Martha, but I have to remind you of the terms of Harriet's will. You have two choices. Donate her valuables to benefit a charitable organization or sell them. You cannot give them away to individuals."

"Are you sure I can't sell them at a deep discount?"

"No. You have a fiduciary duty to sell them at fair market value."

Sometimes the law is unfair. "I'll be in your office tomorrow at two."

At seven-thirty I grabbed a roll of duct tape, loaded Arthur into the car, and drove to Lucy's. To my surprise, she had Birdie in tow. Lucy snapped her seat belt and twisted around to look at Birdie buckling herself into the backseat. "When I told Birdie what we were going to do tonight, she insisted on coming. Right, hon?"

Birdie sat next to the dog and patted his head. "Martha dear, I just had to join you. It's going to be so satisfying to collar this perp."

I didn't want to hurt her feelings, but she could be a real liability to my plan. "What if we have to struggle or make a fast escape, Birdie? I don't expect that to happen, but you never know. Are you sure you're up for it?"

"If there's any trouble, I can defend myself with this." She reached in her purse and held up a pair of fabric shears with seven-inch blades. Her knuckles, enlarged and twisted by arthritis, showed white as she clutched her weapon.

Lucy opened her tote bag and pulled out a Browning semiautomatic .22 caliber pistol, the one she loaned me earlier this year to defend myself. "And I've got this."

That's when I noticed they were both wearing identical black hoodies.

I handed her my roll of duct tape. "You might as well add this to your arsenal."

We drove through the chilly December night and reached Harriet's in twenty minutes. Floodlights illuminated the peeling white bark on the slender birch trees lining her circular driveway. As I pulled my Corolla up to the entrance, a motion sensor triggered carriage lamps on either side of the front door.

I'd never seen the house in the dark. The surrounding trees blurred the sharp lines of the architecture, and the windows stared blank and empty as a corpse. I grabbed Arthur's leash and we all walked to the front door. A dog barked somewhere down the street, and Arthur briefly twitched his ears. My spine tingled. "Ready?" I pulled my knitted scarf tighter around my neck, took a deep breath, and unlocked the door. "Let's do this."

CHAPTER 31

I flipped on the switch in the foyer. The alabaster globes on the chandelier warmed the area with a golden glow, but the rest of the vacant house stayed dark. We stood in the pool of light and Birdie leaned in close.

"What exactly is your plan, Martha dear?" Her voice echoed in the empty space.

I stroked the dog's head. "Arthur and I will greet Emmet Wish at the front door. You guys stay out of sight. I'll take Wish down into the safe room and trick him into confessing. Meanwhile, Lucy will sneak halfway down and hide on the landing behind the door where she'll record everything. Once we get the confession, we'll make a citizen's arrest and call the police."

"What if he resists arrest?" Birdie nervously twisted the end of her braid.

"Arthur can subdue him, and Lucy has a gun. If we have to, we'll tie up Wish with duct tape until the police arrive."

"What about me?" Birdie raised her hand. "What can I do?"

She could barely climb the stairs with her arthritic knees and couldn't move fast in an emergency. No way would I put my seventy-something friend in a position of danger. "You'll stay out of sight, Birdie. In case things get rough down there, we need someone who can call for help. You're our backup."

She drew her cell phone out of her purse and waved it with a smile. "Roger that."

At five minutes before nine, headlights shone through the living-room windows as a car entered the driveway.

"It's him," I hissed. "Quickly, hide."

Lucy and Birdie covered their heads with their black hoodies and scuttled into the powder room directly across from the hidden portal.

Just before Lucy pulled the door closed, she whispered, "Be careful, girlfriend."

I answered the soft knocking right away.

Emmet Wish smiled as I opened the door. The short man wore dark jeans and a black pea coat against the December chill. He thrust out his hand. I recognized his large ring with the red stone. "Hello, Mrs. Rose." He crushed my hand in a too-tight grip.

I shivered and tried not to look spooked. "I'm so glad to see you, Mr. Wish. I've been dying to show you what I found. Please come inside."

"Please, call me Emmet, and I'll call you Martha." He stepped into the foyer and Arthur immediately stood at attention and growled softly.

"What's he doing here?" Wish pointed to the dog.

"Oh, don't mind Arthur. He's just old and cranky. See the white on his muzzle?"

Wish looked around. "Did I pull you away from your family tonight? I hope I didn't cause anyone to be upset by asking you to come here."

He wants to know if anyone else knows I'm here.

I opened my eyes wide. "I live alone. Nobody else knows I'm here." I hoped he didn't pick up on the lie that sounded so hollow to my ears.

He squinted. "Who else knows about the room?"

"Well, the guy who built it, of course." I tried to laugh. "And a few others. But I wouldn't worry about them. They don't know exactly where the room is or how to get inside," I smiled brightly. "But I do. Would you like to see it now?"

I walked over to the stairway and counted up five steps. Like Lucy did earlier in the day, I reached under the front edge of the stair tread and pressed a small button. The tread flipped open and revealed the keypad beneath.

"Amazing." Wish spoke in near reverence. "I would never have found this setup on my own." He looked at me quickly. "Open it up, please."

I shifted my position so he couldn't see the code I punched in. The paneling clicked open to reveal the steel door. As Wish approached the portal, I glanced at the powder room. Lucy had opened the door a crack and I could see her bright orange hair peeking out under the hoodie. I flapped my hand next to my leg gesturing for her to move back out of sight.

"The door won't open." Wish tugged on the handle.

"Wait a minute." I stuck the little key in and activated the override.

The electromagnetic switch clicked. Wish yanked on the door and entered the dark space.

"There's a light switch to your right," I said. "I'll be right down."

He turned on the light, descended quickly to the landing, and opened the second door. When I heard him go the rest of the way down, I knocked three times on the powder room door to give Lucy the all clear.

I kept Arthur right next to my legs as I followed Wish into the secret room.

The insurance agent made straight for the display case where the priceless first editions lay. "So this is where you've been hiding."

Show time. I just hoped Lucy had managed to sneak as far as the landing with her iPhone in Record mode.

My mouth dried out and my voice shook a little. "Sounds like I'm not the only one who's been looking for these books."

He looked up sharply. "What are you saying?"

I took a deep breath. "I think you know. You were the one who searched this house. You were looking for these books because you wanted to sell them on the black market."

His mouth fell open and he merely stared.

"You gave yourself away when you told me earlier about having a client who would jump to buy them. Tell me, did the same buyer who paid you for the Benjamin Franklin watch also want to buy the books and the Declaration Quilt?"

He found his voice. "You don't know what you're talking about."

I crossed my arms. "How did you know about the quilt? It wasn't insured."

"Harriet must have told me."

"You're lying. Dr. Hunter from the Smithsonian mailed a letter about the quilt after Harriet's death, so it should have remained in the pile of unopened mail. Yet we found it on Harriet's desk, opened by whoever searched her house. Opened by you."

"You can't prove that," he snarled.

"I think I can. When I give the letter to the crime lab, they'll be able to lift your fingerprints."

Wish took a step toward me, and Arthur snarled and bared his teeth.

"You'd better stop right there."

Wish looked at the dog and held up his hands. "Okay, okay. Maybe I did search for the books like you said."

"One of your clients was the buyer?"

"Look. I'm in a unique position to know what rich people own and what they want to own. If I find a buyer for something, I'll acquire it for a price."

"You mean Harriet's not the first client you've stolen from? There were others?"

Wish shook his head. "You don't understand. Everyone gets something. The real owner gets fully compensated by the company for the stolen item. My buyer gets his package, and I get a fee."

"So what happened?" I hoped Lucy's phone was picking up every word. "Did you kill Harriet when she caught you robbing her house?"

"No! Harriet was already dead when I broke in. I admit, I came back and searched this house every night for a week. But the disgusting smell got to me, and I just gave up."

"Why didn't you call the police and report her body?"

"How could I explain my presence in Harriet's house in the first place? Even if I made an anonymous call, I'd left fingerprints behind."

"I don't believe you, Emmet. I think you killed my friend, and I'm calling the police."

"Wait!" Wish waved a hand. Drops of sweat gathered on his upper lip. "I can make you rich. You're the only person who's been in this room, right? Well, no one has to know you found the books. My buyer's still very interested. He'll go as high as four million for the set. We can split the amount fifty-fifty. You'll file a claim for mysterious disappearance. Harriet's estate will be compensated for the full amount. Believe me, we'll both be millionaires."

"And let you off the hook for killing my friend? Not a chance."

"I really hoped to avoid this." Wish reached inside his coat and pulled out a small revolver. The dog growled and tensed his muscles, ready to attack. Wish turned his gun on Arthur and wiped the sweat off his lip with the palm of his other hand. "Call off your dog. I don't want to have to shoot him."

I made a stupid decision to bring Arthur. Once before, he risked his life for me and received terrible wounds. Even though the dog would gladly defend me again, I couldn't risk getting him killed. I reached down and patted his head and tightened my grip on his leash. "Easy, boy. Take it easy."

I kept watching the hand holding the gun. "What are you going to do, kill me too?"

He didn't answer. His scanned the room and dried the palm of his free hand on his pant leg. "I'm taking those books. With the money I get, I can leave the country. You're in no position to stop me. Too bad nobody else knows about this room, because you're going to be locked inside."

I had collected enough proof now to make Farkas eat his words. I looked toward the stairway. "Lucy?"

Lucy stepped out from behind the door on the landing, all five feet eleven inches and bright orange hair. Her hands were steady as she aimed the Browning at Emmet Wish. "Drop the gun or I'll shoot you deader'n a doornail!"

Wish turned his head to look at Lucy. His eyes widened in surprise. Then he looked at me with a wounded expression. "I thought you said we were alone."

I shrugged. "You know what they say, 'No honor among thieves.'"

His face darkened, and he turned toward Lucy. She reacted quickly and ducked behind the door. In the small room the gunshot sounded like a bomb. The bullet ricocheted off the steel door and whizzed past my head, only inches away.

I dropped to the floor and crawled under the library table, pulling Arthur with me. Arthur kept trying to lunge out of my grasp. He wanted to attack. Everything in his police training prepared him for taking down a man with a gun.

Any second Wish could fire under the table and kill me. I unhooked Arthur's leash. "Go!"

"Hey!" Wish shouted as Arthur's teeth sunk into his gun arm.

I scrambled on all fours into the open as fast as I

could and hoisted myself up butt first. When I looked up, Lucy had stepped out from behind the door and aimed her Browning. "Drop the gun."

Wish lost his struggle with Arthur and the gun clattered from his hand to the floor. I bent to pick up the revolver. I wished I knew the correct police command. I settled for, "Okay Arthur, let go."

The dog understood me and released Wish's arm. Blood dripped on the floor from his torn flesh. Wish sank to his knees. Arthur stood over him panting, growling, and lunging every time the man tried to move.

Lucy remained on the landing and glared at Wish. "Stop whining. You're lucky I didn't get to you first."

I smiled at my friend. Born and raised in Wyoming. Mother of five boys. Tough.

"Let's get out of here," I said.

We forced Wish to stand and walked behind him as he climbed the stairs. We had to watch where we stepped because he left a growing trail of blood behind. For sure the man would need surgery on his arm. Wish remained oddly silent for a man who was about to go to jail for murder.

"Where's the duct tape?" I asked Lucy.

"In my tote bag upstairs."

"Those wounds on his arm aren't fatal. We should tie him up so he doesn't escape."

Wish reached the top of the stairs first. Before we knew what was happening, he jumped through the doorway and used his good arm to slam the door shut behind him.

Lucy, Arthur, and I were locked in the stairwell, and Birdie was alone with a killer.

CHAPTER 32

Lucy rattled the doorknob. "Oh crap! How're we going to get out of here? Birdie's alone out there. I should never have listened to you, Martha Rose. If we die in here, Ray's gonna kill me,"

"Harriet never would have installed a room where she could be trapped inside." I looked around frantically for a way out. In the dimness of the low-watt overhead light, I spotted a red button on the wall opposite the steel portal. "Here!" I punched the button. The electromagnetic lock disconnected with a click and released the door.

We stumbled into the foyer, clutching our guns. Arthur shot past us. Wish staggered to the front door, leaving a thin ribbon of red behind. He had just begun to turn the knob when Arthur pinned him against the entrance.

Birdie jumped out of the powder room closet holding the shears with both hands and pointed at Wish. "Freeze, dirtbag!" She slowly limped in a crouched position toward Wish, jabbing the air with her scissors.

Wish's mouth went slack. "Are you kidding me?"

He raised his right arm to get a better look at the bloody, open wound. Then his eyes rolled back and he slumped to the floor. Out cold.

"He's probably in shock." Lucy ran to her tote bag for the roll of duct tape. "Good job, Arthur." She glanced at me. "Let's bind him up before he awakes.

We rolled him over and wrapped the silver tape around his wrists. I stuck out my hand. "Give me those scissors, Birdie, so I can cut the tape."

"Oh no, Martha dear. These are my good fabric scissors. I don't want to ruin the sharp edges."

"But you were willing to stab the guy with them?"

"Well, only as a last resort. When I heard gunshots, I called the police. They should be here any minute."

I ripped the tape with my teeth, then bound Wish's ankles together. I wrapped more tape tightly around the wound in his right forearm to staunch the bleeding.

Moments later a cavalcade of sirens approached from a distance. Vehicles screeched to a stop in the driveway. Someone pounded on the front door, and a familiar voice shouted, "LAPD! Open up!"

Lucy and I dragged Wish's body away from the front door. Farkas stood on the porch surrounded by five uniformed policemen—all with their guns drawn. Blue and red lights pulsed in a garish dance on top of four squad cars.

I closed my eyes and let out my breath. "Thank God you're here."

Farkas scowled when he saw the three of us. "We received a 9-1-1 from this address."

I pointed to Wish, lying unconscious with his hands and feet tied together. Red smeared the floor underneath him. "He tried to kill us, but Arthur disarmed him first."

"You'd better call a bus," said Birdie. "He's lost a lot of blood."

Farkas lifted an eyebrow and looked at me. "Really?"

I shrugged. "She's a fan of cop shows."

We spent the next two hours at the West LA Division of the LAPD giving statements. Lucy borrowed my cell phone to call Ray and found someone to give Arthur a well-deserved drink of water. I joined Farkas in a small blue interview room and played the recording of Wish's confession. "You should've listened to me, Detective. I was right about the killer."

"I never said you were wrong. I just told you to back off. After our conversation tonight, I started looking into reports of high-end thefts during the last five years. Turns out your boy sold insurance to a number of the victims. Your hunch about him was right on the mark, and I would have gone after him if you hadn't . . . jumped the gun."

I crossed my arms. "I'm glad you're amused. Thanks to us, you have Harriet's killer, along with a confession."

"Correction." He pressed his lips together and pointed to Lucy's iPhone. "Wish copped to a number of felonies, but I didn't hear him confess to Mrs. Oliver's murder."

"Oh, I'm sure you can beat it out of him."

Farkas squinted at me. "I'm debating whether to throw you and your dangerous gun-toting, knife-wielding gang in jail tonight."

"Guns and *scissors,* Detective. On what charges?"

"Obstruction. Weapons. Assault. Kidnapping. Give me time. I'll think of a few more."

"I've got a better idea." I gathered my purse and hoped I could bluff my way home tonight. "Why don't we all go home and get some sleep? I've got a yoga class in the morning."

Farkas hesitated, then stood and moved toward the interview room door. "Quilting, Mrs. Rose. Stick to your quilting."

Lucy and Birdie sat with Arthur in the lobby. Birdie snored softly with her chin resting on her chest. I touched her shoulder. "Time to go home." We piled into my car and headed for Encino. As soon as I pulled into Lucy's driveway, Ray opened the front door.

"Oh, oh." Lucy's voice became quiet. "That's not a happy face."

I unbuckled my seat belt, intending to get out of the car. "I'll tell him it's my fault. I'll lie and say you had no idea what you were getting yourself into."

"I already told him that."

My mouth dropped open. "You blamed me?"

Lucy wiggled her red-penciled eyebrows. "What are friends for?"

Ray reached her side of the car and opened the door. They stared at each other for several seconds without a word. He took his wife's hand and helped her out of the car. He stuck his head inside and glared at me. "I don't believe either one of you." He slammed the door and I watched them walk inside, Ray's protective arm around her shoulders. No matter what trouble Lucy might have gotten into tonight, Ray would love her.

I backed out of the driveway and steered across the street to Birdie's darkened house. Lucy's husband, Ray, loved his wife madly, even after so many decades together. In contrast, Russell Watson probably never even noticed Birdie's absence.

I helped her out of the car and walked her to her door. "You were great tonight, Birdie."

She gave my arm a little squeeze. "I know. This is the most fun I've had in a long time. Good night, Martha dear."

After a short drive home, Arthur and I walked in my house at one in the morning, and he made straight for the water bowl. I made a pot of chamomile tea to calm my nerves and gave Arthur two dog biscuits. He took them so gently from my open fingers, you would never have known he ripped open a man's arm just a few hours before.

"You're a brave boy, Arthur." I stroked his head.

Adrenaline still pumped through my body as I headed for my sewing room and the emergency package of M&M's I kept in my tote bag for times like this. I changed into my pajamas and sat under my blue and white quilt on the sofa. Bumper jumped up on my lap and settled his furry orange body in the folds. One by one, I fished out the green M&M's from the bag. I always ate one color at a time, saving the brown ones for last. The racing inside my head slowed after a few deep yoga breaths, chocolate, and tea.

I reached over to the coffee table and picked up the keepsake I chose from all of Harriet's possessions, the antique wooden dreidel from Portugal. In just a couple of days, Jews all over the world would kindle the first light of Hanukkah. And

children once again would play with their dreidels
and recall the time when the Maccabees saved our
temple in Jerusalem. Turning the spinning top
over in my hands, I admired the delicate painting
of the Hebrew letters: ש ה ג נ. *A great miracle happened
there.*

Wish claimed Harriet was already dead when he
broke into her house to steal the books. But who
wouldn't lie to avoid a murder conviction? I had
confidence in Detective Farkas. He'd get Wish to
confess to everything.

I sighed. Tonight the team from LAPD's Scientific Investigation Division descended on Harriet's
house for the third time. Farkas promised they'd
close up the safe room and secure the valuables
before they left. I trusted him to keep his word.
Farkas knew how valuable the quilt and the books
were. And anyway, once they locked the safe room,
nobody could enter without the key and the code.

Since we'd solved Harriet's murder, I could now
focus on finding out who really killed Nathan
Oliver and clear Harriet's name. Isabel Casco knew
more than she was telling. She had a lot of explaining to do, starting with why she wore Harriet's ring.

I also needed a plan to get Nico Grimaldi, the
boat captain, to talk. I knew in my gut he had important information in the mystery of Nathan's
death. I needed to be smart, though. Digging up
the past could be dangerous.

If Carl or Crusher and his guys were around to
help, I'd feel a whole lot safer. For some reason,
they weren't available. I doubted Ray would let
Lucy come with me again. Farkas wouldn't help me
because he believed Harriet killed Nathan. The

truth was, I'd have to interview Grimaldi alone. My stomach churned at the thought.

Tomorrow would be a long day. With a huge yawn, I hit a wall of fatigue. Bumper meowed as I pushed him off my lap and moved down the hallway to my comfortable bed. I plumped my pillow, nestled under the covers, and closed my heavy eyes. As I fell asleep, I had a vision of the tower on Paulina's tarot card, where people fell and jumped to their deaths.

CHAPTER 33

I stood at a conveyor belt, sorting through huge piles of old clothes. The more I sorted, the bigger the piles grew. My heart sunk. No matter how fast I moved, I'd never finish the job. Then I floated up into grayness and cat whiskers tickled my face, followed by a rough little tongue on my cheek.

"Thank God you woke me." I stroked Bumper's fur.

The clock read nine-thirty. Too late to attend my Yoga class. My body ached and throbbed all over. The excitement yesterday of finding the Declaration Quilt and books, the terror of being shot at, and the late-night interrogation at the police station—all contributed to one huge fibromyalgia flare-up. To make matters worse, the weather outside had turned cloudy and damp with a promise of rain. I staggered into the kitchen to feed the animals, take my meds, and brew a hot cup of tea.

While waiting for the water to boil, I grabbed a notepad and pencil and jotted down a to-do list: Call Lucy and Birdie. Call Henry Oliver. Talk to

Isabel. Pay Grimaldi a visit. Be at Abernathy's office at two.

This felt like sorting through an endless pile of used clothing. My meds started to kick in about the time I finished my second cup of tea. Time to get going. The sooner I could wind up Harriet's estate, the sooner I could get back to my real life.

I called Lucy first. I'd been close to the Mondellos for twenty years and counted on our long friendship to smooth over any anger Ray might be harboring about the shooting last night. Now past ten, I figured he'd be working and Lucy would answer the phone. I was wrong.

"You're both a couple of lunatics! What the hell were you thinking?"

"I'm sorry, Ray. I knew with a trained police dog and all, we could take the guy down."

"*Take him down?* Who are you? Annie Oakley?"

"No, but Lucy is. And anyway, Arthur did the job for us."

"You almost got my wife killed."

I'd never heard him so angry, and I hated to be the reason. I loved this man almost as much as I loved Lucy.

"No, she didn't."

Lucy picked up the telephone extension. "Nobody forced me to go. I went because I wanted to. Hi, Martha. You okay?"

"I oughta have the both of you locked away." Ray hung up.

"Oh, Lucy, I'm so sorry. I never thought he'd go so far. I feel terrible I put us all in danger. Ray has a right to be angry."

"He'll get over it."

"Have you spoken to Birdie today? Did she tell Russell?"

Lucy chuckled. "I saw her briefly outside a few minutes ago. Russell has no clue she left the house last night. They sleep in separate bedrooms, remember? Anyway, she seemed very chipper. She said, 'I wish I were fifty years younger. I'd join the force.'"

"Thanks again for being there for me last night."

"I'd say *anytime*, girlfriend, except I'd be lying. I promised Ray I'd lay low for a while. See you next Tuesday for quilting."

My pulse sped as I dialed Henry Oliver's phone number. I gave him Abernathy's address and told him to meet me there at two. I hung up quickly before he could start in on me, but my hands were shaking anyway. The sooner I could be rid of the bully, the better.

I let Arthur out in the backyard for a potty break around the time the first raindrops started to fall. Given the prolonged drought in California, we welcomed any amount of moisture. I only wished the rain hadn't appeared on a day I planned to be driving around LA. Traffic would crawl. Before I let Arthur back into the house, I dried off his fur and muddy paws with an old towel. He licked my face.

I left a voice mail for Isabel. Then I called Grimaldi, the boat captain who threatened Nathan Oliver.

A woman's voice answered the phone. "Hello?"

I introduced myself as Harriet's executor. "I'd like to speak to Nico Grimaldi."

"You're too late."

"I'm sorry? Is there somewhere I can reach him?"

"My dad passed away last week."

Oh no. Grimaldi was dead? "I'm so sorry."

The woman's voice caught in her throat. "Why did you want to talk to him?"

What could I say? *Do you know if your father killed Nathan Oliver?* "An old debt."

"Did he owe you money?"

"The other way around. I'm trying to determine if Mrs. Oliver might have owed him some money. For the loss of his boat." I hated to lie to her this way, but I didn't want to add to her grief.

"That's news to me. I thought they settled years ago."

What? Harriet settled with Grimaldi? Abernathy must have known. Why didn't he say something?

"Can you tell me more?"

"Not much. Around thirteen years ago, my father received a large amount of money from Mrs. Oliver. He spoke so highly of her. He said aside from my mother, she was the kindest woman he knew. He named his new boat *Harriet's Heart* after her."

Thirteen years ago. Around the same time Nathan disappeared. Could Harriet have paid Grimaldi to kill Nathan? I pushed that thought away. "Do you know if they had any further contact?"

"No, I don't think so. At least my father never spoke about it."

"Would your mother know?"

"My mother died when I was two. My dad and I have been alone for twenty years. Now he's gone too." She started to cry.

"I'm so sorry for your loss."

After I hung up, I realized I never asked for her name.

So Harriet paid the boat captain. After our meeting with Henry Oliver, I'd ask Abernathy why he led me to suspect Grimaldi could have killed Nathan but never bothered to mention the large sum of money Harriet paid the boat captain around the time of Nathan's disappearance.

My stomach growled. I had skipped breakfast, and lunch was still an hour away. Thank goodness God invented brunch. I removed some leftover vindaloo and a packet of rice from the freezer and stuck them in the microwave. In five minutes I spooned hot chicken in a spicy gravy over the steaming rice. Not the usual egg-and-bagel brunch fare, but it worked for me, especially on a cold morning.

With my tummy in a happier place, I settled in my sewing room to create more wedges for Quincy's quilt. When making a quilt, I liked to stack several layers of fabric and use a rotary cutter and thick acrylic ruler to mass-produce the individual pieces. Working with curves required more careful handling, so I used my fabric scissors to cut each piece separately.

I finished making all forty-eight yellow wedges for the first ring and arranged them in a circle, moving the different prints around until I found a pleasing balance. I looked at my watch, nearly time to leave for Abernathy's office. I tried Isabel's number again and finally reached her. "I caught Harriet's killer last night."

"You caught him? How? Who killed her?"

"Emmet Wish, the insurance agent. He wanted to steal some valuable books. When Harriet confronted him, he killed her." I told Isabel about the trap we set for Wish and how he shot at us.

Isabel coughed. "Good grief. You sure do take chances. But good for you."

"We need to talk about Harriet and Nathan."

She took a drag of a cigarette. "You don't want to go there."

"I sure do. Especially since you told Detective Farkas Harriet killed her husband. I want to know what happened. I also want to know why you have Harriet's canary diamond cocktail ring, the one matching her necklace."

"First of all, I never said Harriet killed Nathan. I let the detective believe what he wanted to. Second, Harriet gave me the ring."

"When? Why would she give you such an expensive piece of jewelry?"

"About thirteen years ago, right after Nathan disappeared, she wanted to thank me for helping her through such a difficult time. I never asked her for a thing. She knew I admired the ring and insisted I take it. You know how generous she was."

I did, but things were beginning to look bad for Harriet. Did the three of them—Harriet, Isabel, and Grimaldi—kill Nathan?

"It seems like Harriet had a fit of generosity right after Nathan's murder. First to Grimaldi, then to you. You either talk to me, or I'm going to the police with what I know."

She coughed again. "Fine. Come by this evening."

An hour later, I sat in Abernathy's office at a large conference table. Dark rainclouds melted into the brooding Pacific Ocean. Henry Oliver wouldn't show up for another ten minutes. I told Abernathy about Emmet Wish and the shooting in Harriet's house last night.

Abernathy's face turned ashen. "I had no idea you were so foolhardy. You could've been killed, but I'm glad Harriet's killer is behind bars."

"I'm a little worried. The detective threatened to charge us with assault and kidnapping."

"The police probably wanted to scare you. They know the DA would never bring charges. Wish showed up willingly, and he pulled the gun on you."

His cell phone chimed and he flipped it open. "Bring him in."

Two minutes later Nina, the assistant, walked in with a tall, dark-haired man in his late forties wearing an expensive suit with a very unattractive scowl on his face.

Abernathy met him at the door and briefly shook his hand. "Mr. Oliver? I'm Deacon Abernathy, attorney for the estate of Harriet Oliver." He turned toward the table. "And this is the executor, Mrs. Martha Rose."

Oliver looked past Abernathy's shoulder and sized me up. I remained seated, maintaining eye contact with him. Oliver merely nodded down his arrogant nose. Abernathy escorted him to a chair on the opposite side of the table; then the attorney took a position next to me. "Mr. Oliver, I'll get right to the point. Neither you nor your sister were named as heirs or beneficiaries of Mrs. Oliver's estate. Neither of you, therefore, has a claim to any of Mrs. Oliver's property or possessions."

Oliver darkened and twisted forward in his chair.

Abernathy held up a silencing hand. "You are here solely at the sufferance of Mrs. Rose, who—despite your rude and threatening behavior toward her—wishes to extend to you the courtesy of an explanation of your legal standing. So, if you have any questions about your rights in this matter, you will address them to me. If not, this meeting is over."

I knew right away Abernathy had taken the wrong tack. Henry Oliver would only view the word "no" as a challenge. Oliver pushed his shoulders back. "Mrs. Oliver possessed some items belonging to me and my sister, things that have been in my family for generations. They weren't Harriet's to give away or sell to strangers, and I mean to have them back."

The belligerent tone in his voice hung heavily in the air.

Abernathy merely folded his hands on the table. "Unfortunately for you, the law says otherwise."

I put my hand on the attorney's arm, and he bent down. I whispered in his ear, "Ask him what he wants."

Abernathy cleared his throat. "Mrs. Rose is a fair person."

Oliver's eyes slid in my direction. I returned a steady gaze and hoped he didn't see the vein throbbing in my neck.

"Despite your shoddy behavior, she's agreed to entertain any reasonable requests. She wants to know exactly what you want from Mrs. Oliver's estate."

Henry Oliver took a list out of his breast pocket and slid it across the table with fingernails that were shiny and perfectly shaped, the kind of man who always looked clean and effortlessly put together. He wanted everything. Even some of the antique wooden toys.

Abernathy looked at me and I slowly shook my head and took a deep breath, and said, "Mr. Oliver,

I cannot possibly give away millions of dollars from Harriet's estate. In my opinion, those valuable items should be in a place where they can be properly conserved, like the National Archives or the National Library. Especially the Declaration Quilt. It's nearly priceless but has seriously deteriorated. The quilt needs to be properly conserved. It's a national treasure."

Oliver glared at me. "That's not up to you to decide."

I ignored him. "I sympathize with your desire to keep the other family heirlooms. I'd feel the same way if they were mine. As a matter of fact, I've already set aside some of the items on your list. They're packed, crated, and ready to return to your family."

Oliver seemed to relax a little as I made tick marks on his list with my pen. I handed the list to Abernathy, who slid it back across the table.

"These are the items you may take, but I can't just give them to you. The law says I must sell them at fair market value."

Oliver narrowed his eyes and clenched his jaws. "Outrageous."

I nodded. "It does suck."

Abernathy stood, signaling the end of the meeting. "Let us know what you decide. If you're serious about buying the items Mrs. Rose has set aside for you, we'll provide you with a fair market evaluation."

After Oliver had stormed out of the office, I turned to Abernathy. "I spoke to Nico Grimaldi's daughter this morning. He died last week."

Abernathy looked surprised. "Too bad. I didn't like the idea of you going to see him, anyway."

"You didn't tell me everything about Grimaldi. You revealed he had a reason to kill Nathan. Yet, you failed to tell me Harriet gave him a large amount of money around the time Nathan disappeared. What were you hiding?"

"I was protecting Harriet and Grimaldi. When I gave you his contact information, I didn't know he'd died. Otherwise, I might have said something then."

"Tell me now. Why did she give him money?"

"Harriet felt ashamed of what Nathan had done to the man. She compensated Grimaldi for the loss of his charter boat business. When you discovered Nathan's body in his own backyard, I knew the police would assume Harriet killed him. If they knew she'd given Grimaldi a large sum of money soon after Nathan's murder, they'd misconstrue it as a payoff and arrest the unfortunate man."

I'd been right. Harriet didn't pay the boat captain to kill her husband. She gave Grimaldi money as an act of restitution. I rose to leave. "So who do you think killed Nathan?"

Abernathy squeezed the corners of his eyes. "I have no idea."

I rode the elevators to the parking garage. As soon as I stepped out, someone walked out of the shadows toward me. "Mrs. Rose? A word."

It was Henry Oliver, and he was pointing a gun straight at me.

CHAPTER 34

Oliver grabbed my right arm and shoved the gun into my side. "Walk to the white Mercedes and get in the passenger seat. I'm prepared to shoot if you try to run away."

I froze while trying to overcome the muddled and frightening pictures in my head. When I didn't move, he tightened his grip on my arm.

Pain shot through my tender muscles. "Ow! You're hurting me."

He pushed me into the car and slammed the door shut. As he moved around the car to the driver's side, I tried to escape, but Oliver had remotely locked my door. Before I could unlock it, he slid into the driver's seat and pointed a gun at me.

My heart raced, and my mouth went dry. "Where are we going?"

Oliver's jaw clenched tightly. He started the engine. "Where do you think?"

Of course there could be only one place he'd want to take me. Should I tell him Harriet's house would be crawling with police and the forensics team from the shooting the night before? Nah. I'd let him find out for himself.

Predictably, the rain slowed traffic to a crawl. As we sat stuck in the intersection of Sepulveda and Wilshire, my cell phone rang. An LAPD number showed on caller ID. Farkas.

"Give me your phone." Oliver held out his hand.

I surreptitiously pressed the Answer icon. "The books are hidden in a secret room. If you kill me, you'll never get inside." I could only hope Farkas heard me and realized I was in trouble.

Oliver grabbed the phone and threw it out the window. "Don't underestimate me, Mrs. Rose." As he spoke, he turned toward me slightly and his jacket fell open. A heavily carved gold watch peeked out of the top of his vest pocket. A ruby glinted on the end of the winding stem. Suddenly, all the pieces fell horribly into place.

"That's the Benjamin Franklin watch." I pointed to the timepiece.

Oliver said nothing.

"You were the one who took the watch from Harriet's bedroom. She never would have allowed you up there. It was you. You killed Harriet!"

"Shut up."

I started to see the overall pattern. Wedge by wedge, like the yellow ring on Quincy's quilt, all the pieces fell into place. Emmet Wish told the truth. Harriet was already dead when he broke into her house.

Words began tumbling out of my mouth. "You were determined to get the books and the quilt and all the family heirlooms back, but Harriet refused to give them up or tell you where she'd hid them."

"I had asked her several times since Nathan's

death for certain things. She kept putting me off. Finally, on my last visit, she confessed to her scheme. She intended to sell them and build a monument to her son's memory."

"So you strangled her in a rage."

"I wouldn't expect you to understand the importance of heritage. People without pedigree never do. I'll never permit the Oliver legacy to be sold to strangers." He glared at me. "One way or another, I'll get what I want."

Not if the police and the SID unit are still at Harriet's house.

I could only pray Farkas understood what I tried to tell him and waited for us at last night's crime scene.

Oliver turned the steering wheel sharply and I realized we were already on Bundy Drive, about one minute away from Harriet's house. Soon my ordeal would be over and Henry Oliver would be arrested for Harriet's murder.

He pulled into Harriet's empty circular driveway. The police and SID team were gone. I was alone with a killer.

My whole world had shrunk down to the inside of this small Mercedes. While we were driving, I hadn't noticed the rain had stopped. I hadn't noticed the street signs passing the windows. I had focused on unraveling the mystery of Harriet's death. Now I must focus on surviving. As long as I didn't leave the car, I'd be safe. If I entered Harriet's house and opened the secret room, my life would be over.

We were hidden from the street and from the neighbors by the trees and privacy hedges ringing her large property. Every house in this luxury neighborhood sat discreetly behind landscaping designed for total privacy. Whatever happened from this point on would happen without witnesses.

Oliver came round and yanked open the passenger door. He pointed the gun and regarded me with cold, dark eyes. "Get out."

I stayed put. The car was safety. The car was life. He grabbed my arm and pulled me out. My knees were so weak I could hardly stand. He stuck the gun in my back. "Move."

For once I made my weight work for me. I slid to the ground. "No!"

Oliver waved the gun. "Get up or I'll kill you."

The rainwater puddle on the driveway soaked the seat of my trousers, and the hard cement chilled my flesh. "You can't kill me. You need me alive to get in the room."

Oliver cursed, then stepped behind me and bent forward. He put his hands under my armpits and tried to lift me. I went as limp as I could, creating a dead weight. He still held the gun in his right hand. The barrel pointed away from me. I reached up under my arm. I grabbed the barrel with both hands and jerked it forward. Oliver struggled to maintain his balance. The gun slipped out of his hand and into mine, firing toward the driveway with a loud pop.

Would the neighbors hear the gunshot and call the police?

"Son of a—" Oliver kicked my shoulder.

"Stop it!" I turned and fired the gun in his direction. The bullet went wild, but he stopped kicking long enough for me to aim at his chest.

Oliver stared down at the gun pointing toward his heart and stopped moving.

I had to figure out a way to stand up. "Back up and keep going until you reach the front door steps."

"You won't shoot me." Oliver's lip curled.

"You're dead wrong. I shot someone several months ago and I'll shoot you now if I have to." Last spring I had defended myself against a killer who came after me with a knife.

"You're making a huge mistake." He backed up.

"Put your hands on your head and turn around."

"I'm not—" I aimed near his feet and fired again. The third blast. Where were the neighbors? Wasn't anyone at least curious?

My body began to hurt, and I felt very cranky. Oliver's hands flew to his head and he faced the house.

"Maybe we can work something out." Oliver's voice became smooth and friendly.

"There's nothing to work out. Now get on your knees and count to twenty out loud."

While he counted, I got on all fours, grabbed the car door handle, and hoisted myself up to a standing position. I leaned against the Mercedes for support and kept the gun trained on Oliver. He reached twenty and stopped.

A car drove up the street. The tires made a swooshing sound as they passed through the puddles without slowing. *Farkas, where are you?*

Since Henry Oliver had tossed my cell phone somewhere on the street near Wilshire and Sepulveda, I'd have to use his. "Reach into your pocket with one hand and pull out your cell phone."

Oliver removed his right hand from his head and slowly reached into his coat pocket. He held the phone up. "Here."

"Like I'm stupid enough to come and get it? Slide the phone behind you." Instead, Oliver tossed the phone in a high arc sending it in the bushes.

Crap! If Crusher were here, he'd know what to do. How was I going to get help now?

"Nice try, Henry. Here's what we're going to do. You're going to stand up. Keep your hands on your head."

Oliver stood and turned around. The knees of his expensive suit were soiled and wet. He spoke calmly. "Without a cell phone, you can't call for help. And you can't hold me off forever. Let me get in the car and I'll leave. You can keep the gun."

"I've got a better idea. Walk down the driveway, hands on top of your head."

"Hell, no."

I aimed at his feet and fired for a fourth time. "Just do it."

I stayed about six feet behind him while he moved down the driveway.

"Walk to the middle of the street and stop."

He walked slowly and stopped in the street. "All I want is what's mine."

"Sit."

Oliver stared at the wet asphalt. "I'm not sitting down in that."

I raised the gun and aimed at his chest. "Down." My arms shook in pain.

Oliver glared at the gun and sat in the middle of the street with his hands on his head. A Volvo came toward us, screeched to a stop, backed up, and turned around. As he drove off, I prayed he'd call the police. A red Mustang came from the opposite direction, and this time it stopped. A teenage boy got out and started taking pictures with his cell phone.

I glanced at him. "Please call 9-1-1. I've got a little emergency here."

"I just posted your picture on Facebook and Twitter."

"Thanks a lot. In case the police miss your tweet, do you think you could also call them for me? Tell them to notify Detective Gabe Farkas. Tell them my name is Martha Rose."

"Sure. No biggie." He looked at his phone and whooped. "This thing is so going viral."

Within three minutes, cars started parking along the roadside. People jumped out and began taking photos and videos as Henry Oliver screamed obscenities at them.

My mouth went dry. I didn't know how much longer I could stand. "Does anyone have a piece of gum?"

A young girl handed me a stick of gum.

I shoved it in my mouth.

"You a cop?"

I shook my head as I bit into a refreshing burst of peppermint.

Another kid asked, "Is this a movie shoot?"

A girl in pink Ugg boots jumped out of her black Audi to get a closer look. "It's some kind of new reality show, right?"

In one final effort to understand why an overweight fifty-five-year-old woman would be forcing a man in a suit to sit down in the middle of a wet street in a fancy neighborhood, gum girl asked, "Is this like a Brentwood version of the video where everyone pops up and starts to sing ' 'Girls Just Wanna Have Fun'?"

I shifted my arms in an attempt to ease the pain. "We're waiting for the police."

Oliver looked around at the crowd surrounding him and then back at me. He removed his hands from his head, stood, and twisted his mouth into an ugly smile. "You can't shoot me now. You might hit an innocent bystander."

He was right. I didn't dare shoot at him with all those kids standing around. *I wish Crusher were here, he'd subdue the guy in no time.*

Oliver turned and grabbed the girl in the pink boots around the neck, using her as a shield. He growled in her ear, "Where's your car?"

"Don't hurt her!" I lowered my gun.

She pointed to the black Audi parked behind her.

He tightened his grip. "Keys!"

"In the car," she squeaked.

Oliver pushed her away and jumped in the Audi. She fell onto the asphalt sobbing.

Finally, sirens approached. Four squad cars formed a blockade across the street in both directions. Officers jumped out of their cars with guns drawn and yelled for people to clear the area.

One of the cops helped the girl to her feet and dragged her to safety behind a squad car. She pointed to the Audi. "He tried to steal my car."

Police surrounded the Audi with guns pointed at Henry Oliver.

"Get out of the car and put your hands on your head!"

"Out of the car, now!"

Oliver opened the door and surrendered.

I handed the gun to a uniformed officer. "Call Gabe Farkas and don't let that man go. He killed Harriet Oliver."

"Right behind me." The cop thumbed over his shoulder.

Farkas pushed his bulk through the crowd of teenagers.

"What took you so long?" I asked. "Didn't you figure out my message?"

"Yeah, I also got the 9-1-1, but there are massive pileups on the 405 and the 10. I got here as soon as I could."

"I caught Harriet's killer. Henry Oliver, her brother-in-law, confessed. He was going to steal the books and the quilt and kill me, but I managed to wrestle the gun away."

"You got some fancy kung-fu training I don't know about?"

"No, I just sat down and refused to move."

"Yeah, my wife complains I do the same thing. You okay?"

"He only bruised me. I'm wet and cold and my body aches." Fog settled over parts of my brain and I started sweating. "I guess you'll want to tape off the driveway as the new crime scene. What is this, the fourth time in two weeks? Must be a record." I thought about my dream that morning. "You've been here so many times. It's kind of like sorting through mountains of used clothing, don't you think?"

Farkas looked at me funny and his lips moved, but I couldn't hear what he said through the loud ringing in my ears. A strong pair of arms grabbed me as my body turned to rubber. Then everything went black.

CHAPTER 35

I woke up on the ground with Farkas staring at me, eyes wide with concern. "You scared me, Mrs. Rose. You okay?"

"How'd I get down here?"

"You fainted for a couple of seconds. It happens sometimes when people go through a shock."

I sat up and took stock of my body. My right arm throbbed where Oliver grabbed me, and I was stiff and sore from head to toe. For once, being overweight had prolonged my life. If I'd been down to my goal weight, Oliver could easily have lifted me and forced me inside Harriet's house. I might be dead right now. The enormity of my narrow escape hit me and tears spilled down my cheeks.

Farkas helped me to my feet and offered me a tissue. "Maybe we should have a doc take a look at you."

I didn't want to be "checked out" by a doctor in a cold hospital emergency room. I just needed a warm quilt and some rest. "I'm not sick. It's the stress of the last few days. I just want to go home."

Farkas put his hand under my elbow. "If you're sure you're okay . . ."

"I'm fine."

"I'll drive you home, then. You can give me a statement on the way." The detective escorted me to his white sedan and helped me inside. He set a recording device on the console while he drove. Fortunately, we didn't hit gridlock heading north toward Encino.

I carefully laid out the whole story of Henry Oliver and his obsession with the family heirlooms. "He threatened me, kidnapped me, and would have killed me. He expressed no remorse at killing Harriet. He merely viewed her as a woman without pedigree."

Once we arrived at my house, Farkas made sure I got inside before he left.

I swallowed a Soma and soaked in a hot bath until the pain subsided and my butt warmed. I put on my pajamas and warm socks and cuddled with Bumper on my sofa. Two hours later a knock at the door woke me.

Lucy and Ray stood on my porch with a casserole dish, a salad bowl covered with Saran Wrap, a baguette wrapped in aluminum foil, and a bottle of wine. Ray bent to kiss my cheek. Thank God he'd forgiven me. "You look a lot better now than you did on your YouTube video."

I stood aside to let them in. "What video?"

"Richie called to tell us he recognized you on this video that's gone viral. He said in the first hour you got over a hundred thousand hits. Now it's populating Facebook. Everyone's calling you Grannie Oakley. You're famous for singlehandedly capturing a killer."

I groaned. "I'm not a grandmother yet. Do I really look so old? I want to see the video."

I watched myself standing like a gray-haired Rizzoli with two hands on the gun. The girl gave me the peppermint gum. Oliver stood and grabbed the young woman in the pink boots. Then he threw her down and jumped into the Audi. Before he could escape, the police arrived and took him into custody. One of the officers removed the gun from my hand. My mouth moved in conversation with Farkas. He reached over to break my fall as I slid to the ground. A minute later I sat up and cried. Then when I stood, the crowd started clapping.

I smiled. "They clapped for me? I don't remember them clapping."

We ate salad while Lucy piled our plates with hot lasagna smelling like garlic, oregano, and melted cheese. Ray poured deep red Chianti into our glasses. I helped myself to a slice of sourdough bread toasted with garlic butter and parmesan cheese. After my day, I deserved all these calories.

A half hour later I looked at the clock and remembered my date with Isabel. "Oh crap! I have to go to Abernathy's and pick up my car. I've got to be somewhere tonight."

Ray frowned. "Not a good idea."

"I feel so much better after such a delicious dinner. I'll be fine."

While Lucy cleared the dishes, I got dressed. We piled into Lucy's vintage caddy and as we reached the end of my street, an Eyewitness News van approached from the opposite direction. Ray slowed the car and the van parked in front of my house.

"The media's gotten hold of your video, Grannie," Lucy chuckled.

Ray shook his head, eyes on the rearview mirror. "You're in for it now."

"Drive!" I ducked down in the seat when the NBC News van headed our way.

The Mondellos chauffeured me safely to my car in Abernathy's building, where I was abducted just hours before. I drove to Isabel's condo on Eleventh Street in Santa Monica. She answered the door holding a drink.

"Martha. I wondered when you'd get here." Isabel looked at me with weary eyes. She took a deep breath and her long white silk caftan whispered as she stepped aside to let me in. A cloud of Chanel N°5 swirled around her. Even with super-short hair, Isabel managed to exude feminine elegance.

She held up her glass and Harriet's ring sparkled on her finger. "Drink?"

I shook my head. Isabel led me to the living room. We sat on the white leather sofa. She put down her glass and reached for a pack of cigarettes on the coffee table. "You look terrible."

I told her about Henry Oliver kidnapping me and confessing to Harriet's murder. "I've got bruises to prove it." I rolled up my sleeve.

Oliver had left large black finger marks where he grabbed my arm and a red blotch on my shoulder where he kicked me.

She clicked a green plastic lighter and puffed until the tobacco on the end of her thin brown cigarette glowed orange. "He really did a number on you. I saw Harriet look exactly like you do—too many times—from Nathan's abuse."

I shuddered. "It seems violence runs in the Oliver family. Did she ever fight back?"

"She was terrified first, for her own safety, and then for her son's. She spent her life trying to placate that monster."

I folded my hands in my lap. "Are you ready to talk about the night Nathan was killed?"

Isabel took a deep drag on her cigarette, leaned back, and blew out a long stream of smoke. "Two years after her son's death, I finally told Harriet what I knew about Jonah's accident. The same evening, a Friday, she apparently gathered the courage to confront Nathan, which sent him into a rampage.

"I got a call from Harriet around eight. I rushed over. Huge black bruises showed on her arms and face and neck. He'd beaten and choked her. He sat in the living room, holding a tumbler full of scotch and an empty bottle of Macallan on the table beside him. When he saw me, he shouted obscenities."

I flashed on Henry Oliver also spewing curses in the middle of the road earlier today.

"I threatened to call the police." She picked up her glass and stared at it. "Nathan drained his drink and threw the glass at me. It narrowly missed my head and shattered on the wall. Then he exploded out of the chair and came after me. I tried to run, but he caught me and backhanded me in the face so hard I fell to the floor."

After my near-fatal encounter with his brother, I knew Isabel spoke the truth about the violence. What kind of hatred and family secrets would produce two such brutal siblings?

Isabel took a large gulp of vodka. "Nathan just laughed and grabbed a fresh bottle of scotch. He called me a whore and told me, 'Get out. Say good-bye forever to your friend.' Then he went back in the living room and sat down."

By now, tears streamed down Isabel's face. She looked at me and her lips trembled. "I knew Nathan meant to kill Harriet. I tried to take her with me, but she just stood there, too terrified to move. So, I went in the dining room, picked up one of those heavy old candelabras, and walked behind his chair. He didn't even notice me. I smashed him in the head." Isabel took another large drink and started to weep.

Farkas said the fatal blow to Nathan's skull came from behind and above. Isabel's story made sense, especially when I also remembered seeing the big dent on the bottom of one of the candelabras.

"Oh my God."

She carefully dabbed under her wet eyes with a tissue, trying not to smear her mascara and eyeliner. "What else could I do?"

"Whose idea was it to fake the suicide?"

"Mine. I didn't want to go to jail. I convinced Harriet to bury the body in the backyard. We chose a spot in the lawn near the fence and I called a friend. We took turns digging all night until the grave was deep enough."

I blew out my breath. "He must have been some good friend."

Isabel nodded. "Nico Grimaldi and I had become pals after Jonah's funeral. He didn't hesitate to help when I called."

"Did you know Grimaldi died a week ago?"

Isabel wept softly. "Yes, I didn't go to Palm Springs like I said. I stayed with Nikki, his daughter, and helped with his funeral. She contacted me today right after you talked to her."

"What did Harriet do while you and Grimaldi cleaned up?"

All that vodka had finally begun to work its magic on Isabel. She slowed her speech. "Nathan had hurt her pretty badly. We all agreed: If she went to the hospital, the police would come snooping around. So, we put her in bed to rest while we worked. Nico and I scrubbed the living room. Nathan's blood was all over the chair and the rug and on the nearby lamp and table. Drops of red even landed on the ceiling. We washed down everything we could, but some things, like the chair and the rug, couldn't be salvaged. Nico took an ax to the soiled furniture. He put the pieces in bags and drove straight to the dump."

"Wasn't anyone curious about the hole in the backyard or the missing furniture?"

Isabel broke into a phlegmy cough. "On Sunday I drove to Costco and bought a bunch of plants. We made a flower bed over the grave. Looked like it'd always been there. Harriet called her gardeners and let 'em go. They never returned to the house, so they never knew the ground had been dug. The new gardener she hired the following week didn't know the difference."

"Didn't the housekeeper suspect something was wrong?"

"Harriet also let the housekeeper go over the phone so she wouldn't return and see the disaster inside the house. She told the new housekeeper the living room was being redecorated."

"Whose idea was the suicide note?"

"Mine. I figured if everyone thought he drowned at sea, they wouldn't look for the body."

Isabel had thought of everything. She protected both herself and Harriet from a monster and committed a nearly perfect crime.

"How did you get Harriet's cocktail ring?"

Isabel emptied her glass. "Harriet insisted on giving me the ring for helping her. She also insisted on helping Nico get back on his feet."

"What caused your falling out two years ago? She ended your friendship so abruptly."

"Harriet couldn't stand the guilt." Isabel's shoulders sagged. "As time went by, she wanted to go to the police and tell them what happened. But she knew if she did, she'd get Nico and me in trouble. I pleaded with her to sell the house and get on with her life, but Harriet said the day Jonah died, so did she. The more depressed she became, the more she pulled back. Finally, one day she just cut me off. I could never get her to return my calls."

Isabel blinked back tears. "So now you know the truth. Are you going to turn me in?"

I knew all along Harriet wasn't a murderer, and I'd been determined to clear her name. But if the truth came out now, Isabel might go to jail for saving the life of a friend. There was no statute of limitations on murder. Where was the justice in that?

I leaned forward. "You came to Harriet's defense. I'm not sure how the law will look at this, but as far as I'm concerned, you rescued her. I'll leave the decision up to you whether you go to the police, Isabel. If you do, I know a fancy attorney who owes me a huge favor."

Isabel walked me to her door and gave me a boozy hug. "Thanks, Martha."

I walked in my door at ten, exhausted. All I could think about was collapsing into bed. Thankfully, the street in front of my house was empty, suggesting the reporters grew tired of waiting for Grannie Oakley. However, I suspected they'd return in the morning.

CHAPTER 36

Arthur's barking woke me. I slept for ten hours straight. I threw on my blue chenille bathrobe and shuffled into the living room to see why Arthur had raised the alarm. Two news vans were parked in front of my house, and when a couple of reporters saw me looking out my window, they hurried toward my front door, microphones in hand.

I ignored their knocking. I took care of my animals and put on a pot of strong Italian roast coffee. Most of the calls on my answering machine were from the local news stations looking for live Grannie Oakley interviews. Abernathy left a message advising me not to talk to the press because of my involvement in Harriet's murder investigation.

My daughter, Quincy, also left a message saying she'd seen the video. I called her right back.

"Mom, what happened yesterday? Are you okay?"

"I'm fine. The man on the video kidnapped me, but I managed to escape."

"Who was he?"

"It's complicated. I'll tell you the whole story later. It's over now."

"No, Mom, it's not over," she wailed. "That video has gone global. Naveen just got off the phone with his parents in Mumbai. They saw you on YouTube, Mom. They're convinced our family's involved in organized crime."

I laughed. "That's ridiculous. I've only been involved in *disorganized* crime."

"Not funny. The Sharmas pushed up their visit and will arrive next week. You have to come to Boston and convince them you're just an ordinary mom."

Unfortunately, that train left the station four murders ago. "I'll do what I can, honey."

The fifth time someone knocked, I snapped and yanked open the door. "Stop disturbing me. I have nothing to say to you people."

A young man with perfect blond hair thrust a microphone in my face. "Come on, Mrs. Rose. How did it feel to be kidnapped?"

I glared at him. "Go back to journalism school until you learn to ask more intelligent questions."

An African-American woman snickered, and then asked, "Would you mind telling us how you got involved in the Oliver murders?"

"Since I'm a witness, I can't talk to you. You'd be better off asking the detective on the case, Gabe Farkas. Now, you can hang around all you want, but you'll be wasting your time." I smiled at the young woman. "My daughter is a reporter for NPR. I know a decent journalist when I meet one. Good luck with your story."

The phone rang again around noon. *Maybe I should get an unlisted number.* "What!" I expected to hear from another television producer.

"Mrs. Rose? This is Dr. Evelyn Wong from UCLA

Hospital. I'm calling about a patient, Mr. Joseph Levy."

Yossi was a nickname for Joseph. She meant Yossi Levy. Crusher. My stomach dropped. Horrible scenarios sped through my mind. Motorcycle accident. Gunshot wound. Worse. "Oh my God. Is he all right?"

"An ambulance brought him into emergency early this morning. He's been through surgery, but he's conscious now and asking for you. We've admitted him. Just ask for directions to his room at the main desk on the first floor."

Thank God. Crusher wasn't dead. I smiled with tears in my eyes as I pictured him on his knees in front of me the night he proposed. He had been so funny. Why did I say no? Why didn't I trust him? Crusher couldn't be more different from the Oliver brothers. He was gentle. Swect. Honest. Did I make a huge mistake turning him down?

I grabbed a jacket and ran to my Corolla parked in the driveway. Thankfully, the reporters had given up on me. I sped three miles west on Burbank Boulevard and hopped onto the freeway. Thirty minutes later I parked my car in the visitors' lot and rushed to the main entrance of the hospital. I got directions to Crusher's room, knocked softly on the door and walked in. Soft daylight bathed the pale yellow walls. The air smelled pungent with antiseptic.

Crusher lay in bed, a mountain of injuries. Angry bruises and cuts distorted his face and lips. His right leg was wrapped in sterile dressings and elevated. A white cast enclosed his left arm, and an IV pole held two bags of liquid dripping through a tube. I pulled the chair next to his bed, sat down, and gently touched his good hand.

"Yossi?" I whispered.

He rolled his head toward the sound of my voice. His swollen eyes opened in narrow slits.

"Babe." He gave my hand a small squeeze.

My heart lurched. "What happened to you?"

"A little fight."

Ogg the caveman.

The door opened. A man with a scruffy beard swaggered into the room. He wore jeans and a brown leather jacket. A blue and gold badge with the letters ATF and an eagle on top hung from a strap around his neck. He nodded once at me and walked to the other side of Crusher's bed.

What was Alcohol, Tobacco and Firearms doing here?

"Yo, Levy. How's it going, man?"

Crusher lifted his right hand and they bumped fists.

Crusher knows this guy?

The agent looked at me and grinned. He thrust his arm across the bed and shook my hand. "Andy Black, ATF. Levy and I go way back. This guy's a legend."

Crusher looked sheepish through his cuts and bruises. He turned to Black. "This is Martha. She doesn't know yet."

"Know what?"

Crusher avoided my eyes.

This can't be good.

Crusher nodded once at the ATF agent.

Black looked at me and tugged nervously at his right earlobe. "We've been undercover for five years, trying to stop arms smuggling to Al Qaeda and Hamas. The big take-down happened last night in San Pedro. My man here"—he pointed at Crusher—"took on three guys at once."

My head seemed to briefly disconnect from my body as I tried to absorb this information. For a moment I thought I'd walked into the wrong room. Crusher finally looked at me and tried to smile.

I pointed to the ATF agent. "Is this man saying you've been working for him undercover?"

Black snorted. "It's the other way around. I work for Levy. He ran this op."

If Golda Meir had risen from the dead and walked into his room to say *"Well done!"* in Hebrew, I couldn't have been more shocked.

"Yossi? Is this true?"

"Yeah."

So much for gentle, honest, and sweet.

"So the bike shop, the Valley Eagles, the last four months, you and me—that was all part of some elaborate sting?" My voice quivered and hot tears threatened to spill down my face.

"Not all." He reached over and took my hand.

"Even Carl and Malo? Are they agents too?"

"Malo yes. Carl is civilian. IT guy."

"And me? Was I just a convenient part of your cover?"

Crusher's face swam through my tears. I didn't know this man after all.

I'm such an idiot! How could I have allowed myself to be deceived by a man once again?

"Uh, maybe I'll come back later." Black ran his hand over his cheek and left the room.

Crusher squeezed my hand. "You and me. As real as it gets."

"How can I believe you now? I trusted you, and all the time you were living a lie. When were you planning to tell me you were a federal agent?" I tried to pull my hand away. He wouldn't let it go.

"Not how I planned to tell you. Couldn't blow my cover. *Only* thing I lied about." His grip tightened. "I love you, babe."

A nurse dressed in scrubs printed with tessellated cats bustled into the room. She took a syringe from a tray and injected the IV line. "Time for your pain meds," she smiled.

Crusher's grip on my hand loosened and his eyes closed. I waited until he was breathing deeply and walked out of the room, head reeling.

I left the hospital and drove home, unsure of what to believe. I didn't know a person could be so grateful to find someone alive one second, only to want to kill him the next.

CHAPTER 37

That night marked the first night of Hanukkah. I placed the special nine-branched silver candelabra on a table at the front window and lit one flame. I thought about all the past holidays and how my daughter's innocent little face shone in the magic of the candlelight. If she married Naveen Sharma, would she ever celebrate Hanukkah again?

I turned on the television and saw a snippet of my video on the evening news, along with my brief non-interview from the morning. *I really should lose some weight.* Shortly afterward, Uncle Isaac called and gave me an earful.

"I'm perfectly fine, Uncle Isaac. Nothing to worry about. You know how the news exaggerates everything."

"Where was Yossi Levy during all this mishugas?"

"Fighting terrorists."

"*Vus?*"

"I'll explain later. The crisis is over. Harriet's killer is in custody and I'm safe."

"Were you wearing your *hamsa?*" He referred to the hand of God symbol of protection.

I touched the tiny golden charm hanging from a chain around my neck. "I always do."

I had plenty of excuses to avoid Crusher for the next few days. I spent time confirming the details of Dr. Naomi Hunter's upcoming visit and appraisal of the Declaration Quilt. Calls and e-mails to Susan Daniels kept me up to date on the success of the estate sale and auction. In the end, Harriet's jewels and collectibles raked in nearly three million dollars.

Quilty Tuesday arrived again, exactly three weeks after I accepted the job of becoming Harriet's executor. I had accomplished a lot since then. I laid her to rest beside her son. I uncovered embezzlement. I caught a serial thief. I solved her murder. I helped Detective Farkas arrest her killer. I located the body of her missing husband, Nathan.

And I'd keep Isabel's secret.

Once the quilt and books were safely on their way to Washington, I'd hire a contractor to fix Harriet's house in preparation for sale. Julian Kessler had finished his audit of Harriet's finances and found no further problems, so I felt comfortable working with Abernathy again. With his help, I hired a broker to sell off the rest of Harriet's properties. I expected the bulk of her estate to be disbursed within six months. Then I'd truly be finished.

By Tuesday, I'd made a decision about Crusher, aka Yossi Levy, aka Ogg the Caveman, aka Federal Agent Joseph Levy. Four months ago, he told me he had "hidden depths." I'd thought he was talking about a spiritual life, not an undercover career catching arms smugglers. If he lied to me about who he was, he probably lied about being in love with me. I'd be a fool to think otherwise. So I decided to make a clean break.

Before I drove to Birdie's for our regular Tuesday morning sewing group, I made a quick visit to the hospital. When I got to Crusher's room, the head of his bed was raised almost all the way up. His voice was deep and confident as he spoke in Hebrew to a dark-haired man in a black suit. They stopped as soon they saw me.

"I'm sorry. Is this a bad time?" I took a step back.

"No." Crusher beckoned with his good hand. The swelling on his face had gone down and the bruises had begun to turn from angry purple to green with yellow edges. "Come in."

Crusher took my hand and tried to kissed it, but I pulled away. "Martha Rose, this is Ambassador Gideon Singer from the Israeli Embassy."

Singer put his hand on his heart and bowed quickly. "A pleasure. I came to congratulate our friend here and to say *kol hakavod*."

The Israeli *Ambassador*? On a personal visit! Okay, so Gideon Singer wasn't Golda Meir risen from the dead. Nevertheless, a high-ranking representative had just told Crusher "Well done!" in Hebrew.

After some small talk, Singer smiled graciously and left the room. I sat next to Crusher's bed. He closed his eyes and took a deep breath. "You smell like flowers. You're beautiful. I was afraid you wouldn't come·back."

"I shouldn't have, after all the lies you told me."

"I didn't want to worry you."

"And yet now I'll always worry about whether you're telling the truth. Today I find you with the

Israeli Ambassador. A couple of weeks ago you joked about how I should work for the *Shin Bet,* the Israeli secret service. So I've got to ask. Are you involved with them too?"

Crusher looked at the cast on his left hand and said nothing.

"Okay. I get it. Secret agent, spook, spy, whatever. I'm over it. I'm over you."

He raised his head, eyes pleading. "I was only trying to protect you."

"Then why do I feel betrayed? You picked the wrong person to lie to, Yossi."

"As soon as I get better, I'll make it up to you."

I suspected Crusher would bide his time and try to con his way back into my good graces. He was a patient man. After all, didn't he just spend the last five years preparing a trap for the bad guys? Not going to happen. I came by this morning to say I've decided to give up men for the rest of my life. Especially you. From this point forward, I'm a Jewish nun."

"Babe. Does this mean I can't come and stay with you at the convent while I recuperate?"

"Are you kidding?"

Crusher moved slightly and winced in pain. "I've got two busted ribs, a broken wrist, a bruised kidney, and a bullet wound in my leg. They say I can't go home unless I have someone to care for me."

"I feel badly you're wounded, but not that bad. Maybe you could stay with your friend Ambassador Singer."

"You're killin' me."

I stood. "Good-bye, Yossi, whoever you are." I left his room and headed for my car.

The inside of Birdie's house smelled like freshly baked coconut ginger cookies and coffee. I sat in the green chenille chair with the wide arms.

Lucy wore ninja chic today with black leggings and a black tunic sweater. She looked up from pinning a seam together, and the gold hoops in her ears flashed in the light. "Where's Arthur today?"

"Oh, Arlo picked him up on Saturday. He stayed long enough to tell me he'd broken up with his girlfriend. He had to coax Arthur into the car. The dog kept looking back at me like he wanted to stay."

Lucy chuckled. "Probably because you're way more fun than Arlo is."

"Yeah, I kind of failed to mention his dog dug up a dead body and took down a man who was shooting at us. I figured what Arlo didn't know . . ."

"What's going to happen to the Declaration Quilt?" Birdie brushed a wisp of white hair from her cheek.

"The curators are coming this week to authenticate the quilt. If they're satisfied it's the real McCoy, they'll arrange for safe transport to Washington DC. Eventually it'll be displayed along with the Declaration of Independence in the rotunda of the National Archives."

"And they'll pay two million for the quilt?" she said.

I shook my head. "I've decided to donate everything since Harriet's estate doesn't need the money. The name *Harriet Gordon* will be inscribed on a plaque right next to the quilt. She'll be remembered by everyone who views it. The books go to the National Library, and the Oliver family papers will go to the historic Touro Synagogue in Newport, Rhode Island."

"What about the Benjamin Franklin watch, dear?" Birdie picked up a green fabric leaf and began appliquéing with tiny, invisible green stitches onto a creamy background.

"The DA wants to keep the watch as evidence until after Henry Oliver's trial. Then it will go to the Smithsonian."

"And the other lovely heirlooms?"

"Estella cried when I told her how much she'd have to pay to get all the things she wanted. But, in the end, she agreed to buy back the china and the silver candelabras—especially after I promised to get Susan Daniels to reappraise them at the lowest possible value."

Birdie raised an eyebrow. "I know you put more things in those crates than just the candelabras and china. There must be all kinds of antique silver pieces and porcelain in there."

"I don't want the trouble of repacking those shipping containers. I'll send them as is. The extra pieces were uninsured, so there won't be any official record of them, anyway."

And I want to send the weapon that killed Nathan far away from the LAPD.

Birdie took a sip of coffee. "I hope Estella appreciates what you're doing for her."

"What did you find out about the cocktail ring?" asked Lucy.

Isabel had been through enough. *I'd never share her secret with another soul, not even my best* friends. "Oh, didn't I tell you? Harriet gave Isabel the ring as a gift."

"For helping to get rid of her husband?" Lucy was no fool.

I avoided looking at her. "The police are satisfied Harriet killed Nathan."

"What else do you have left to do, dear?" Birdie refilled my coffee cup.

I summarized the business arrangements Abernathy and I were working on. "There's plenty of money for the Jonah David Oliver wing of Children's Hospital. The rest will be disbursed among Harriet's other charities."

Lucy bit into a cookie. "Did you find out why Yossi and the others suddenly dropped out of sight?"

"Can you believe this?" I put down my needle. "Yossi headed a clandestine operation for the ATF, and most of the Valley Eagles were part of it. They used the bike shop as their cover." I told them about the guns, Hamas, and the call from UCLA Hospital. "His whole life was a lie."

"I don't believe it." Birdie's hands flew to her mouth. "All this time Yossi Levy headed a joint op for the ATF and the Israelis—and you never suspected a thing?"

"Well, how would Martha know something like that?" Lucy clucked her tongue.

"I thought all those boys got special tattoos to identify them in case they got killed. I'm sure I saw something like that on an old episode of *Get Smart*." Birdie tilted her head and looked at me. "Did you ever see anything like an ID tattooed on his body, Martha dear?"

I just stared at her.

"That's old school, hon." Lucy glanced at Birdie. "Nowadays they implant chips in the armpits like they do for dogs. Then if the guy shows up in the morgue, the coroner just passes a bar-code reader over him."

Seriously? "I swear, I'm going to walk out of here if you don't stop." I closed my eyes and rubbed my forehead. "He lied about who he was. He pretended to fall in love. He even proposed marriage. I was an idiot to fall for his bull."

"Don't get upset, dear." Birdie tried to comfort me. "Yossi had every right to protect his cover. I'm sure he hated to lie to you, of all people. Didn't he say he just wanted to protect you?"

Lucy pursed her lips. "Birdie's right. He was sweet to shield you from the dangerous part of his life. He may have kept you in the dark about working undercover, but I don't think he lied about his feelings. I've seen the way he looks at you."

Why are my friends taking his side? I shook my head. "It doesn't matter anymore. I'm over him. Can you believe he had the nerve to ask if he could recuperate at my house?"

"Just how badly hurt is he?" Birdie put down her sewing and leaned forward.

I described his injuries and his surgery.

"So he has a wounded arm *and* a wounded leg?" Lucy scowled. "Who's going to help him while he's recovering? He can't get around on his own yet."

I shifted in the chair and cleared my throat. "He said he doesn't have anyone else."

Lucy locked eyes with me. "Have you forgotten all the times you went to Yossi and asked for his help? Did he ever once refuse you?"

I squirmed a little more and my cheeks warmed.

Lucy was right. I relied on Yossi for help and protection, yet when he was hurt and vulnerable, I refused to return the favor. "No, but I never lied about who I was!"

"Get over yourself, Martha. You owe him."

"But he betrayed me." I bit my lower lip.

"Yossi Levy is not your ex-husband, and he's not Arlo Beavers. He lied because of the important job he had to do, not because he cheated on you with another woman. Yossi almost lost his life protecting this country from criminals and terrorists."

"Exactly," Birdie spoke eagerly. "Yossi's a hero. He deserves our support and understanding."

By now my ears and neck were burning. I closed my eyes and leaned back, feeling smaller and smaller.

"You must let him stay with you, Martha dear." Birdie's voice became gentle. "I'll help you take care of him. I'll cook lots of healthy soups and bake bread fresh every day. What about you, Lucy?"

"I'll help you with his laundry and changing bandages. I piled up lots of nursing experience raising five active boys."

I tried one last time to derail the Crusher fan club train. "I have to fly to Boston next week."

Lucy smiled brightly and wiggled her fingers in air quotes. "No problemo. While you're away, Ray and I will come over and stay with him. They can watch sports together."

Birdie bobbed her head rapidly. "Good idea."

I rolled my eyes.

"With our help, Yossi can recuperate at your house for as long as he needs to. What do you say, girlfriend?"

Just shoot me!

Please turn the page for a quilting tip
from Mary Marks!

CHOOSING YOUR FABRICS

Choosing fabric for a quilt is the most important part of quilt making. You will cut up perfectly good materials into small pieces; then you will sew them back together again into a new design. Since you are going to all that trouble, you want the end product to justify all your efforts. You want the colors and the patterns to blend together in one harmonious whole.

However, you don't want your choices to be so harmonious that the quilt turns out to be dull and unremarkable. Like every great recipe, you need to have a few ingredients that add power and interest. So here are a few hints about mixing fabrics that I've found work for me.

Color: Get acquainted with the color wheel. Find out which colors complement each other and use them together. For example, I love blues, so I find that if I want a contrast that's not too jarring, I'll combine blue with orange, its opposite on the color wheel. If I want the contrast to be a little more dramatic, I'll combine blue with yellow, a color that's close to orange, but just different enough to be noticeable. Remember, a little bit of a complement goes a long way. Of course you can combine blue with any color. Each combination evokes a different feeling. Experiment with the colors you like and see what pleases your eye.

Pattern: Unless you are making an Amish-style quilt, you will be using printed fabrics. Try to vary the scale of the print. For example, I love flower prints, especially calicos with ditsy little flowers scattered all over. But a quilt made with nothing but small flowers can be chaotic to look at. So I often combine those small-scale calicos with large-scale flower prints. The larger prints give the eye a chance to rest, and the overall design is clearer and less confusing.

Graphics: Try to include some stripes, checks, plaids, or polka dots with your more traditional prints. The geometric shapes provide a pleasing contrast and add just the right amount of spice. Black and white graphics can be even more interesting. Try to be as judicious in their use as you would be when seasoning your recipe with salt and pepper.

Background: I love traditional quilt block designs. The geometrics of squares and triangles can be combined in an infinite way with colors and patterns. But not every element of the design can feature a strong pattern. Some of your fabrics need to play a more subtle role. These quieter background fabrics will allow the flavors of the featured fabrics to come through, and provide that overall balance you're looking for.

Finally, it's your quilt. Experiment with the colors and patterns you like. Make sample blocks if you're not sure whether the fabrics work for you. If they do, great. If not, try something else until you're satisfied. There are no right or wrong choices, so go forth and create!

Please turn the page for an exciting sneak peek
of Mary Marks's next Quilting Mystery

SOMETHING'S KNOT KOSHER

coming soon!

CHAPTER 1

I looked at caller ID and smiled. My best friend, Lucy, often rang in the middle of the afternoon to chat. I fully expected to hear that her youngest grandchild had made the honor roll at Encino Elementary. I certainly wasn't prepared for the shocking news.

"Turn on your TV, Martha. Channel seven."

"Why? What's up?"

"It's bad. I'll stay on the line."

Her voice held an urgent tone I didn't like. I dashed to the living room and grabbed the remote. A local newscaster stood on the sidewalk on Ventura Boulevard next to yellow police tape. "This brazen robbery occurred two hours ago in front of a dozen customers and employees of First Encino Bank. Witnesses said a single masked gunman forced everyone to lie on the floor in a back room and then pushed a hostage to the vault.

"A minute later, witnesses reported hearing four gunshots. The robber escaped carrying a duffel bag. When the police arrived, they discovered the body of the hostage inside the vault.

His name is being withheld pending notification of next of kin."

My pulse hammered in my throat. "Oh my God, Lucy. Does Birdie know? That's Russell's bank." Birdie's husband Russell was the vice president of First Encino. "Who got shot?"

"I'm here with Birdie. I was visiting her when the police came to notify her."

"Notify?" My stomach turned a flip. "Russell?"

"Yes. He's dead, Martha."

"I'll be right over."

Russell Watson hadn't been one of my favorite people. He didn't treat Birdie with the tenderness she deserved. Still, his shortcomings didn't justify murder. I couldn't predict how long I'd be gone, so I made sure my orange cat Bumper had enough food and water to last for a while. Then I grabbed my keys and jumped in my new Honda Civic. Less than five minutes later, I pulled up in front of Birdie's house behind a familiar silver Camry.

Lucy Mondello and Birdie Watson lived right across the street from one another in a more up-scale part of Encino. My name is Martha Rose, and the three of us have been quilting together every Tuesday for sixteen years. We were so comfortable with each other, we didn't bother to knock before entering. I rushed up the stairs of Birdie's front porch and pushed the door open.

A pair of cozy, overstuffed green chenille chairs faced a slip-covered sofa in the living room of the California bungalow. Dressed in matching yellow blouse and trousers, Lucy sat next to Birdie on the sofa, hugging the older woman's shoulders with a comforting arm. Birdie wore her signature blue denim overalls and white T-shirt.

Across from them, a woman in a blue FBI jacket with yellow letters sat in one of the easy chairs. LAPD homicide detective Arlo Beavers sat in the other. My ex-boyfriend. In his mid-fifties, with a shock of gray hair and a white mustache, he appeared fit and handsome as ever in his suit and tie. Just the sight of him made my toes tingle. We exchanged a brief glance; then I rushed to sit next to Birdie and grabbed her hand.

"I'm so sorry, Birdie. I can't believe Russell's gone. You know you're not alone, right? You've got Lucy and me."

Birdie sniffed and reached a shaking, blue-veined hand toward the tissue box on the coffee table. She nodded and blew her nose. I was saddened to see how the shock and grief transformed her normally cheerful face. Her mouth hung slack and her eyes brimmed. She looked all of her seventy-six years.

"I know, Martha dear. I'm glad you're here." Silent tears spilled down her cheeks as she twisted the end of her long white braid.

I nodded at the agent, but looked at Beavers. "Do you know who did this? Why did they have to kill Russell? Why couldn't they simply take the money and run?"

Beavers pursed his lips under his mustache and shook his head once.

Agent Lancet wore her brown hair pulled back into a severe, no-nonsense bun. "We don't have much information at this point. It's still early." She stood slowly and handed her business card to Birdie. *Kay B. Lancet, Special Agent FBI.* "We'll do everything in our power to catch the people who killed your husband, Mrs. Watson. Meanwhile, if you can think of anything to help our investigation, please call that number. I'm very sorry for your loss." The heavy rubber soles of her boots squeaked on her way to the front door.

Beavers also rose and turned to me. "Can I speak to you outside?"

I followed him out the front door, curious. Agent Lancet drove away in an unmarked black SUV. We hadn't spoken since December, almost seven months ago, when I babysat for his dog while he took his new girlfriend to Hawaii. He turned his face toward me and his eyes softened. "How have you been, Martha?"

Those dark eyes. Why did I still find them irresistible? "Fine, until now. I'm still in shock."

He nodded. "Yeah. Nobody's ever prepared for a thing like this. Listen. Since this is a federal crime, the LAPD is offically off the case. But I know Agent Lancet. We go way back. She allowed me to come here as a courtesy when I told her I knew the wife of the vic. Can you think of anyone who might've wanted Russell Watson dead? Did he have financial problems?"

"I haven't a clue. Why do you ask?"

"Just trying to cover all possibilities."

"Well, Russell wasn't the warmest human being on the planet. He probably managed to piss off a few people in his time, but don't we all? Shouldn't you be asking Birdie this?"

Beavers ran his fingers through his thick gray hair and blew a puff of air out of his mouth. "Kay did ask, but Mrs. Watson couldn't think of anyone. Maybe when the shock wears off she'll remember more. I figured she might've mentioned something to you and Mrs. Mondello in passing."

I shook my head. "Sorry." I turned to go inside.

He put up a restraining hand and cleared his throat. "Are you still seeing Levy?" Beavers was referring to Yossi Levy, aka *Crusher.* Crusher and I had gotten together—sort of—after my breakup with Beavers. Seven months ago, Crusher—an undercover ATF agent—caught a bullet in a shootout and almost died. After I turned down his latest offer of marriage, he left LA for a new undercover assignment in parts unknown. I hadn't heard from him since, but I didn't want to admit that to Beavers.

I answered with a question of my own. "Are you still dating what's-her-name? Kerry? Arthur's veterinarian?" Arthur was Beavers's German shepherd. I loved that dog.

"No, I broke up with her awhile back. She was too . . . possessive."

I jerked my head up and snorted right in his face. "Look who's talking!" When I dated Beavers a year ago, he'd become jealous and demanding. When I refused to be manipulated, he broke up with me.

Beavers had the grace to stare at the ground, and said, "I'd like to take you out to dinner sometime. Just to catch up. Maybe start over. . . ."

Did I hear him right? He wants to pick up where we left off? "I can't think about that, Arlo. The only thing I want to do right now is go back inside and help my friend." He nodded and backed away as I turned around and pushed my way through the front door.

Lucy studied my face as I closed the door noisily behind me. Her perfectly penciled red eyebrows raised in question marks. I kept walking and bit my lip. I'd discuss my love life at a more appropriate time. Like when pigs came to Passover.

I headed toward the kitchen. "I'll make us a pot of coffee."

The items Birdie used every day were conveniently displayed on open shelves or behind glass doors in her old-fashioned kitchen. The coffee press occupied a permanent spot on a counter paved with colorful Mexican tiles. I turned on the fire under a kettle of water on her large cast-iron stove.

The aroma of cinnamon and molasses led me to a freshly baked ginger cake cooling in a square jadeite dish. Birdie loved to bake in the mornings. Surely the present crisis justified my indulging in a slice. I'd think about Weight Watchers later.

I returned to the living room with a tray of steaming mugs and plates of cake. Birdie gratefully accepted coffee but declined the food. "I couldn't possibly eat anything, Martha dear. But you girls help yourself."

Lucy stretched, arching her back like a tall, red-headed cat. "So what did Arlo talk to you about?" she asked, forking a piece into her mouth.

"He asked if anyone would want Russell dead." I avoided looking at Birdie. "He also asked if you were having financial problems."

Birdie wrinkled her forehead. "Yes, Agent Lancet asked me the same questions, but I couldn't think of anybody who'd wish Russell harm. I mean, I wouldn't have been privy to something like that, anyway. Russell never talked about his work." She sighed. "As for financial problems, I wouldn't know about that either. He never bothered me with such things."

I understood what Birdie meant. She and Russell lived in a sterile marriage. They coexisted in separate bedrooms and didn't share much of a life. Why she had settled for such a loveless arrangement had baffled Lucy and me for years. All Birdie would ever tell us was, "He has his good points."

"Still," I persisted, "did Russell seem worried lately? Did he act any differently? Show some signs that something was bothering him?"

Birdie thought for a moment. "Well, he did get a phone call a week ago. Afterward, he was more snappish than usual." A look of alarm clouded her face. "Do you think the call's connected to his death?"

"Who knows? I mean, Arlo's question was odd. When a crook uses a gun in a bank robbery and kills someone, it's usually not personal. Right? So why would he ask if anyone wanted Russell dead? It's almost as if he thinks Russell was a target."

Beavers' question suggested Russell Watson's killing was deliberate. If so, did Russell know the masked man? Did he have problems? Did he scheme to rob is own bank? Did something go wrong at the last minute that got him killed? I hoped not, for Birdie's sake.

Birdie looked off into the distance, wrung her hands, and muttered something I couldn't understand. She looked more fragile than I had ever seen her. Poor thing would be mortified if she learned Russell was involved in some kind of heist. I didn't want the FBI's suspicions to add to her distress.

I wish I knew more, but getting Beavers to part with any facts wouldn't be easy. He's always been super professional. Conscientious. He never once revealed confidential details about a case when we were dating. Could I convince him to make an exception now because of Birdie?

Persuading Beavers to reveal information would take a lot of finesse on my part, but I owed it to Birdie to try. I'd start with that invitation to dinner.